Midsummer Night

Midsummer Night

SIX FANTASY NOVELLAS

Charlie N. Holmberg
Julie Wright
Annette Lyon
Jane Redd
Amber Argyle
Luisa Perkins

Mirror Press

Copyright © 2019 Mirror Press
Print edition
All rights reserved

No part of this book may be reproduced in any form whatsoever without prior written permission of the publisher, except in the case of brief passages embodied in critical reviews and articles. These novels are works of fiction. The characters, names, incidents, places, and dialog are products of the authors' imaginations and are not to be construed as real.

Interior Design by Cora Johnson
Content editor: Michele Holmes
Copyeditors: Kelsey Down, Haley Swan, and Kristy Stewart

Proofreaders: Lisa Russo Leigh and Lisa Shepherd

Cover design by Rachael Anderson
Cover Photo Credit: Deposit Photos #77816602, Deposit Photos #36297481

Published by Mirror Press, LLC

ISBN: 978-1-947152-65-6

More Timeless Romance Anthologies

Winter Collection
Spring Vacation Collection
Summer Wedding Collection
Autumn Collection
European Collection
Love Letter Collection
Old West Collection
Summer in New York Collection
Silver Bells Collection
All Regency Collection
Annette Lyon Collection
Sarah M. Eden British Isles Collection
Under the Mistletoe Collection
Mail Order Bride Collection
Road Trip Collection
Blind Date Collection
Valentine's Day Collection
Happily Ever After Collection
A Yuletide Regency Collection
Kissing a Billionaire Collection
Midsummer Night Collection

TABLE OF CONTENTS

Illusions of Love 1
by Charlie N. Holmberg

Dancing with the Moon 41
by Julie Wright

The Truest Treasure 99
by Annette Lyon

The Isle of Rose 155
by Jane Redd

Lady of Shadows 217
by Amber Argyle

Fire and Fountain 285
by Luisa Perkins

Illusions of Love

by Charlie N. Holmberg

One

EVEN IF CELTIN DERENG were a magicless, talentless pauper, Aster would still be in love with him.

She hadn't meant to fall in love with him, of course. When she'd arrived at the estate two years ago to take the assistant position, she'd been so nervous she barely saw the magician as a human being, let alone a man. Celtin—that is, Master Dereng—was one of the top magic wielders in the country. He'd worked for the regent himself, though his employ and residency was at Trundon House. Which was very nearly royalty, as Lord Trundon was eighth in line to the throne.

Drummond, who had gotten Aster the position in the first place, claimed the number would never be more than a number, but it was still impressive to the daughter of a small-town doctor. A very *lucky* daughter. Such job opportunities were uncommon for the lower classes, especially for women. But it just so happened that Aster's childhood friend, Drummond, showed a spark for wizardcraft in his adolescence and caught the eye of Celtin—Master Dereng—some eight years ago. And so when the magician's previous assistant decided he wanted to be a lawyer instead, Drummond had put in a good word for Aster. The rest was history.

Aster was very good at her job. She kept the library

organized, the potions labeled, the powders sorted, and Celtin punctual to all his appointments. She booked carriages and made sure the famous magician ate three meals a day. She tidied the workspace and cleaned up every glass vial Drummond broke, if she didn't catch them first. She always loomed close when Drummond worked with glass, unless he was mixing chemicals. Then she stayed as far away as the room would allow.

For now, their laboratory was in the basement of Trundon House and would be until construction on the detached one near the woods was complete. It was an overlarge cellar lit and warmed by magicked sconces. Tan cobblestone comprised the floor, walls, and ceiling. Shelves and cabinets took up nearly all free space, and old rugs—still worth a fortune—lined the floors to keep out the chill. A year ago Aster had taken up the work of rearranging those rugs so the largest sat beneath the long worktable near the entrance. Drummond had a habit of tripping over the smaller ones. Neither he nor Celtin had ever commented on the arrangement, but she knew Drummond was grateful.

Today, she organized powders, baubles, and fabric squares on a cloth-lined tray, checking her list on occasion to ensure she hadn't forgotten anything. Tonight, Trundon House was hosting a ball. It was to be the party of the year, in celebration of the eldest son's twenty-fifth birthday. However, those in the household knew it was also a means of introducing Garron Trundon to the local women as well. Twenty-five was getting old for a bachelor, if Lord Trundon had anything to say about it.

Master Dereng was thirty-one. Not that Aster ever pointed it out.

The door opened with a loud creak, and Celtin pushed his way into the laboratory as though summoned, his pace quick. The suddenness of it caused Drummond to jump and throw his pestle halfway across the room. He cursed under his breath, then glanced at Aster and mouthed an apology.

Aster simply rolled her eyes. She was quite used to Drummond's foul language, even before she joined him at Trundon house. It was one of many things he often got in trouble for back home.

Her eyes moved to Celtin. She worked with him for hours every day, so his sudden appearance didn't quite send her heart racing, just... *stretching*. Like it could cross the room and curl up next to him. He was a man who didn't appear remarkable *at first*, but further study proved otherwise. He was of an average height and trim, and he dressed well. Today his cravat was a pale lavender and his waistcoat a modest shade of blue, though its lapels were bold and embroidered. The silver chain to the watch he always carried hung from his pocket. He wore his hair unfashionably long, dusting his shoulders, and yet Aster could not imagine it ever being cut. She might cry, were he ever to shear it. The large, gentle waves—almost the color of graphite—were so sprightly they reminded her of fledgling feathers. So soft to the touch. At least, Aster imagined they were soft to the touch. She knew her place well enough not to cross that line. And she respected Master Dereng, however much she might pine after him.

"Drummond"—he slid his toe under the fallen pestle and kicked it upward, snatching it with his free hand—"I appreciate the focus, but don't forget the world still exists around you, hm?"

Drummond took the pestle. "Sorry, sir."

Waving away the apology, Celtin strode to the bookshelves at the back of the room. Grabbed a thick tome from one and began thumbing through it, then set it back and grabbed another. "Aster, where's the Tolwick volume? On color manipulation?"

Abandoning her tray, Aster hurried to the shelf and grabbed a red-spined book level with Celtin's elbow. "Right . . . oh." She crouched, scanning spines. Moved to the next shelf. "The red one?"

"I thought it was brown." He pulled a pair of spectacles from his pocket and sat them on his nose. "Leather."

"Tolwick's not leather," Drummond called over his shoulder.

Celtin pulled out another book, then set it back. "Tolwick is one of the greats. Of course it's leather." He selected another book. "What is all this? Why is Abel next to Patrickson?"

Aster had a feeling this conversation would happen. She paused her search. "You wanted them rearranged by year published last week." Though in truth, she liked Celtin's subtle eccentricity. She liked that he didn't think like everyone else.

"Did I?" He leaned back, tapping his chin. "Was I very tired?"

"Especially tired." Aster hid a smile.

He sighed. "I think it was . . . 1730?"

"He died in 1737, didn't he?" Drummond called. "Didn't write much in his old age."

Celtin turned about. "You're paying attention to your history lessons now? What's next? Aster to tell us she's joining the circus?"

"I have been working on my tightrope," Aster chimed with utmost seriousness.

A single, dry laugh escaped the magician's throat. "I would very much like to see that." He glanced at her, his brown eyes sparkling. "But I would rather see the Tolwick volume. It has the clasp on it . . . about three inches thick."

"Three inches . . ." Aster snapped her fingers, then crossed the room to the table where her tray sat. A book was wedged under its back leg; it had been wobbling a fortnight ago when Drummond was labeling his brews, and he'd grabbed the book and shoved it under there. Crawling under the table in the most ladylike fashion she could muster, Aster pushed up with her back and carefully slid the volume free.

"Red leather," she said upon emerging, straightening her hair and skirt. "We were both right."

Celtin blinked. "You're using the work of one of the greats to prop up a table?"

Drummond glanced over, then furiously began grinding the tapis root.

Aster smirked. "Something like that." She needn't explain; Celtin had already shot a look toward his apprentice, though the exasperation was entirely feigned. He so rarely lost his temper—another quality Aster admired. When she'd first started, she'd given the magician plenty of reasons to shout at her. He never had.

As for the book . . . Celtin was known for finding creative ways to fix problems. He might have done far worse to fix the table.

"The way you scrambled for it," Celtin began, "I very much suspect the circus." He smiled at her in a way that made her feel like a butterfly, and when he took the volume from her hand, his thumb just brushed hers. Aster clenched her jaw to keep her face from betraying her. Tucking the book under his arm, he headed for the door. "Aster, the tray to the drawing room, if you would."

"Just a moment!" she called after him as he headed up the stairs into the main house, forgetting to close the door behind him.

Grabbing a rag, Aster went to the workstation and wiped up spilled powder from Drummond's accident.

"Don't know why I'm so nervous," Drummond mumbled over his half-crushed tapis root.

"Are you?" Aster looked him over. Drummond was tall, taller than Celtin, and wide. The kind of man you'd hire to guard a cell or the like. Though he was of an age with Aster, twenty, and had the build of a soldier, his face was that of a fourteen-year-old boy. Pale as winter, without the slightest hint of stubble. His father hadn't been able to grow a beard until he was nearly fifty.

Celtin shaved by choice.

Clearing her throat, Aster said, "I think the whole house is nervous. We're not even attending the party, but we're responsible for our share. Though Cook said if we come by an hour before, she'll slip us some pastries."

Drummond smiled at that, though his eyes didn't leave his work. "She say how many?"

Aster grinned. "I suppose that depends on whether or not she's looking."

Drummond nodded. Slowed his crushing. "But I am going tonight. He asked me to."

Aster wasn't surprised. Celtin was, of course, the entertainment for the evening. There would be musicians and dancing and food, but Lord Trundon planned an intermission to showcase Celtin's specialty, which was colorwork with illusions. That was what he'd just run off to do—final discussions for the event. Drummond likely wouldn't do any of the show directly, but he'd be just off stage, ready to hand up needed supplies. Likely adding sound effects.

Celtin was a master of performance.

"You'll do wonderfully." She patted his large hand and offered him a smile.

Drummond rubbed the bridge of his nose. "I'll do good enough. S'all I want, good enough."

Returning to her work, Aster added a small vial of indigo to the tray before picking it up. "We can go over the show after I deliver this, if you'd like."

The apprentice let out a long sigh. "I would. Thank you, Aster."

Beaming, Aster took up the tray by its handles and carefully ascended the stairs into the house, careful not to knock anything over. She weaved between busy servants in the kitchen, then took the narrow servants' stairs up to the first floor. The ballroom was located here. Liveried staff bounced back and forth, dusting alcoves, arranging chairs, hanging decorations. Aster was careful not to bump into them, and, fortunately, they watched out for her as well. Down the long corridor carpeted sky blue, around the corner, where the hustle and bustle died down. The drawing room was the last door on the right, just before the mahogany staircase that led to the family's sleeping quarters. The door was cracked a finger's width.

"—mention it," Mr. Garron Trundon, the eldest son whom the ball was for, said as Aster turned to push the door open with her back, "because while the party's thinly disguised purpose is for me, I think you might want to look at the wares yourself."

Aster paused. She shouldn't eavesdrop, she knew, but those words *did* make her heart quicken. She strained to listen.

She recognized Celtin's scoff. "I'm perfectly capable of choosing a spouse."

Aster's grip tightened on the tray.

"Then why haven't you?" Mr. Trundon asked. His footsteps moved closer, rather than farther, from the door.

Oh Lord, please tell me I'm mishearing. Celtin to find a wife at the ball? *Her* Celtin? Not that he was *hers* in any sense outside being her employer. But her fingers chilled around the tray's handles, its weight doubling. She couldn't bear it if Celtin got married. She'd never . . . she didn't think she could work under him if he did, however much she loved her position. Seeing him with another . . . she'd rather go back home to work the farm.

Celtin didn't answer.

A soft *smoosh* indicated one of the two men had dropped onto a sofa. "You have to mingle either way. As long as you let me pick first, there's no harm in it."

"I—" Celtin began.

The tray grew unbearably heavy. Aster pushed open the door, ending the conversation before Mr. Trundon could inspire Celtin to his plan. She hoped her face didn't give her away. As expected, the chat stopped immediately. Celtin even glanced away and cleared his throat.

Mr. Trundon lounged on the settee, looking every bit relaxed.

Pasting a smile on her face, Aster said, "Here's the tray. My apologies for not knocking." She gestured to her full hands. Did her voice shake? She swallowed and set the tray on the closest end table, then straightened a few items to make it look pristine before curtsying to Mr. Trundon. Looking at Celtin, she asked, "Will there be anything else?"

The magician seemed uncomfortable. At the conversation, or at being interrupted? Aster tried not to wring her hands.

"That will be all." He tugged on his cravat. "Thank you, Aster."

Nodding, Aster excused herself. She thought, briefly, to leave the door cracked and wait outside, but thought better of it. Pulling until it latched, she quickened her step and hurried toward the laboratory. Servants bustled around her, pinning, hanging, and arranging the last preparations for the party, but Aster didn't hear them. She barely saw them.

The stairs leading down to the laboratory stretched long. She stopped just outside the laboratory door. Leaned her forehead on the wood and closed her eyes. Her heart still hadn't calmed.

Women from all over the county and beyond were coming to tonight's ball. And Celtin was of a station for nearly all of them. And who wouldn't be mesmerized by his countenance, his stance, that graceful way he moved? Even if one didn't like his long hair or, perhaps, the cut of his nose, they would easily be won over by his prestige and his talent. *Everyone* would see his display tonight. Aster had witnessed most of it herself—she'd helped with the story—and it was breathtaking. The ugliest, foulest man could win over the crowd with a show like that.

She didn't want to lose him. Truly, even if he never looked at her twice, she'd be happy to remain his assistant until the day she died. To be around him, even if she was never close to him. That would be enough.

But it was foolish of her to hope the present would be the future. That they'd always stay this way, her, Celtin, and Drummond. Celtin would want a family soon enough and settle down. Drummond would finish his apprenticeship and get his own residency. And Aster . . . well, maybe Drummond would take her in. There was that, at least.

Morose, she pushed open the door. It seemed heavier than usual. It took her whole body to close it again. At least the slowness of it all didn't startle Drummond, who still ground that tapis root. His knuckles were red with it.

She studied him, thinking of the show tonight. She knew everything he needed to have prepared so it would go smoothly. Maybe he'd even keep an eye on Celtin for her. Take note of the ladies attending, and . . .

And . . .

An idea pushed its way into her head which was equally appealing and terrifying. As though sensing it, Drummond looked up. His brow furrowed. "What's gotten into you?"

She met his eyes. Stepped away from the door. "Drummond—"

He dropped the bowl and pestle. "Oh no, Aster. You've got that look again. Last time you got that look, I was in the stocks half a day."

She paused and planted her hands on her hips. "You were not."

"You're right." He stepped around the worktable. "*Last* time I had to copy one hundred pages on alchemy. The time *before* that was the stocks."

A worm of guilt niggled at her gut. It *had* been her idea to buy those fireworks. And before that, to see if a person could ride a cow just as well as they could a horse. But Drummond had still lit the wick and saddled the animal.

"Please, Drummond," she clasped her hands under her chin and closed the distance between them. "Please just hear me out."

She glanced back at the door, ensuring it was shut.

Letting out a long breath, Drummond rubbed the bridge of his nose again. "Fine. What?"

She swallowed. "I . . . overheard Celtin and Mr. Trundon talking."

"You were eavesdropping."

"I was opening a door and caught a few sentences." She tried to sound indignant, but her the tremor in her voice made her sound like a child scolded. She knew Drummond had heard it, for he relaxed suddenly and concern lined his forehead. Rubbing a chill from her arms, she explained, "Mr. Trundon was talking about Celtin finding a wife at the ball."

His shoulders drooped. He knew, of course. Working in such close quarters, without a woman around to gush her thoughts to, Drummond knew the whole of it. "I'm sorry, Aster."

"Well." She coughed, banishing the quake from her voice. "That's the thing. There will be lots of eligible women at the party tonight. What's one more?"

He eyed her. "I think they'll notice if you go. You don't have a dress, besides."

"I have plenty of dresses, they just—never mind, that. I'll just slip in, and no one will know. Not even Celtin."

"How would Celtin not know?"

Aster looked at him hopefully.

Drummond cursed and, this time, didn't apologize for it. "Please tell me what I'm thinking is wrong." He threw up his hands. "But of course it's not. Because you're Aster, who couldn't sit demurely in a corner for a day if the queen herself asked you to."

"You've practiced under him for eight years!" She clasped her hands in pleading. "You're practically a magician yourself. All I need is a few illusions—"

"You want me to mask you so you can go to the ball? And do what, exactly? Shake your hips in front of Master Dereng?" He winced and said, "Sorry," at the same time Aster barked, "Keep your voice down!"

She turned away, wringing her hands. "I just . . . if I can win him over . . ."

"You'd still have to confess if you did," he pointed out. "It couldn't be a long-term ruse."

She nodded. "I know. But I don't have time to work it all out. The ball is in *four hours*, Drummond. It's risky, but by the time I think of something else, it might be too late. At worst, I can just . . . distract him. To buy myself more time."

Drummond leaned against the worktable. "And a year and a half hasn't been enough time?"

She flushed. It had taken her only six months to realize how utterly astounding Celtin Dereng was. The whole week after admitting it to herself, she'd barely been able to say a sentence to him without stuttering. "I can't just . . . *declare* myself. He's my employer." *And above my station. And busy. And wonderful.*

Drummond ground his teeth.

"Please? He'll be occupied the rest of the night. I'll set up everything you need for the performance, and that will leave us enough time for the spells."

"I can't—"

"You can, if you take your time."

Drummond studied her. Folded his arms. Considered. For a terrifying moment, she was certain he would say no. That she'd be spending tonight in her bedroom surrounded by pastries, eating her anxiety until Celtin declared on the morrow that he'd met the love of his life, and then Aster would have to sweep up the broken pieces of her heart and find a reasonable excuse for why she had to go back home.

When Drummond sighed, again, elation filled her from her crown to her toes. She knew the cadence to all Drummond's sighs, and this was a good one. "Fine. *Fine.* But the show prep first, understand? And get your church dress. It's easier to mask something that already looks close to what you want."

Aster bit down on a squeal and hugged him. "Thank you. Thank you thank you thank you."

He peeled her off. "And if we're caught, you're putting *your* head on the chopping block."

But Aster was already dancing away, pulling out all the supplies Drummond would need for the show.

Two

WERE ANYONE TOLD THE regal woman standing in the gilt hallway was actually the magician's assistant, they would never doubt Drummond's talents.

Her gray Sunday dress now shimmered green. The illusion of lace trimmed its hem and the bodice. He'd even added volume to her sleeves and the light patterning of cream-colored lilies to the skirt. She wore the simple chain necklace he'd given her for her birthday last year, but now it appeared as pearls around her neck. She'd styled her hair herself, pinning it up simply but elegantly, but Drummond had turned her dark brown locks a soft shade of blonde. Aster had suggested auburn, but her friend had insisted it was too close to her natural color and likely to give her away. Admittedly, the honey color *was* quite fetching.

The changes to her face had sounded slight when he explained them, but when she'd looked into the hallway mirror, she hadn't recognized herself. Her nose was a little rounder, the bridge straighter. Her skin color was lighter. Her hazel eyes glimmered a blue so bright she almost turned back for the laboratory to demand they be changed. Surely such bright eyes didn't look real! But the longer she stared, the longer they seemed to suit. And if anything could be a distraction to Celtin, it would be vivid blue eyes, just like the ones the Trundon women had. Men certainly tended to trip over themselves around them.

Aster's brows were thinner and higher, her eyes sharper and less round. Her cheekbones were prominent, as was her chin. Not something she would have chosen for herself, but they worked well with the other additions.

She was no longer Aster, the magician's assistant. She was ... well, she needed to figure that out, didn't she? But she would feign shyness around anyone but Celtin. She wasn't here to socialize or dance. She had one night only to win him over. And after that ... she'd figure it out, one way or another.

She wished she'd had more time to plan as she entered the ballroom. The place was full of people in finery. Not two steps within the door was a group of people around her age chatting with one another. A woman laughed while fanning herself. A man offered to take his companion's empty champagne flute.

No champagne, Aster told herself as she pushed through, her green-enchanted skirts rustling as though they were entirely real. Drummond really had outdone himself. She'd be a fool to undo his hard work by letting herself get silly with alcohol.

Chairs lining the walls of the ballroom held mothers and grandmothers, as well as a few maids too shy to interact. An empty seat called to her, but Aster turned away. She needed to find Celtin. Find him, then ... say something. Something general, that Aster wouldn't know. But what about Master Celtin Dereng was common knowledge, and what was her own? That he was renowned, yes, and that he worked here. That a lot of the decoration lighting the ceiling and windows was of his own making—surely that wasn't a jump to make—and that he'd be performing tonight. Everyone knew he'd performed for the queen. She could bring that up. Yet Aster also knew he tired of talking about his work, and surely every person he conversed with tonight would ask after his magic. Aster needed to stand out. She needed to talk to the person, not the magician.

The musicians played a waltz in the corner. The music was lovely. Pausing by a pillar, Aster let the notes wash over her as she scanned the room. But with so many clusters of people and the main floor occupied by dancers, she couldn't find him.

She headed toward the refreshments, moving aside to let two women pass. A small group of three lingered by the next pillar, two women and a man. Aster caught a snippet of their conversation.

"And you hale from Wetherby?" the man asked.

The woman—a beautiful creature with hair pale as beeswax—nodded. "Just north of Leeds."

"I hear the industry there is booming."

The woman shrugged. "Perhaps. But it's the poppies that have everyone talking."

Aster pushed past, memorizing the information. *Wetherby. Leeds.* To her left, an older woman cried out, "Oh Mr. Gurney, what a pleasure it is!" and to her right, "—and my daughter, Meriwether."

And so, by the time Aster reached the far side of the room, she'd become Meri Gurney from Wetherby, just north of Leeds.

She declined a drink offered by a servant and scanned the room a second time, clutching nervous, gloved fingers to her breast. They were real gloves, made more pristine by Drummond. She couldn't very well risk someone feeling her fingers through an illusion and suspecting her.

A tenor behind her startled her. "Are you hoping for a dance partner, miss?"

Aster turned around, meeting the eyes of a tall gentleman

with a kind face and broad shoulders. His waistcoat even matched her dress. He looked to be a couple years her senior.

She understood, suddenly, the use of a fan, for she would have liked to hide behind one just then. "I'm afraid I'm quite poor at dancing. Simply looking for a friend." She curtsied, hoping it was quick enough not to look unpracticed. She *had* practiced ... for about two minutes before leaving the laboratory.

The man looked a little chagrined, but nodded politely and moved on. Aster let out a long breath. Hopefully he was merely bold, and she'd not need to worry about further requests to take to the floor. What she needed now was—

Celtin. She spied him conversing with two men just behind the waltzers. Her pulse quickened, and she thanked her gloves for hiding moistening palms. *It's now or never, Aster. Don't let Drummond's efforts go to waste.*

She pushed confidence into her bearing and made her way toward Celtin, easing around groups, avoiding elbows and servants carrying silver trays. As she neared, she hung back, knowing it would be rude to interrupt. Her mind kneaded itself with what she would say.

You know him, Aster. Talk to him like you would any day. But not about work. And not about his work. Or Drummond.

You're a refined lady from Wetherby who enjoys poppies and the countryside. You're very interested in magic, not that you have a single bone for it in your body. But take the first chance to steer away from magic. Show him substance.

The two men took turns shaking Celtin's hand before departing. Celtin turned toward the dance floor. Aster thought she saw two women headed his way.

Time for courage.

"Master Dereng!" she called, lifting her voice just enough so she didn't sound like herself. Celtin turned toward her.

Forcing grace into her legs as she approached, she added, "It is Master Dereng, isn't it? You match the description."

He didn't answer immediately. Instead he studied her face, then dropped his eyes down to the lace at the bottom of the gown and back up to her hair. That was good, wasn't it? If he thought her pretty, she was already halfway there.

"I am," he said slowly.

She curtsied. "Forgive my boldness. I'm Meri Gurney, from Wetherby. Just north of Leeds. I was hoping to make your acquaintance."

Nodding, he said, "I know the place. I was there last summer."

Oh, he was! She remembered scheduling that for him. He'd been gone eight days.

He tilted his head slightly, studying her. "You've got quite a few cotton mills up there, now."

"Oh yes, the industry is taking off." *Thank you, beeswax woman.*

He nodded, a glint of amusement in his eye. Why was he amused? "And how are you taking to it?"

"Oh, well," she thought for half a second, "I think it's wonderful. Every new factory opens up dozens of jobs for the locals."

"I'm glad you feel that way." He ran his thumb along the chain of his watch. "I've heard many complaining that the factories foul up the air and draw in crowds."

That gave her pause. Would Meri Gurney prefer bright summer fields to encroaching city factories? Well, she did now. Aster couldn't backtrack unless she wanted to sound a fool. "Well, that's unfortunate. My estate has not yet been directly affected." Seeking to steer the conversation elsewhere, she said, "I'm sure you tire of the conversation, but I'm very intrigued by what you do." She didn't have to try to sound genuine; she loved Celtin's work. "I very much look forward to your performance tonight. I was unable to watch when you were in town last, and I've been looking forward to it ever since receiving Lady Trundon's invitation."

It was the lady who sent out the missives, yes? Aster thought she recalled one of the maids mentioning it.

A small smile quirked his mouth—perhaps the night was too early for him to be exhausted by the topic. "Then I shall endeavor to make it my best. Miss Gurney, you said?"

She nodded. The waltz ended, and applause from the guests thundered around them, forbidding conversation a moment. As she grasped for a new topic of conversation that wouldn't give her away, Celtin asked, "Since you're here, Miss Gurney, would you do me the honor of the next dance?"

Lord pray Drummond's spells hid the blood draining from her face. "O-Oh, you're so kind." She cleared her throat. "Unfortunately, I am a terrible dancer. My sisters all agree. Stiff ankles."

His lip quirked again. She loved that expression, that amused yet kind expression that lit up his eyes. "It's a simple quadrille. You'll catch on."

"I-I don't think—"

"You're a smart one," he insisted and held out his hand. His ungloved hand.

Aster couldn't help herself. She lifted her own and let him take it. She blinked and found herself on the dance floor, lined up with other women dressed similarly to herself, Celtin across from her. And the music played so beautifully.

She tried to follow her line. The women stepped forward, then back. The men followed suit. Then partners linked both hands and rotated a full circle. She was half a step behind all of them. Turn around, link hands again—

Celtin whispered, "Then you'll step and trade places with the woman on your right, repeat, and trade back."

They broke apart. Aster did as Celtin instructed and kept up. When she returned to Celtin, the dance changed, but only for eight measures. Then it repeated itself. It was rather mathematical in its execution. And, indeed, simple enough that she felt rather graceful by the third repetition.

He took her hands again as they turned about. She couldn't help but notice the way their fingers joined. Again, she prayed that Drummond's illusion hid her true face, for she could feel heat pricking her cheeks just as easily as she felt the heat from his fingers seeping through her gloves. *Never* had she interacted with Celtin thus. They'd worked together for two years, having reason to get close, but not like this. He'd never had a reason to dance with her. She'd never had a reason to ask if he would.

But *he* had asked, and his brown eyes watched her as they moved. She thought she could feel his gaze on her skin even when they switched partners. *Drummond, you clever man.* He'd been with Celtin four times longer than Aster. He'd know what sort of women the magician conversed with, or even courted. He'd likely matched Aster to them. He had certainly seemed confident in his style choices when he enacted the spells.

But had she succeeded in wooing him intellectually? She'd have to find a second chance to wrap him in conversation. After the dance?

They pulled together for the last turn, but Aster couldn't bring herself to engage him then, though the couples beside them chatted. Celtin was so close. So warm. And even in this crowded room, she picked up his scent of sage and lemon. This was so different from the laboratory. These simple dance steps were nothing like when she'd been close to him before, transcribing, handing him ingredients, helping him brainstorm. She couldn't take her eyes off him.

She felt like a little girl who'd finally blossomed into a woman. And she wanted it to last forever.

But it was not hers to have. The music came to a close, and seeing the other women in the line curtsy to their partners, Aster quickly followed suit. As the dancers cleared the floor, Celtin took her hand in his and pressed a kiss to the back of it.

Aster's blood ran so hot, she was sure she'd faint.

"Many thanks, Miss Gurney," he said. "If you'll excuse me, I must prepare for the show."

"And keep your word," she murmured.

He raised an eyebrow. "Oh?"

She smiled. "To make it your best."

He mirrored her grin and nodded. "But of course." Releasing her hand, he departed into the crowd. It took several seconds for Aster to realize she stood, gaping after him, in the middle of the dance floor. Coming to herself, she quickly fled as newcomers filled the space.

Now she did allow herself an empty chair at the edge of the room and again wished for a fan. He'd taken to her, hadn't he? Aster wasn't incredibly experienced with men, but he'd asked her to dance, and she was sure the kiss on the back of the hand was not mandatory. She hadn't seen anyone else do it . . . but then again, she hadn't paid attention to anyone but Celtin.

Did he think her clever, what she'd said about the show? She could be cleverer than that. So long as she didn't sound like Aster.

She spent the next song trying to string together astute things to say. Topics she thought Celtin might bring up and ways she could reply to them, editing out anything only Aster would know, or idioms she used frequently. Slowly, moment by moment, Meri Gurney formed a soul. By the time the song finished and the lights dimmed, Aster almost felt the disguise was a real person.

She was up from her chair in an instant, pushing with the rest of the crowd toward the stage previously occupied by the musicians. Not too close—Celtin was known to borrow color from bystanders on occasion, and she couldn't risk him accidentally pulling off her illusion. But she pushed close enough to see most of the stage, if she stood on her toes. She had the thought to drag a chair over, but surely Meri Gurney was too polite to try such a thing.

Aster had seen Celtin perform before, and she'd seen several pieces of this production. She'd helped him write the story. But she rarely got to see him perform in such a refined capacity, before an audience of gentlemen and ladies, in a room so beautifully gilt. And on a stage! Someone stepped on her toe and rushed an apology, but she hardly noticed. The moment the first light appeared between hung maroon curtains, she was entranced.

It was a pale blue light, wavering like smoke off a candle. Celtin appeared behind it; he'd changed his waistcoat to the azure one she'd mended two weeks ago. In that faint light, even his hair took on a bluish hue, like the ocean after a storm.

It was perfect.

"It begins on an island," he crooned, and while he had a strong voice, Aster detected a feather of magic amplifying it to the room. Celtin waved his hands, and the blue light grew in intensity and size, spreading out over the stage, rippling as though swarmed by waves. The crowd oohed and ahed, but Celtin was only getting started.

A glimmer of gold formed in the middle of the ocean. If one were to look closely, they would see sparks of the color flowing from offstage, where Drummond knelt behind a curtain. That gold color came from *real* gold, provided by

Lord Trundon. The shimmer spun and grew, forming a sandy beach. Browns and greens flowed after it to form plants, trees, and houses. Celtin paused, hands on his hips, scanning the room. Then he shrugged and lifted his hands toward the maroon curtain overhead, pulling color from it to form the shadows of people. The curtain was left translucent, and the audience chuckled.

Aster did too, despite expecting it.

"The island was in the middle of the earth, surrounded by an ocean larger than any we could know," Celtin's rich baritone sang. "The ocean brought them life. Not only sustenance"—more colors flew out from what Drummond had prepared, forming fish and whales coursing through the water—"but trials and blessings."

Rain began to pour over the island, coalescing from the air overheard. The entire stage darkened as black clouds—that color stemmed from the soot Aster had spent weeks collecting—churned overhead. A spark of lightning ripped through them, causing many in the audience to gasp. But seconds after the storm descended, it lifted. Through waving hands, Celtin formed a brilliant rainbow that stretched the entire width of the room. It looked *real* and received much-deserved applause. A sudden seagull passed through it, not of Celtin's creation, and from behind the curtain, Drummond called, "Cuh-cah!"

Aster snorted, then quickly covered her mouth. No one seemed to notice the unladylike sound—they were too busy laughing. She hadn't expected the seagull.

"But one day," Celtin moved his arms before him as though stirring a great cauldron, and the colors and light swirled with the gestures, "from the depths of the ocean came a fantastic beast unlike any before seen."

The blue of the ocean darkened with the black of the

clouds, forming the masterful shadows and details that made Celtin so popular. The great dragon formed, filling the entire stage. It was blue, gray, and black, with a long, fanged face so terrifying Aster shied away, despite knowing it was only an illusion. It resembled a serpent, but with half a dozen fins and two muscled legs. Its eel-like tail hung off the stage, and thin tendrils of lightning pulsed around it. Each time the power flashed, the pale mane covering the first third of its body rippled. It was *alive*, it was magnificent, and for a moment, Aster thought it looked directly at her.

Or, rather, at Meri Gurney.

"It rose from the depths!" Celtin's voice strengthened, and the dragon surged upward, causing many to shriek. "And took up the island on its great back. It swam south, to the place of its winter rest. But the winter would destroy the island and all that lived upon it. The beast *had* to be stopped."

The dragon melted away as the island grew, lending to the effect of looking at it through a telescope. Many people, now with defined faces, hair, and clothing, gathered around. Their speed and gestures related their panic. One tall man, his body speckled silver, stepped in front of them and put up his hands.

"Their bravest warriors would leap from the isle's tallest mountain in an attempt to reach the beast's head," Celtin explained. With the coaxing of his crooked finger, red flowed in from the audience. A man let out a startled sound, and those around him chuckled; Celtin merely winked. The color might have come from a waistcoat or sash, something that could be left modestly translucent. He'd return the color when the show was over.

The gathered warriors now wore red garb, the color worn by soldiers. They ran to the edge of the island, armed with spears and harpoons, as guns would do nothing in the midst of the sea. They hesitated. Aster waited with bated breath.

The first leaped, and the current instantly swept him away. More gasps dotted the audience. The second leaped and swam hard, but lost his spear. The next three jumped together and got a spear into the dragon's great neck, but could only hang on for dear life, for they had not the strength to swim closer.

Several of the warriors deserted, shucking off their red uniforms and hiding amid the island trees. A man behind Aster booed.

Then, finally, the last warrior stood on the mountain peak. Aster clutched her hands together under her chin, blood racing with excitement.

The warrior backed up for a running start, then leaped farther than all the others. He dived into the foray and, with the use of two arrows, began to climb up the serpent's back.

The visual telescoped in on him, the stage darkening as the serpent dived deeper into the ocean. Still the warrior carried on, one hand over the other until he reached the serpent's mane. He clutched it in handfuls. Lighting sparked, shaking his body, but onward he went. "For my people," Celtin whispered. Then again, louder. "For my people!"

The warrior reached the dragon's head and, grabbing one of its eyelids, forced it to turn back.

"You will return my island!" Celtin sounded angry. "Or I will kill you and let you sink to the bottom of the sea."

The serpent laughed, though the disembodied voice wasn't Celtin's, which earned more gasps. Aster recognized Drummond's voice. "If I sink, so will you."

"No, the warrior said," Celtin made gold light pulse at the warrior's heart, "for my homeland sails with the strength of its people. As God is my witness, we shall live, but you have no such promise. Choose your life, dragon."

The dragon continued to sail. A few in the crowd whispered one to another. But, after several long seconds, Drummond the Dragon answered, "I will turn back for your valiance."

The colors and light shifted as the entire visage rotated, casting dancing lights across the ballroom ceiling. "But," the monster continued, "tell me your name so I might know to fear it, that others of my kind will not risk their souls with such thievery."

The warrior stood tall as the dragon breached the surface. "I am Ann of the Island."

Many gasped. A smile so large it hurt Aster's face, and she clapped as the warrior removed a red helmet and a cascade of golden hair rippled behind her in the wind.

Celtin had wanted a surprise ending. Aster had suggested making the warrior a woman. She hadn't known Celtin would use the idea.

For a moment, as cheers erupted from the audience, Aster felt herself up on that stage, garbed in red, her hair flowing freely behind her. The monster conquered. And, indeed, the woman warrior looked remarkably like Meri Gurney. Was that coincidence, or had she inspired Celtin to make a last-minute change? Hope like fire swirled inside her. The room went dark, earning a few exclamations from those around her. Within seconds it brightened again, and the stage was empty, everything returned to normal, the colors and light snuffed out. Even the overhead curtain hung in its full maroon splendor.

A second applause filled the room. Aster joined it, holding her place while the other guests spread out in the ballroom and the musicians took their seats. She searched for Celtin. Where had he gone?

It took a moment, as Lord Trundon took to the floor with his son to speak to the guests, for her to notice a cluster of people near the southmost exit. She caught a hint of graphite hair among them.

Not wanting to cross the ballroom and upset Lord Trundon, Aster took the long way around, hurrying best she could through the onlookers without drawing attention to herself. Around a pillar, past the refreshments . . . she nodded politely to the first man who'd asked her to dance, then exited the ballroom and came back in through another door to avoid a gaggle of matrons.

Celtin was at the center of a social hurricane. Even with Lord Trundon taking the floor, many guests swirled around the magician, asking him questions, remarking on his display, pointing out symbolism and whatever else excited them. Celtin addressed them all politely, from what Aster could see—she only got glimpses of him here and there before a woman's head and a man's shoulder blocked her view.

She opened her mouth, closed it. Raised a hand, as though to be seen behind the group, but more people from the stage side joined in. One young woman who was all legs and beauty elbowed her way over with a woman whom Aster assumed to be her mother trailing behind her. Several people allowed her passage; she must have been someone important to earn such deference.

Within moments Celtin's full attention was on that woman, her lovely face, her bejeweled ears and neck. And yet the rest of the crowd would not part for Aster. And why should they? She was a nobody.

A nobody who was supposed to be distracting Master Celtin Dereng from women like this one, who laughed behind gloved fingers in a way so elegant Aster felt like she'd been slapped.

She backed off. It was no use to fight the crowd. She'd simply . . . wait. She'd charmed the magician earlier, had she not? And yet just as she had thought the warrior woman in the showcase looked like Meri Gurney, she also resembled this wealthy woman giggling over Master Dereng's every word.

The night is barely half over, Aster. She searched for an empty seat close by. Lord Trundon finished his sentiments, and a round of applause sounded across the ballroom. A few chaperoned young women approached Mr. Trundon, the eligible bachelor of the evening.

If only he were the only one.

Taking a deep breath, Aster spotted a free chair away from other guests and started toward it. She bumped shoulders with another woman, unsure if the contact was due to her distraction or if the other lady had simply been walking too close.

"My apologies," Aster said, turning to see the very woman she'd emulated earlier, the one from Wetherby with hair pale as beeswax.

The woman offered a tight-lipped smile. "I don't recognize you. Charlotte." She extended her hand almost as though expecting Aster to kiss it. Aster clasped it instead, then released it. "Meri," she said. "From—" She couldn't say Wetherby! This woman would know her otherwise.

Fearing a great pause, Aster used the first place she could think of: her hometown. "Wisbech St. Mary."

"Oh." A soft laugh passed Charlotte's pink-painted lips. "No wonder I don't know you! That's a backwater little place in the Fens, isn't it? All . . . farms and such?"

Aster's skin warmed. "There is a lot of farmland, yes. Lord Trundon brings in his wheat from there."

Her smile was condescending in a way Aster couldn't put her finger on. "Well, next I eat bread, I shall think of you, Miss Meri."

She offered a curtsy and headed toward Celtin and his fans.

Aster watched her go, her chest tightening. Finding her chair, she sat at its edge, wringing her gloved fingers together. *That was unnecessary,* she thought, glancing back Charlotte's way. The other woman had already merged with the cluster.

An ache formed in her chest, and she rubbed it with a knuckle. *Celtin.* His title was earned and not inherited, so he was not restricted to the laws of society like Mr. Trundon was. He could marry whomever he wanted, even a backwater doctor's daughter from upriver.

And yet seeing him so at ease with the social elite, Aster had to admit Drummond was right. She'd been in love with him for a year and a half. Eighteen months to win him over, and never once had he looked her way. Why would he do so now? And even if she did catch his eye tonight . . . would he not be angry when she came clean? Aster certainly would be. Celtin was slow to anger, yes, but Aster was stepping beyond her bounds. She risked her employment and his trust with this ruse. She couldn't possibly reveal her deceit in hopes of shifting his heart to the true her, assuming Meri Gurney could claim it in the first place.

Best to keep the lie to a minimum. Best to leave while she was ahead.

Blinking away pricks in her eyes, Aster stood, smoothed her hair, and hurried to the closest exit with her head held high. No use having some gentleman follow after her and ask her what's wrong, or offer her a carriage. She lived in the servants' quarters. Hard to explain that, dressed as she was.

She had nearly reached the stairs when she heard her name. The false one, that is. "Miss Gurney!"

Her heart lodged into her throat when she turned to see Celtin catching up to her, a little ragged but no worse for wear. He straightened his waistcoat and offered her that handsome smile of his. "Leaving already? You've not told me if I kept my word. Did you enjoy the performance?"

More pricks. *Pray Drummond's blue eyes mask them.* "Oh, I loved it." She tried to push enthusiasm into her voice, for she genuinely adored the show. She adored everything about it, including its creator. "It was truly spectacular."

Celtin's brows drew together. "Are you all right?" He lifted an arm to touch her, but settled it instead on his pocket.

She managed a smile. "Quite well, just tired."

"Not too tired for another dance, I hope."

Her heart twisted so hard, her breath caught. She glanced to the stairs. "You are a remarkable dancer and an excellent teacher, Master Dereng." Her voice grew soft, so she forced more air into it. "But I think it best you dance with the other women. I don't belong here."

She curtsied and hurried away, dodging any more questions he might have. Leave Celtin to be the noble gentleman she'd tried to avoid!

But of course he would be. Because he was Celtin. Beautiful, kind, unobtainable Master Dereng.

She could not go straight to her rooms. She was no magician; only Drummond could take off her disguise. So she took the servants' stairs to the laboratory, avoiding others best she could. She paced the length of the room three dozen times before Drummond came in, carrying a crate of all his show supplies.

"Drummond!" Aster exclaimed, and her friend dropped everything in his arms. Translucent bobbles and bags scattered over the floor.

"Sorry," she added, rushing over as Drummond, after seeing her, whipped around to shut the door.

"What are you doing down here?" he asked.

"I left early. This was a stupid venture and not worth the risk. Just"—she shook out her skirt—"take it off, please?"

He sucked his cheeks in, but came over to remove the

spells, starting with her hair and working down. "Did something happen?"

Aster shook her head. "Nothing happened." *And nothing ever will. How silly this was, trying to merge my daydreams with reality. I have enough.*

Her chest hurt.

He pulled the last of the illusions off her dress, turning it into simple but nice-enough church attire. Aster pulled the pins from her hair and pocketed them before combing through the brown-again locks and braiding them over her shoulder. An appropriate hairstyle for an assistant.

"Thank you," she said, grateful when Drummond did not pry further. She helped him pick up the baubles and return them to the crate before making her escape. But as she pulled open the door, she said, "Drummond, when you get your residency ... you'll take me on, won't you? It's a bother finding an assistant, let alone training one."

He looked taken aback. "But of course I will, Aster. I wouldn't leave you behind."

She smiled, or thought she did, and took the stairs two at a time.

The kitchen was empty; the last of the refreshments must have gone out. Aster snagged a crust of bread, but immediately thought about wheat and the Wetherby woman from upstairs and tossed it aside. She wasn't really hungry, besides.

With no need to rush or hide, Aster took her time winding through the dark halls. Taking the serving stairs up, then up again. No one else had retired just yet; the bedrooms were dark, the windows lit by moonlight. Choosing a detour, Aster trailed down the hallway to the balcony at its center. The night air bore a light crispness. She breathed it in, letting it cool her as she strode to the stone railing. The ballroom was just beneath it, and its music, accented by distant conversation, drifted upward. Closing her eyes, she listened to it, imagining her feet executing the dance she'd shared with him. Meri Gurney had gone home and moved on with her life, but Aster had stayed behind to cherish the memory. She replayed it in her mind to exactness, ensuring she wouldn't forget the steps, the song, the touch.

Drummond would be done with his apprenticeship in a year or two. Then they'd move on, together. Drummond with a wife of his own, Aster following his children around the house, preparing his materials for work or entertainment or whatever Drummond decided to specialize in. It would be a good life. Good enough.

She opened her eyes just in time to see a yellow spark in the air that mimicked a butterfly before it winked out. She sighed. A finding spell—Celtin used them when he needed assistance and she wasn't around. Even in the middle of the night, on occasion. Only minutes would pass before he found her. Probably to clean up backstage after the guests left. Normally she'd take initiative and head over, but she wanted a few more minutes of music and starry sky. It calmed her.

A quarter hour passed before another set of footsteps sounded on the balcony. "A little dark to enjoy the view, isn't it?" Celtin asked as he approached.

Steeling herself, Aster turned toward him and smiled, trying to ignore the stretching of her heart. "I suppose it depends on what you're looking at. For the gardens? Yes. But I find it difficult to see the stars in daylight."

He smiled and leaned against the railing beside her, glancing heavenward. They stayed like that for a few breaths before he added, "The performance went well."

She hugged herself. "I would have loved to have seen it."

Letting out a long breath through his nose, the magician drummed his fingers on the railing. "Aster, we need to talk."

The seriousness of his voice put a fright in her, and looking at his dark eyes, her pulse hammered.

He averted his gaze to the shadowed gardens. "A clever attempt, but I'm afraid I'm very familiar with Drummond's work."

There were no spells large enough to hide the flush that consumed her like a wildfire. She stepped back from him and covered her face with both hands. "Oh God above."

"I don't think you fooled Him either." There was a lightness to the joke, but Aster wilted under it, wishing she could seep through the balcony floor and puddle in a corner down below.

He let her stew there, not demeaning her or accusing her, just allowing her humiliation to fester like a fever for who knows how long. Hands still over her face, she confessed, "Drummond was so careful..."

"He was. He's very talented, which is why I took him on in the first place. But I know his style. I also know your figure. He failed to disguise that."

Aster dropped her hands. Mortification consumed her by the second. "I-I'm so sorry, Master Dereng. I only meant to... I didn't think it any harm if I stopped at the ball for only a moment. I shouldn't have done it! It's not Drummond's fault. I bullied him into it. He was so stressed for the performance he didn't have the energy to withstand me—"

Celtin laughed. "Oh, I believe it." He put both hands on the railing, then pulled away from it. Slipped one hand into his pocket before changing his mind and letting it run along the chain of his pocket watch instead. "What I wish to clarify" —he met her gaze—"is that I hope your endeavor means I would not be mistaken in our mutual... feelings."

She felt as though she'd swallowed a mouthful of snow. "M-Mutual?"

He ran a hand back through his hair. "I have . . . been in a difficult predicament this past year. Because of our situation, that is. I did not want to put you in an impossible place." His expression softened. "I would not want you to accept me because I am your employer and have power over you. Yet I did not want to make your work life challenging were you to refuse."

Aster gaped. Certainly she was mishearing things. The music below was louder than she realized and she was mishearing things.

Mutual? *Accept* him?

"I've been trying to find a way around it. I wasn't sure, you understand. Drummond aside, you tend to be, well, kind to *everyone*. But when I saw you downstairs, disguised and approaching me . . ." He dropped his hand and balled it into a fist. "Do let me know if I'm being utterly ridiculous, Aster. If I am, I'll make the excuse that I've drunk too much and we'll go on tomorrow as though this never happened."

Speech failed her. She stared at him, his beautiful face, his earnest eyes, listening to him as though everything he'd said moved through molasses. It took her too long to hear his words. Too long to understand them.

An awkward chuckle passed his lips. He stepped back. "Perhaps I *will* have a drink."

She shook herself. "I . . . no, Celtin. I mean—" She was so flustered, so hot and so cold, she could barely think straight. "That is . . . I'm a little backwater, you know. I'm not sure I understand?"

His lip quirked. "You are hardly backwater, Aster."

"But if you could be plain."

He chuckled. "Now, you know I am very bad at that." But he closed the distance between them and took her hands in his own. In a voice just above a whisper, he asked, "Tell me why you came to the ball."

She warmed under his gaze. "Just to . . ."

She hoped he'd cut in and say something, but he didn't. And so her fever brightened.

Ashamed, she averted her eyes. "I overheard you talking to Mr. Trundon. About finding . . . a wife at the ball. And I didn't want you to—"

To her embarrassment, her voice thinned. She swallowed against a sore lump and finished, "I didn't want you to find one. Not one of . . . them."

"And yet dolling yourself up like one of them was supposed to earn my regard?" He lifted a hand and brushed a stray hair behind her ear. Her skin burned where he touched it. She dared to meet his eyes.

"But you said . . ." She took a deep breath. "I had already earned it . . . ?"

He smiled, so soft and reverent, so lovely. "Indeed."

She could cry. She did, a little—she had to blink to clear her vision. She released his hands and poked him in the chest. When confusion graced his features, she said, "I'm making sure you're not an illusion. It would be just like Drummond to play a trick on me."

Lifting a hand, he placed a knuckle beneath her chin. "I assure you, I am very much real."

His eyes—there was something in his eyes Aster had never seen before, not toward her or anyone else. Like magic, but of a different kind. He was warm and smelled like sage and lemon and his breath tickled her nose as he drew closer.

In that moment Aster remembered her courage, the courage that had paid off after all, and standing on her toes, she met his lips and shivered at the contact. Her heart erupted and heat flashed through her, making her feel very much like those fireworks that had gotten Drummond in trouble. But she was not the only one taking courage, for Celtin curved his hand around the back of her head and pulled her closer, taking her lips between his, and Aster could have died for the bliss of it.

Three

Dearest Drummond,

You were right; the Tower of Pisa is not nearly as large as that painting makes it appear to be. But it is still quite a sight! Another century and it will be kissing the cobblestones. That's what the locals say, at least.

Rome is an amazing place and I'm almost sorry you're not here to enjoy it. But good news! You'll have extra time to copy over those books. Celtin and I have decided to stay another month. You could call it a honey-many-moons, perhaps? But of course I'm joking. We're only extending a week! (Yes, I do think I'm quite funny.)

Today we're to Florence where we're meeting up with Celtin's sister. My sister-in-law! Not six weeks ago I didn't think I'd ever have one. How the time flies! I hope she likes me. I've none of your spells to trick her into doing so.

All right, Celtin just left the room. So I'll rush to tell you he thinks you'll be ready to test in six months. SIX MONTHS! So forget the copies and get ready! Of course I'll help you when I get back. I'll sleuth what I can to give you a head start. It's the least I can do to repay you.

Best Wishes!
Aster Dereng
P.S. My cousin Alisse—you remember her, yes?—would

make a wonderful assistant. I know you'll be needing one, and since I can no longer fill the position . . .

Charlie N. Holmberg is the *Wall Street Journal* bestselling author of The Paper Magician series, which *Publishers Weekly* called a "promising debut." Short-Listed for the 2015 ALA Fantasy Reading List for *The Paper Magician*, she is also the author of *Followed by Frost, The Fifth Doll*, and *Magic Bitter, Magic Sweet*. Charlie is a board member for the *Deep Magic* ezine of science fiction and fantasy. She is represented by Marlene Stringer at the Stringer Literary Agency. Visit Charlie online:

www.CharlieNHolmberg.com

Dancing with the Moon

by Julie Wright

"Walk with me," the ghost whispered as it flickered and reflected the moonlight. "Let me touch your hair and hold your upturned hand. Let me rest my arm over your shoulders as I light the path before us and stretch your shadow to its limits behind us. And then let us dance."

One

Grace

"I FOUND A GHOST!" Grace's sister, Annabelle announced at dinnertime. Since Annabelle had barely celebrated her sixth birthday, the news created far less alarm in the three other members of the family than it might have otherwise if it had come from an older, more reliable source.

The announcement elicited little more than a murmuring comment from their mother—who usually enjoyed Annabelle's tales.

Even Grace, who often indulged her young sister by pretending to believe the ludicrous things the child conjured from her imaginings, maintained her focus on her brother as he recounted his experiences working for the cobbler in the neighboring village of Easton. He explained in detail the way the leather had to be worked and shaped and cut in order to make a sturdy yet pliable pair of shoes.

Not that Grace cared at all how shoes were made, but she'd missed her brother during the many months he'd been away learning his trade. Being that they were barely a year apart and they'd had twenty-three years to get used to one another, being without him had created a hole in her, and she determined to fill it with as much of his presence as possible before he had to return to the cobbler's shop.

Grace felt selfish for wanting to ignore her sister for a moment. Annabelle had been born three months after their father had died. She'd come into the world at a time when Grace should've been marrying and rearing children of her own.

Their mother's pregnancy had been a surprise to them all since their parents were not young people. Their father should never have left their mother in such a fragile pregnancy. The delivery almost killed her and left her crippled. If only he'd sent Shem to do the hunt in his place.

But he hadn't sent Shem. He'd gone himself and never returned. With their father passed on, Grace and Shem adjusted their own lives in an effort to prolong the lives of their mother and newborn sister. And then Shem left to learn his trade because he could no longer put off the business of being a man. The task of caring for their family fell to Grace, and she'd felt the loneliness in her duty. A woman of twenty-three years should've had a husband to help her.

But who wanted a wife who came with such complications as a dependent mother and small sister?

"It was a really *real* ghost!" Annabelle insisted when she realized no one believed her.

"Shh! Annabelle! You can tell us about your baby ghost later," Grace said.

"But my ghost isn't a baby. It's a man ghost. A man like Shem."

"You say you saw a ghost, Anna-belly?" Shem asked, his mouth curving up into a wry grin, likely realizing he'd bored the little girl with the details of his work. "Was it terribly frightening?"

Annabelle frowned and swept back the stray strands of nearly white blonde hair that never seemed to stay in her braids no matter how tightly Grace wound them together. "No," she said. "It was bothersome and in my way when I tried to feed the hens. I told him he shouldn't be in our feed shed. But he didn't care that I told him to shoo away. He only looked and looked at me with great big, pale eyes." She held her fingers up around her eyes as if the action could make her own blue eyes larger.

Grace and Shem shared a look over their sister's head. "A man in the feed shed?" Grace asked, her heightened voice proving how much such news alarmed her.

"I'm sure it's nothing but a fairy story," their mother said.

Grace closed her eyes, took a breath, and counted to three before responding. Her mother had been as absentminded and as irresponsible as Annabelle since their father had gone.

Grace worked in the village most days teaching the magistrate's children their letters and numbers so that her sister and mother had food on the table and clothes on their backs. Was it so much to hope that her mother keep a clear head for even the smallest things such as a strange man in their feed shed?

"Mother," Grace started to say, but Shem interrupted.

"What did your ghost look like, Anna-belly?" he asked.

Annabelle shook her head, making the acorn shells Grace had looped at the end of her braids click together. "His hair was white, as if the moon had kissed his head. And his face was mist."

"You missed his face?" Grace asked.

"No!" The child was clearly tired of explaining herself. "I saw *through* his face, like the mist at the waterfall."

"You can't see through faces, darling," Grace said, trying to remain calm over the fact that a man had taken shelter in their feed shed. At least Shem had come home for a few days so she didn't have to face this alone.

"I know!" Annabelle slapped her tiny palm on the table. "That's what I'm trying to tell you! That's why he's a ghost!"

"Want to check the shed now?" Shem asked Grace.

"If we plan on sleeping soundly tonight, definitely now." They both stood, and Grace grabbed her mother's walking staff.

"You're both overreacting," her mother said while remaining seated at the tiny wooden table. "It's a fairy story."

"It's not a fairy story!" Annabelle insisted, looking cross with her mother as well.

Grace and Shem ignored their mother and sister, took a lantern, and went outside. A few feet away from the door, Shem pointed at Grace and then made motions that indicated he'd open the door while she stormed inside with the walking staff. Grace narrowed her eyes, shook her head, and motioned that she'd open the door. They stood still, neither of them budging until Grace tucked the walking staff into the crook of her arm. She made a fist over her open palm. Shem readied himself with his own fist over palm. They bounced their fists on their palms twice before making their choices. Shem chose scissors. Grace chose paper.

She lost. Sometimes she felt certain Shem cheated somehow, though she knew there was no way to cheat. With a sigh, she gripped the walking staff in both her hands and gave Shem a sharp nod.

He yanked the door open, and Grace leaped inside with a yell. She frowned at the space between the shelves lined with preserves and grains. Frowned because anywhere a man could fit remained empty.

Grace turned, half expecting that the whole situation was a big joke and she'd find Shem laughing at how silly she'd looked flying into the room with her teeth bared. But Shem wasn't laughing. He lifted the lantern higher, and his own face frowned.

"Do you think Annabelle's telling tall tales, fairy stories, like Mother said?" he asked.

Grace shook her head. "She seemed sincere, but if someone was here, they're gone now."

Satisfied, they closed it up again and made their way back to the house.

"Will you be all right on your own tomorrow?" he asked before they entered the house.

"We'll be fine. Honestly, Shem. I'm a full-grown woman. If I can't keep the other women of our household safe, then what good am I?"

He laughed. "All right. If you're sure." He entered the house and called to Annabelle that they'd vanquished the ghost.

Grace's foot hovered in the air just above the stone step of the front door. The hairs on her neck rose, and her skin prickled with the knowledge that someone watched her. Someone stood behind her. If she turned, she felt certain she would see.

She didn't turn.

She didn't want to see.

Grace would not believe in ghosts.

Two

Arell

HE'D TRIED TO SPEAK to them. To communicate. To demand answers. To get their attention.

But they didn't hear him. They didn't see him. They didn't even acknowledge him. So Arell went from attempting communication to watching to see what they did. He'd watched them from the moment the man and woman walked out of the house right up until the woman shut the door on him, cutting off the light from their lantern and the glow of the lamps and fire inside.

The sliver of light that smuggled its way out between the cracks in the shutters was not enough to shake the incredible cold that made him feel like a pail of milk left out in a metal bucket during the harshest of winter nights. His veins were nothing but ice, his breath little more than frost.

But the cold wasn't the worst thing that had been done to him.

The worst was that Arell didn't know where he was. He didn't remember how he'd come to the shambles of a farm in which he stood. One moment, he'd been making the rounds on his night watch at the king's palace, and the next, he stood blinking in bright morning light in a part of the land that didn't look in any way familiar. The palace stood on the firm foundation of rock atop the tallest of five hills, where it kept watch over its people in the valleys and along the surrounding hills. Arell had been walking the walls, his boots clapping against the stone.

And then he wasn't.

Something had happened. Something had dragged him to the farmlands so far from his home in the palace that he could not see the hills that should have been in plain view no matter where he stood in the city.

But what?

What had happened to alter everything he knew? Arell closed his eyes to try to think, to recreate the last moment he remembered. He took slow, even breaths and focused on the last fragmented memory. Odd how the memory was more sound than anything else. His boot heels clacking against the stone. The flap of a bat wing. The breeze lifting the rustling leaves down at the ground. And another sound.

His mind felt as though a thick fog shrouded his every thought past the moment he'd turned to the foreign noise. All he remembered after that was finding himself in a shed full of tools, animal feed, and small barrels containing water.

He growled, snapped his eyes open, and turned back to the house where the man and woman had gone. If he could ascertain his location, he could make his way back to wherever it was that he'd lost himself.

He'd tried asking the child earlier, but she'd sniffed at him as though he was something to be scraped from the bottom of a boot. She'd made no indication that she'd heard his question, and the only words he'd received from her were demands for him to move out of her way. The child was certainly determined and hadn't seemed at all afraid of a man on her property.

He thought of the prince who wandered the palace

grounds as if he were already king. The young girl had the same sense of confidence as the young prince. Strange to find such confidence from a child born to the relative poverty that would accompany life on a farm.

Arell shivered and looked up at the sky crowded with stars. No moon. The detail made him frown. Hadn't there been a half moon just the night before when he'd been atop the wall?

He was sure there had been.

How could such a thing change in one night when the moon had been waxing and waning by marked degrees for millennia? How could it change in an eyeblink?

It couldn't. Arell knew it couldn't. Yet it had. And the cold. The cold was a thing unbearable. Yet he knew from the position of the stars that it was still a season of warmth regardless of what changes had come over the moon.

The summer months made a man shed clothing like the coming winter made a tree shed leaves. He'd only worn his jacket during the night watch because it was part of the uniform, and it showed others in the king's employ that Arell was ranked and therefore had access to all the palace.

Arell moved to wrap his coat tighter around his body when he realized he wasn't wearing it.

He grabbed at the clothing he wore, realizing he was in full dress uniform as if he'd been on his way to a ball.

Being dressed in such attire confused him almost more than finding himself away from the familiar hills of his kingdom.

Arell needed answers. He looked to the closed door of the farmhouse. The thatch sagged as though exhausted by years and weather. The light escaping from around the door and shutters had faded. The lamps had been extinguished, and the fire had died enough to be little more than the glow from the last embers.

Had he really taken so long before deciding to knock and announce himself and get those answers he desperately needed? He was a soldier in the king's personal guard. His position depended on him making decisions immediately. And it felt like he *had* been quick and decisive, but the light from inside told a different story.

Time had passed.

Well, no more time wasted. He lifted his hand and rapped his knuckles hard against the wood.

And then he sucked in a deep breath.

Because he no longer stood outside the door. He was inside . . . in a woman's bedchamber.

He let out a curse, and the woman in the bed sat up straight.

Three

Grace

GRACE FELT THE PRESENCE as soon as it arrived. It brought with it a bone-shivering cold that sank through the many layers of blankets.

"Who's there?" she demanded to know.

"I'm Arell of the king's guard."

The voice splintered like ice, making Grace wrap her blankets more tightly around her.

"What king insists on a member of his guard entering a woman's bedchamber?" Grace felt pride at not letting the fear cause her voice to quaver. She squinted to try to see the owner of the voice but saw nothing aside from the darkness. The voice penetrating the darkness froze the room, every consonant like ice cracking, every vowel a slushy snowfall.

Someone was in their home. Someone had entered uninvited and certainly unwanted. And that someone brought with him a stinging freeze.

"No king sent me. I don't know how I came to be here, but I must return to my post. I protect the king. My absence will be felt."

"Now, see here. Your absence is something *I* would very much like to feel. There is no reason for you to be in my home. I want you to leave." Grace said the words as forcefully as she could manage without chattering her teeth with the brittle cold. Annabelle had said she'd seen a ghost. And Grace could no longer doubt the child's declaration. For what, but a ghost, could turn her room into winter? What but a ghost could be a disembodied voice? "Where are you? Show yourself to me."

"I'm standing right in front of you!"

The strength of his words and the frustration that obviously came with them felt like a wash of ice water over her skin. She gasped with the shock. "I see nothing. No one stands before me." Her words were insistent, but she knew she was wrong. She felt him more vibrantly than she'd ever felt anything in her life. His presence was a riot of color and cold in her mind. "Show yourself to me!"

Her demand was met with contemplative silence before he said, "I don't know how to make myself clearer to you. Can you really not see me?"

She focused on his direction, staring into the cyclone of space that seemed to belong to him and him alone. "I see nothing."

"How do you not see me when I'm here? I'm here!" His arctic frustration bit at her.

"You're making the room so cold!" She gasped again, the shiver working through her.

"I am doing nothing," he said. "I feel as though I'm entombed in ice. This place is wretched. How can you stand the cold of your land?"

"Because I was warm in my bed until you woke me. And it seems that the air around where you say you stand becomes colder still when you raise your voice."

He stayed silent another moment. Grace believed that, whoever he was, he was not the sort of man to act without thinking first. And that was a quality she admired. Her father had been the sort to run headlong into action without ever thinking of what those actions might mean for him later—let alone what those actions might mean for his family. She was quite sure that her father's impetuous determination to act recklessly led to his death and the family's subsequent poverty.

"You can hear me and feel my cold, yet you cannot see me?"

"Yes." She loosened her grip on her blankets. His calm demeanor warmed the room marginally enough to allow her to relax. That bit of warmth stirred something else in her—compassion instead of fear.

"Where am I?" he asked.

"You're in my bedchamber of my family's home—my father's name was Blackstone. But I believe you're meaning more generally rather than specifically?"

"Yes. Thank you. I'm sure it seems odd that I'm uncertain of my own location, but it has been a very strange night. I have no memory of leaving the palace."

"That is strange," she agreed, "but no stranger than my not being able to see you. Our home is located in the city of Daven on the western ridge of the southernmost part of the Tenali kingdom. Are you at least in the right kingdom? You mentioned being a member of the king's personal guard. It makes me wonder which king you might mean."

He heaved a great breath, and with it, the air warmed again—not by a lot, but enough to show he felt relieved. "I'm in the right kingdom, but the western ridge of Tenali? That's the farthest from the palace one can travel within our borders. I have to return immediately!"

The frigid blast made her jaw clench. "Stay calm!" she insisted. "You're freezing me!"

"I'm sorry. I only—I just need your help."

The way he phrased his plea led Grace to believe he was

not the sort of man who was used to asking for help. "How am I to help you?"

"I need to return to the palace at once. Something has happened. Something—"

"Be calm!" she insisted again. "Tell me what you remember. We can sort this out. But perhaps we should do it by the fire. I'm going to freeze, otherwise. Go to the fire. I'll meet you there."

"Why are you meeting me? Why not come with me?"

If he hadn't already announced himself to be a member of the king's personal guard, she would have thought him afraid. How could anyone in the king's personal guard be afraid to step out alone into a different room? Yet his voice conveyed the curl of fear tightening around his vocal cords.

"I'm in my nightdress, sir. If you're any kind of gentleman, you'll leave so I can put on a robe."

The room warmed a few degrees more, as though the ghost had blushed.

And then he was gone. She was certain he'd left because the temperature rose immediately; the chill of him simply vanished.

She waited a moment before finding the strength of mind to be able to swing her legs down to the floorboards and slip her feet into her slippers. She pulled on her robe and then, in a moment of decision, grabbed her wool shawl and wrapped it firmly over her shoulders. If she planned on meeting a frigid ghost, she planned on being prepared.

It never occurred to her to go to the room shared by her mother and young sister to see if her mother could help her. Grace had spent too many years protecting and comforting them to feel that there was any way they could ever offer her protection or comfort. She considered going to her brother's room and waking him but realized she had no desire to bring him into what her mother had called a fairy story. So little in her life belonged to her and her alone, and even if her sister had met the ghost first, Grace was the one he'd asked for help. Didn't that mean he belonged to Grace?

I should be frightened, she thought. *I should feel dread and terror right to my toenails.* But she only felt a sincere desire to help—a sincere desire to understand and to offer aid that might be in her power to give.

She stepped carefully over the floorboards, avoiding the ones that groaned with the greatest agony to avoid alerting anyone else in the house. She stopped once she'd turned the corner to the parlor and the fire. The room should have held a lingering warmth from the hot coals, but all the warmth had been sucked away.

The ghost was in the room.

She steeled herself against the things she could feel but could not see and then hurried to the fire to coax it back into a warm glow. Her actions would require her to chop more wood later in the week when her brother had left, but she couldn't be in the ghost's presence and have no fire. She'd catch her own death, and then the household would have two ghosts to worry about.

The thought made her smile to herself.

"Do you think my situation is amusing in any way?"

The voice startled her, even though she knew of his presence. "No. I was simply thinking my own thoughts." She wondered if he understood the truth of his situation. Did he know he was dead? Did he understand that very likely at this moment, someone was mourning over his cold body and preparing it for burial? He'd likely be buried in a churchyard somewhere if he was a commoner, but as a member of the king's personal guard, he might be given a place in the palace mausoleum.

Perhaps he'd been dead for a long while and had already been interred. That would explain how he'd traveled so far. He said he'd been gone only a night, but that seemed unlikely. No one could travel such a distance so quickly. Besides, her sister had said she'd seen him in the feed shed earlier that day. However long it had been, Grace felt certain he required her guidance to understand and accept his situation. The sooner he accepted that he was well and truly dead, the better off he'd be.

Once the fire was sufficiently roaring again, she turned to where the voice and the cold originated. It appeared he'd settled in her mother's chair. She fixed her gaze on the chair, which prompted him to ask, "Can you see me?"

"No. I'm sorry. I can only hear you and feel the cold. But why don't you tell me everything from the start? What last memory do you have while things were still normal and what are all the events that led you to my room?"

The tale he spun was rather disappointing. He'd been on the palace wall doing the night watch when he heard a noise, and then he was here on her farm, at her house.

"But what was the noise?" she asked when he'd finished explaining everything.

His silence told her he considered her question so he could answer to the best of his ability.

"A door opened." The words came out with an exhausted sort of triumph as if it had taken a great deal of energy to find his answer, but he felt immense pride that he *had* found it.

"A door?" She felt marginally sorry that she sounded so incredulous. "Didn't you say you were on a wall? Where is there a door on top of the wall?"

He didn't become impatient with her the way many people did when she asked questions. Instead, he explained that the wall surrounding the palace was several feet across and had passages that led up to it from within the wall itself. Doors marked each passage along the wall.

"Was it another guard, perhaps?"

His answer to this question took much longer this time. "No. I wouldn't be relieved from my duty until morning. No one would've been coming for such a purpose. And no other guard would've been on the wall who wasn't already stationed there for the night."

"Do people usually visit the wall? Is it unheard of to receive a message from someone or another while you're on duty?"

"It's not unheard of, but neither is it usual."

"Do you remember receiving a message?"

His long silence provoked another shudder from her. His focus and his frustration at trying to remember sucked away the heat from the fire.

"The king's advisor!"

He blurted the words with such force and so unexpectedly that Grace jumped.

He continued. "The king's advisor had come to the wall."

"In the middle of the night? It must have been an urgent message for him to have come at such a time." Grace wished she could see this man, this ghost. She wished she had a face to put with the deep timbre of voice.

"The message wasn't for me."

"Then who?"

"It was for Simmons, one of the other guards. Norton, the king's advisor, whispered Simmons's name and then thrust out something for me to take. He thought I was Simmons."

That was where the story finally became interesting. Grace leaned in closer to the voice. "What did you do?"

"I took the package."

"And what was it? Something secret?"

He groaned. "My head hurts from digging so hard for my own memories."

Grace frowned, wanting to explain to him that his head couldn't very well hurt since he was dead, but who was she to say what did or didn't happen when one died? Maybe heads could hurt. He'd already professed to being cold, and she'd felt enough of his ice to not doubt him. "I'm sorry for your pain. I'm only trying to help you, not make you unwell."

"I know. And I thank you for listening. Things feel clearer now with you listening to me than they did when I'd been alone. Norton told me to make sure the royal family all received a portion of the contents of the package he'd given me in their dinners."

Grace shook her head. "Well, that's bad."

"Is it? Why? I can't remember anything else beyond that yet. Why is that bad?"

"No one delivers dinner instructions to a member of the family's personal guard in the middle of the night under the cover of darkness. What does the guard have to do with the food served within the household?"

His heavy sigh felt as though it had put the fire out entirely. "You're right. Of course you're right. I know I must seem terribly insufficient as a guard to not see that immediately, but I'm not exactly myself right now. Something has happened, and my thoughts have yet to catch up."

Grace checked the fire to see that it still crackled and burned. She added another log and pushed the coals around. Should she tell him that the something that had happened was that he'd died? Did he really not know?

"It was a packet of poison for each family member, wasn't it? That's the only thing that makes sense, doesn't it?"

She felt sorry to have to agree with him, but really,

nothing else made sense. The royal family had their enemies. She assumed all royal families did. Grudges from neighboring kingdoms or from family members more distantly connected to the throne or those who'd been titled and then stripped of their titles for some such or other reason. A royal family didn't have to do anything wrong at all for others to be envious or poorly behaved. Grace nodded her agreement with him because it was the very first thought she'd had.

"And if this man Norton realized you weren't that other guard," Grace started, trying to figure out how to say it gently. "Well, you would've been a liability at that point."

"Do you think they knocked me unconscious and then dumped me off here?"

No. That wasn't quite what Grace had been thinking. "I was thinking of how Norton might have wanted you more permanently removed."

"Do you think they're coming back for me to finish me off?"

Grace groaned inwardly. "Well, they might if they felt you hadn't already been handled."

"Then they should've just killed me in the first place—" He cut off, and the room turned to a cold that made Grace ache. "You think they've already killed me. You think I'm dead and that's why you can't see me."

"I'm sorry," Grace said. "This isn't the best news for you to hear, but you should consider the possibility that perhaps you—"

"I'm not dead!" the ghost shouted. The flames froze in the fireplace, and the air sliced her lungs to ribbons for the tiniest of instances before the room was suddenly intolerably hot and the flames popped and crackled out of their frozen encasement.

She knew what that meant but waited a moment before

trying to call to him. "Ghost?" She should have used his name and *would* have if she'd known it. Some part of her thought maybe he'd given her that information upon entering her room, but she'd been so frightened at the beginning, she couldn't be certain.

Regardless, he didn't answer.

Her ghost was gone.

Four

Arell

ARELL HAD BEEN FURIOUS with the farm woman for daring to insinuate that he could be dead. Wouldn't a man know if he were dead or not? Of course he would! Farm people and peasants in general were the worst, most superstitious, lot.

But it truly frightened him to consider the haze of jumbles in his mind. The gap between what he'd managed to remember at the wall and showing up in a shed troubled him. Days' worth of travel had to have existed between those two events. At least three—more likely four.

And later, he'd never knocked on that farmhouse door. He'd never properly been invited into the house. He'd been at the door and then in that woman's room. Then when she'd asked him to leave her room so she could put on a robe, he'd been afraid to go, afraid of getting lost along the way.

Arell had been quite proud when he'd found himself by the fire. He even imagined he could feel its warmth. And when he'd grown angry with the woman for daring suggest he might be dead, he hadn't left the house. He'd not exited by any door that he knew of. He simply wasn't there any longer.

He wanted to blame the woman—curse her for his misfortunes—yet he felt the injustice in it. He'd gone to her for help and then yelled at her for trying to offer the only help that seemed reasonable to her. Calling her a superstitious peasant was hardly fair. She had a faultless beauty and resolve to her. And when she'd mentioned needing to put on a robe, he'd realized where he stood and the temptation such a location actually offered him when faced with her dark hair tumbling over her shoulder in a single smooth cascade.

And she wasn't afraid. Well, maybe at the very first, but she'd shaken off that fear rapidly and instead moved to kindness and action. She'd have made a good soldier with such qualities.

And then by the firelight, when he'd been able to see into her blue eyes, he felt that no jewel in all of the kingdom could flash as brightly in the sun as her eyes did in the firelight.

He then remembered that those eyes could not look on him.

She couldn't see him—not even in the smallest degree. Logical sense, not superstition, persuaded her to think of him as a spirit.

But that didn't make him dead.

He fumed over her accusation for several moments longer before thinking to look around him and get his bearings. He hadn't left the farmhouse. But he wasn't in it any longer either. So where was he?

The dark. He was in the dark.

Arell wasn't afraid of the dark, but this dark was something new. It encircled him entirely. And the cold. The cold was indescribably painful as it crushed in on him from all sides.

He closed his eyes, since he couldn't see anyway, and forced himself to focus. Everything required this painful, mind-splitting focus. And even with that, he felt like he existed in a haze of confusion.

He was normally sharp and on top of things; that was

how he earned his place in the royal guard. But since finding himself on that farm, nothing had been clear.

The wall.

It all came back to the wall.

And then he was there.

He was back! On the wall. In the part of the kingdom he knew he belonged: at the palace.

He took several deep breaths to steady himself against the overwhelming dizziness that came over him. It was daylight.

How could it be daylight? How could he be back at the palace when he'd been on the western ridge of the kingdom? But how could he have been in Daven when he'd been at the palace just before that?

He looked around, feeling relief to be where he knew his place and his world. Perhaps it was all just a dream. He'd imagined everything he'd seen and experienced before. That had to be it. Nothing else made sense. Though he hated to think that the beautiful woman he'd spoken to by firelight didn't actually exist, he hated the idea that his entire life had been upended even more.

Home. He was home.

And everything was going to be all right.

He turned to head down from the wall, go to his rooms, and change out of the dress uniform he still wore.

Arell frowned. The clothing. He was wearing the same full dress uniform he'd been wearing at the farmhouse. Then he noticed something more troubling. The flags flying in the guard house were black—black for mourning.

The woman by the fire had told him that the package Norton wanted to give Simmons could possibly have been meant to harm the royal family. Had that happened? Had the family he'd sworn to protect been murdered?

Noises farther down the wall caught his attention, and he

rushed to the men in the distance. His captain, Wilton, and the first lieutenant, Langley, spoke together in hushed tones. They didn't look up at his rapid approach. They didn't answer when he called their names.

And when he reached out to touch them, his hand did something it shouldn't have. It passed right through his captain's arm. "I'm here!" he cried out to them. "Please see me! I'm here!"

"Poor Arell," Langley said.

At hearing his name, Arell hoped that he'd made contact with the man—that Langley could finally see him.

"He was such a healthy man that it seems strange, doesn't it? He didn't take with drinking and pipe smoking," Langley said. "For him to die, to fall down dead with no cause or reason, feels suspicious, sir."

"You think someone killed him? And how, when there wasn't a mark anywhere on his body?" Captain Wilton asked, lowering his voice as he looked around to verify they were alone.

But they weren't alone. Arell stood right next to them. He shook his head, an overwhelming sense of panic flooding him. "I didn't die! I'm right here!"

Langley suppressed a shudder and looked to the sky. "Maybe a storm's coming. A wicked cold wind like that is a sign."

"A sign of what, Lieutenant?"

"A sign that something's not right here." Langley rolled his eyes. "I know how foolish that sounds, but something nefarious is happening. I can't pretend all is well when all is not well."

"You're right that not all is well. But what's wrong isn't some conspiracy in the kingdom. What's wrong is that a man who was trusted and loyal and a friend to us all—a man who was in his prime—is gone. How could such a thing ever be right?"

A single bell rang through the air.

It was not the bells of twilight or the bell that chimed the hour, since those bells were accompanied by smaller bells that sounded like a celebration. The single bell tolling was the bell of bereavement. But only one short blast—not the seven in a row that it would have been if he'd been freshly entombed. It meant he'd been entombed for seven days. Today was the seventh.

Arell had been gone seven days—eight if one counted the day it would take to prepare his body. He looked hard at his comrades. "Where am I?" he demanded to know. "Where have they placed my body?"

But just as the little girl could not hear him and the farm woman had not seen him, these men could neither see nor hear him.

"Where?" he shouted.

The two men frowned and shivered and tucked themselves tighter into their uniform coats.

"Definitely a storm coming," Langley said.

Arell made his way to the wall passage, but before he could take real steps, he was in the passage. "I'm not dead." He chanted this again and again. But he thought of the crypts in the mausoleum where those who died while serving the royal family were kept. And then he was there.

How could he do that if he were not dead?

No. Do not think such thoughts. But there in the low light of the mausoleum where the only illumination came from the stained glass windows at the top of the high walls, he saw what he'd expected but hoped not to find.

A stone on the wall that was fresh with no watermarks from drainage issues or droppings across the top from rodents. A fresh stone covered the resting place of the man for whom the bells of bereavement tolled. And his name was carved into its surface.

"I'm dead!" he shouted to the empty mausoleum. He stood staring for what seemed an eternity, but what did he know of time any longer? Days could pass in an eyeblink.

He could go from hearing a noise in the dark to being dead over a week later with barely a thought.

He stiffened.

The noise in the dark.

The king's advisor called out to Simmons, who had also been on duty that night. Whatever had been in that package had been worth killing Arell over, and if the farmer woman was right, it would end with more bells of bereavement—six sets a day for the six members of the royal family.

And then Arell was in the apartments of the king's advisor. Norton sat at his desk, reading something from a book with aged and torn pages. "I can hear your panic, so you might as well show yourself to me."

Arell startled. Could Norton see him? But before he could answer or confront Norton in any way, Simmons stepped out of the doorway shadows.

"People are suspicious!" Simmons spat out. "They keep asking me questions because I was on duty with Arell that night. They think I know something."

Norton shrugged. "To be fair to those doing the asking, you *do* know something."

"But I didn't kill Arell!" Simmons said.

"And to be fair to me, I didn't kill him either."

Arell frowned. He'd seen the black flags and heard the bells of bereavement. He'd seen the stone with his name on it over his crypt. Did Norton mean someone else killed him?

Who else would have done such a thing?

"Well, he didn't kill himself," Simmons, who'd never been short of sarcasm, said.

"The man's not dead."

"What?" Simmons said.

"What?" Arell said.

"But I saw the body," Simmons said.

"I saw my crypt!" Arell shouted.

The two men shuddered violently in response to Arell's anger.

Norton frowned in Arell's direction but shook his head and turned his attention back to Simmons. "He's not dead because he's been spelled."

"Spelled?" Simmons frowned. "Like magic?"

"Yes. How else could I best one of the guards? It cost me a lot to get that spell. I carried it on me at all times in case of an emergency. And what a waste!" The man narrowed his eyes at Simmons. "You were assigned to that wall, Simmons! You were meant to be there to accept the delivery and to get your lady friend in the kitchens to do the job I've paid you both to do. But where were you, Simmons? Because I can tell you where you weren't. You weren't at your post. One would imagine you purposely changed places with Arell. One would imagine you're trying to back out of our deal."

Arell knew he needed to pay attention. He knew he needed to hear and commit every word to memory. But the shock of discovering he was dead and then of discovering he was not dead had proved so great that finding focus came with difficulty. What did it mean that he was spelled? What spell could induce a man to look dead enough for him to be buried? And why could he walk about like a spirit or ghost if he was not dead?

"I don't like the insinuations you're making, Norton. I'm not backing out of our deal. The change of guard wasn't my doing and not something I had any choice in obeying. You know Captain Wilton changed my orders. If I hadn't obeyed, I would've been dismissed immediately for the night, and it would've cast suspicion on me. And your little spell over Arell has already brought enough suspicion to the garrison. This whole plan has gone to sewage."

Norton jumped up from his chair and shoved Simmons against the wall. "And whose fault is that? Who failed to be where he was to be? And even now, you're in my rooms—a place no member of the guard has any reason to ever be. If anyone saw you come to me, what kind of suspicion would befall you then—especially once the royal family is dead? Take care with your insults, boy! I made a man look dead enough to lock away into a crypt and to blast the bereavement bells for all to hear. Think what I wouldn't hesitate to do to you if you cross me."

To Simmons's credit, he didn't look away from Norton's piercing stare. "It's been a week, Norton. If Arell wasn't dead when they put him in that crypt, after a week of no food or water, he's dead now. So you arguing that he isn't dead is dead wrong."

"I told you, he was spelled."

"So what? He just sleeps for the rest of eternity? What spell can condemn a man like that?"

"There's a time limit. There's a time limit on everything. As the moon becomes brighter, he will become dimmer. When the moon phases full, he'll expire, unless moonlight actually touches the body—which it won't with him locked away under stone. But we're not talking about him anymore. He sealed his fate the moment he drew a sword on me. There are other lives in question. And they also have an expiration date. If the family is not dead by feast day, then the kingdom of Vestat will withdraw their offer, as we will have proven ourselves men who cannot get important work done. If we fail, you will never be captain of the guard because Arell's fate will be very similar to your own, do you understand?"

"Perfectly. So the feast for the princess's birthday?"

"Yes." Norton handed Simmons a packet—the same one he'd handed off to Arell that night on the wall. "Take this with you and leave. And I don't care what circuitous route you must take or who you must kill to keep from being seen leaving my quarters."

Arell lunged for the packet, trying to hinder Simmons in any way from carrying out such a horrible deed.

He fell through the men and their hands joined by the packet of poison. He fell hard and felt as though he'd never stop falling. When the sensation of flipping head over feet came to a stop, he found himself in the throne room. It was late at night, and the room was empty. He must have ended up there in his desperate need to save the royal family. How could anyone discuss murder so casually, especially when several of the targets were children? They were going to kill the princess on her eighth birthday. What monsters could do such a thing?

But they wouldn't do such a thing.

Arell would stop them. He had to.

He found himself tugged back to the crypt. The waxing moon shone light through the stained glass windows, casting a light that unsettled Arell. He wasn't done, but he may as well have been. No one could see him. No one could hear him. And it seemed he had no power over anything in the physical world.

His body was imprisoned behind the stone that bore his name. And his spirit might as well have been imprisoned along with it for all the ability he had to influence the world around him. What good was it to know of the pending slaughter of a good and loving king when no one could hear him confess such knowledge?

But someone *could* hear him.

The tugging and falling sensation didn't stop for a long time. And when it did, he was in the feed shed on a farm on the west ridge of Tenali.

Five

Grace

GRACE DIDN'T HEAR THE ghost again when she awoke the day after he'd become so angry and abruptly left her. She pressed her sister, but Annabelle hadn't seen or heard from the ghost either. She checked the feed shed that morning, but it was quiet and warm with the rising sun. She walked through the house and searched for any unusually cold pockets of air, but the air in the house remained warm and cozy. Maybe the ghost had finally accepted his fate and gone on to whatever afterlife awaited him.

He didn't show up the next day either.

Grace couldn't say why that disappointed her. Perhaps it was because his was the first male conversation she'd received in the last several years that wasn't from either a relative or an employer. And in spite of his frigid temper, he'd been nice.

"My life has truly taken a pathetic turn if I'm daydreaming about a dead man that I've not even seen," she said to the feed shed after checking it a third time.

She turned to leave and walked straight into a blast of urgent, icy air.

"I need you!"

It was him. Her ghost had come back to her. "What's wrong?" She felt foolish for such a question immediately after voicing it. *What was wrong?* As if a man being dead wasn't enough to be considered wrong?

"I'm not dead!" he cried out.

Or a man in denial about being dead wasn't enough to be considered wrong. She shook her head. "You poor, dear man. I can see why you don't want to believe this about yourself, but—"

"I'm not! I've been cursed and put in a crypt, but I'm not dead. I'm not. But I will be if you don't help me."

"I don't understand," Grace said and then looked harder in his direction. Had she seen something? A glint of an outline shifted in and out of her view. As he spoke, his profile shimmered like water in the sunlight. She could see him in a sense and was not disappointed by the little she saw. He had a strong profile. She imagined from the little she saw that he was handsome.

"A lot has happened since yesterday," he said.

"You mean since two days ago."

"Two days? So much time lost already. The king's advisor had bargained with one of the other members of the guard to poison the royal family. He's cursed me to appear as one who is dead. They placed me in a crypt, and the bells of bereavement are ringing, and the black flags are waving. But they will be ringing and waving for the entire royal family if we don't arrive back at the palace in five days. Please go fetch your brother. I'll need him to accompany me to the king's palace. Time is of the very essence, so we must go immediately!" He moved toward the barn, where the only horse the little farm owned was stabled.

Grace didn't follow. When his silvery silhouette turned back, she gave him a look that surely indicated she didn't think he was in his right mind. She hated to be rude, but . . . "First, my brother is no longer with us. He's learning his trade in another city. So if you want help, you'll have to ask me, and you'd better do it nicely if you want my help since you've insulted me by assuming my brother is the only one who is capable of being useful. And second, what kind of access would a guard have to poison the family? That doesn't make sense."

A wisp of a smile formed. "You see? I wondered that very thing. Only it took me longer to get there. I'm not myself at the moment. That's why I need you. You and, apparently, not your brother at all. I need someone to help untangle my thoughts. The guard in question is in league with one of the cooks. I need someone—you—to go with me to the palace and revive my body so I can warn the family before it's too late. We must leave at once."

He turned to go again, but when she wasn't following a second time, he stopped and said, "I know it's a lot to ask, to have you leave your home and family. But the duration of this journey will be short, and lives are at stake, Miss . . ."

"Blackstone. Grace Blackstone. Don't you find it odd that you want me to travel all the way into Tenali, and yet you didn't know my name?"

"I know it now, Miss Blackstone."

"Call me Grace. If I'm to travel all that way with you, we should be able to use our birth names, should we not?"

Her ghost lit up, his outline shining and his presence slightly warmer. "Then you'll go?"

"You did say lives were on the line. I'm not the sort of woman to turn my back on real need."

It was exactly for that reason that she'd never left the boundaries of her village. She didn't leave because her mother needed her. Her sister needed her. And Grace had never been able to turn away that need.

But now, she'd spent several days listening to her brother

telling her of the things outside their village, considering that she might never be able to make a match and have children of her own to teach, which would leave her teaching the village children for a bit of coin for the rest of her life. She would never have a life that belonged to her—except this small part. She would go and find her ghost's body and help him, if she could. She would do it because even when she returned home again, the adventure of what she'd done would live on in her memory, free to revisit whenever she wished. The bills were paid. The garden was bursting with fruits and vegetables. Her mother could handle things for a few days.

"I have to set my family to rights before I leave, but yes, I will help you Mr. Ghost."

"Mr. Ghost?"

"I apologize. I do not remember your name."

"My name is Arell Kiran." His pale silhouette bowed. "You may call me Arell."

She smiled at the thrill of excitement that filled her along with a new sense of purpose. She sent Annabelle with a message for the farmer's son who lived next door, who in turn must take the message straightaway to the village in the morning and put it in the hands of the magistrate so the man would know Grace wouldn't be available to teach his children for a while. The message further explained that she'd send word when lessons would be available again.

When Annabelle left to deliver the message, Grace explained to her mother that she needed to take a brief journey but would be back as soon as she could be. There was much arguing and questioning, but Grace shared little of the information the ghost had given her. Her mother only relented when Grace declared she needed a break. A minute to herself to think.

"Don't you feel you owe me that, Mama? Don't I deserve a few days in light of the many years I have given you?"

No argument could be given in response to Grace's question, because her mother did owe her.

Annabelle had returned in the meantime and followed Grace into her room after she'd made her mother promise to not neglect the garden or her sister, though Annabelle often insisted she could take care of herself.

"But you haven't said where you're going!" Annabelle complained as Grace hurried to pack a bag with things she would need for the journey. The ghost might not require food or bedding, but she surely would.

"There are people who are unwell. I'm going to help them."

"That doesn't tell me anything!" Annabelle swept back the stray strands of blonde hair from her face and then propped her fists on her hips.

"Are you not ready yet?" The ghost, Arell, was suddenly in her room, dropping the temperature enough that Annabelle shivered.

She looked hard in the direction of the cold and gasped. "It's the ghost! You're going with the ghost!" Her pale eyebrows furrowed together. "Why are you going with the ghost, and where are you going?"

"She's a clever child," Arell said.

"She is clever, too clever sometimes."

"Did the ghost just call me clever?" Annabelle looked pleased.

"Can you not hear him?" Grace asked. When her baby sister shook her head, Grace nodded. "Well, prove the ghost right, and be clever by being a good girl while I'm gone. Mind your chores and listen to Mama."

"Is the child not afraid of me?" Arell asked.

"She's excited, not afraid."

"Did he call me a scaredy baby?" Annabelle asked.

"No, dearest. No one would ever say anything like that about you. I'm taking the ghost home so he can find peace. And don't tell Mama about the ghost. She'd never understand. Promise?"

Annabelle gave a solemn nod.

Grace cinched up her bag of belongings and kissed her mother and sister farewell. She tried not to cringe on the outside along with the twinge of guilt on the inside. She shouldn't leave them. It wasn't responsible. But was letting a ghost stay a ghost responsible? Was letting the royal family die without warning anyone responsible?

She prepared her horse and tied her bags of provisions to the saddle. She'd brought a bedroll and enough food to hopefully not need to dip into her coin purse. Being willing to help didn't mean she was willing to let her family go hungry come winter.

She looked toward the source of iced air at the barn door. Her traveling companion made her feel as though winter had already come. *I shouldn't be doing this,* she thought. What kind of woman leaves her family to go off and do the bidding of a stranger? But what kind of woman would she be if she stayed?

She pulled herself up into the saddle. "So how does this work?" she asked.

"Work?"

"You're far too cold to be on the back of my horse. You'll freeze her where she stands."

He paused, considering. "I'd suggest I meet you at our destinations, but a woman shouldn't be traveling alone. Can you not blanket the horse?"

"And what of me? I will also freeze if you ride behind me. Besides, no one can see you. It's the same as me traveling alone." Her horse sidestepped and pawed at the ground, anxious to be moving now that she had a rider. "Easy, Maisy. Easy, girl." She might have been talking to herself as well as the horse for all the worry she felt bubbling and brewing in her belly.

"And what do I do if you're injured or harmed along the way? How would I know how to find you if I leave you?"

"How did you know to find me the first and second time we've crossed paths?"

He didn't answer, likely because he didn't know. Grace tsked, feeling as anxious as Maisy to be on their way. She felt if she stayed too much longer, then she might change her mind altogether. "Fine." She slid off Maisy and hurried to the house where she gathered up the three quilts from the trunk at the foot of her bed.

She used two of the quilts to cover the horse and then wrapped the third over herself. She felt the weight of his cold settle in behind her—not a physical weight, nothing that would actually add to Maisy's burden, but the tangible cold had an emotional weight. She hated to admit how much safer she felt knowing he'd not left her to travel alone.

She released a self-deprecating breath. Safer? Traveling with a ghost?

"I'm truly not dead," he said as if he heard her thoughts.

Maisy hardly seemed to notice the cold as she nickered and stamped her impatience to leave.

"Of course not." With no more excuses, Grace clucked her tongue and coaxed the mare forward.

Once they were out past the surrounding villages and on the first roads leading to Tenali, Grace slowed Maisy's gait to an easier walk. She needed to save the animal's strength so they didn't kill the poor thing.

"It's brave of you to be willing to help me. Honestly, it's brave of you to have not run screaming when I first entered your room."

She laughed. "I did entertain that idea for a brief moment, but that would have required me to leave my blankets. As cold as you'd made my room, there was no way I had any intention of leaving the little warmth left to me."

He laughed as well, the sound silvery and warm. She got the feeling laughing wasn't something he did very often.

He fell silent immediately after, which only deepened her belief that he'd lived a rather solemn existence. "I'm sorry about ever entering your room. I was standing outside the door of your home and was about to knock. My only thought was to ask for help, and suddenly there I was with you."

"Well, you went to the right place in my household if it was help you were after. My mother happens to be afraid of the dark, and my sister, while not afraid of the dark and not really afraid of anything else either, is still just a small child."

"What of your brother? Was he not there that night?"

Grace felt the niggle of resentment that came when she thought of her brother and shoved it away. "He was home then, but just to visit. He had to move out a while back to learn his trade. Right now, the only person he helps is himself."

She hadn't meant to say the last out loud.

"You're angry with him."

Grace twisted in the saddle to try to meet the ghost's eye, though she couldn't see more than a sliver of his shape. "No! I'm not angry. He should have left years ago to make his own way."

She didn't add that *she* should've left years ago to make her own way as well. It didn't matter.

"What of your father?"

Grace pressed her tongue against her teeth as she formed the words in her mind before letting them escape her mouth. She didn't want to disparage her family. She loved them, after all. "He went on a hunting trip and didn't return. He was the sort of man to jump into the fray of any situation—even dangerous ones, I suppose. The townsfolk say he was filled with life, that he gobbled up every opportunity put in his way during the course of a day. Exuberant and energizing, they called him."

When Arell didn't answer, Grace thought she must have done a good job at hiding how she felt about her father's exuberance.

"I always imagined that if I had a wife and child, I'd be less likely to jump into any so-called fray. I mean no disrespect to your father, but even now, with my own life, I'm cautious—at least as much as a member of the royal guard is able. When other people depend on you, it's more responsible to think before jumping."

Grace wanted to reply, to either defend her father or to agree completely. Since she was torn as to which she wanted most, she said nothing at all.

"But truly, I mean no disrespect."

"No. It's fine for a person to say their mind. I'm the one who meant no disrespect. I love my family. The burden of being the eldest daughter falls to me, which means it's my brother who must learn his trade for our survival. And I must stay in the home for the same reason. Any bitterness that may come from that is a failing of mine, not of theirs."

They crossed the bridge over the river, and Grace felt as though the universe played a cruel joke on her. "This bridge, for example," she said. "I've never crossed it before. I'm now officially farther than I've ever been from my front door. And I've always wanted to travel to Blosen to see the glass blowers. I've heard there is no sight on earth like it. We'll be traveling through the heart of that city. The irony is that I'll still not see the majesty of their arts."

"I'm sorry," Arell said, making her feel even worse. She

didn't mean to complain or be bitter. She didn't mean to say any of it out loud as she had, but her feelings felt scoured like a pot drying on the sideboard.

She laughed again and rolled her eyes at herself for being such wretched company. "Apologies? No. That will not do. For a man to apologize because he asks that his life and the lives of an entire family be put before some silly woman's desire to see the whimsical will not do at all. No. *I* am sorry. Your situation is in every way horrible. And I will do my best to put it to rights."

She was sure she'd merely imagined it, but it felt as though his arm had come around her and squeezed ever so slightly. But that couldn't have happened because she would have felt the cold of his touch, and she felt only warmth.

They shifted among a walk, a trot, and a canter to protect the horse from wearing down while continuing forward. They followed the road alongside the river, which meant that they remained with a steady supply of water while they traveled. Arell assured her they would maintain their water supply because they would be following one of the tributaries to the river all the way to the palace. It was a trade route that was well enough traveled to keep them on good road.

And they talked.

About everything.

About the royal family, about the king and how he worked hard to be fair to everyone, about the queen and how she spent more time playing with her children than throwing parties, which some courtiers liked and others didn't. They talked about Arell's family and how his mother had died in childbirth and his father had been a soldier. Arell had grown up in the guard house and could hold a sword before he'd lost his first baby tooth. When his father became sick and followed Arell's mother in death, the other soldiers had kept Arell, figuring the boy was one of their own.

"They're my family, you see," Arell said once they were camped in a clearing off the road well enough to keep them from becoming interesting to anyone of the bandit variety who might be passing by. "That's why this business of Simmons betraying them is so hard for me to understand. Sure, Simmons is newer than most of the men within our ranks, but he's one of us. How could he do such a thing?"

Grace shrugged from where she was seated on her bedroll. The night was warm enough to not need a fire as long as Arell stayed a short distance away and Grace managed to stay bundled. Arell had said lighting a fire might draw attention. He worried because his limited appearance would make it look like Grace traveled alone. "Who can say why some people make choices that hurt others and ultimately themselves? What if they would stop only long enough to consider the consequences of their actions?"

"I'm sorry," Arell said. "I've done all the talking, and we've been gone the better part of a full day."

"Don't apologize. It's interesting to talk to someone when the conversation isn't with parents and has nothing to do with their children and how well those children are learning their letters or when it isn't with older ladies from town and has nothing to do with how my mother is faring or when it isn't with younger ladies in town and has nothing to do with when my brother might return or if he might be interested in the young lady in question."

Arell laughed. And as it had so often throughout the day, the sound warmed her.

"So your brother is a catch, is he?"

"To many, it would seem he is. Our family is far from wealthy, but my brother is a handsome one—handsome enough to make him hard to ignore."

"Must run in your family."

Grace felt heat flash up her neck. He thought her handsome? "Excuse me?"

Arell stammered before saying, "He likely takes after one of your parents? Your father, maybe? I didn't see your mother, but often young men favor their fathers in looks."

Her cheeks burned even hotter at that. So, he hadn't meant the compliment to her. She felt foolish for thinking such a thing and grateful to have no campfire to give away her blush. The conversation, which had been energetic and seemed incapable of stopping, finally wilted into the darkness between them.

Grace yawned, though she felt too invigorated by her circumstances to be tired, and explained they should try to get some sleep. "That is, if you do sleep. Do ghosts sleep?"

"I'm not dead," he reminded her.

"No. I know, but you're not here either." She shook her head and felt as though she might never say another intelligent thing again. "Anyway, I need to sleep. Goodnight, Arell."

"Goodnight, Grace."

She slid into her bedroll and looked in the direction of her ghost. He seemed brighter, more visible in the moonlight. She snapped her eyes shut when she realized she considered him handsome even if he didn't return that feeling. *Don't be a fool,* she thought. *Ghosts are not handsome.*

But no matter what she told herself, she knew that her ghost was, in fact, very handsome. And her feelings regarding that fact had little to do with his looks.

Arell

ARELL WATCHED GRACE AS she slept—or pretended to sleep. He'd embarrassed her by insinuating that she might be attractive, but he couldn't help what she was. He shouldn't be noticing how she looked, the way her every movement enchanted him.

She managed her horse well, an area in which few enough women in his acquaintance had any skill. She was a considerate master of the animal. Her horse had repaid the kind consideration with miles. They'd made it farther than he'd hoped. And yet there was still so much land to cover. So much was at stake if they failed to reach their destination in time.

So why was he wasting time watching the way her dark hair fell over her pale cheeks? Why was he wishing he could brush that hair out of her face so that he could see the curve of her jaw? Why was he wishing she would open those eyes that looked like pools of cool blue water?

Not that he needed anything cool. He was cold enough. But with her nearby, even the cold felt bearable.

He'd told her that he'd ended up in her room when he'd tried to knock on the front door for help. What he didn't tell her was that he'd remembered being in the dark, feeling the cold of his crypt all around him. He remembered feeling a desperate need to find help at that moment. The next thing he knew, he was at her farm. It was as if the universe knew she would help, that it equated such service with her.

And why not? What an incredible person she was to be willing to agree to this journey, even to be willing to believe his outlandish tales. Not one woman had ever caught his eye or his interest so intensely in all his life before now. But not one woman had ever been as full of service, compassion, and intelligence as this one woman.

He felt more anxious than ever to be restored to his own body, to be able to actually touch her cheek, to hold her warmth close to him, to taste her perfect, rosy lips—*Stop it!* But his mind didn't stop thinking of her, not even when he turned away and looked up at the sky and the ever growing moon. *Not enough time,* he thought. *We don't have enough time.* Not enough time to spare his life and save the royal family. Not enough time to spend with this woman who'd undone him and bewitched him even more deeply than Norton. Norton's bewitching was the work of a spell. But the feelings this woman brought out in Arell were greater than any magic.

He watched her the whole night as the moon lit up and shadowed different parts of her face as it swept across the sky. Her beauty, fearlessness, and strength awed him. He'd known several women who'd lost fathers and mothers and had the duties of eldest daughter. He'd not known of one who stayed in the family home and worked to keep the family secure. They'd all married and moved on. Sure, they'd drop occasional coins and small services to their family, but did he know of any who assumed the role of mistress over the home the way Grace had done?

He couldn't think of any.

He inched closer to her throughout the night, wanting to see her more clearly, wanting to memorize her in every detail, from the small mole on her earlobe to the crease just over her brow, there as if she even slept with great concentration. He realized he'd crept too close only when her body shivered and her breath exited her slightly parted lips in a white puff of frosted air. He drew back, but the damage was already done. She stirred and opened her eyes.

"The sun's coming up!" She leaped from her bedroll and hurried to tie it up and get her provisions back onto the saddle. "Why didn't you wake me?"

Arell blinked at her and didn't answer. What could he say? The truth of him not waking her because she was so achingly beautiful and he didn't want to stop looking at her made him sound like the worst sort of fool.

Luckily, her panic to be moving overrode her need for an answer. They were on the horse and trotting away within moments.

Grace ate hard bread and nuts and dried berries from a pouch hanging from the saddle so they didn't have to delay a moment stopping for her breakfast. Arell wanted to allow her to do most of the talking since he'd dominated the conversation the day before. He wanted to show her he was not so shallow as to think her thoughts unimportant.

But was he shallow? He'd been appalled at the disrepair of the farm when he'd seen it the first time, but when he'd gone back, he saw only her. Yes, he'd asked for her brother's help, but it was her face that had filled his mind when he knew he needed help to wake him from the spell placed on him.

Her.

She was something special. Something different. Something worthy and of worth all at the same time.

She did talk to him, telling him of herbs she planted to help those who were sick. Laughing when a woman in Daven had called her a witch because she'd fed another old woman a broth she'd made that had cured the old woman from shaking and coughing. "I'd imagine Mistress Ryern was only angry because she wanted her mother-in-law to die so that she might lay claim to the lovely silver serving set."

Grace seemed to laugh over every wrong done to her. She found humor in the worst of her situations. With each new story she told him, he felt as if she tied a cord around his heart and pulled him toward her.

In the short time Arell had known her, he'd come to admire her.

Later that day, when they came across several riders coming from the other direction, Arell had panicked. No one could see him. By all appearances, she was a woman traveling the roads alone. The men formed a line with their horses across the path to keep her from getting around them, but she reined in her horse and kept control.

She didn't panic and bolt off into the woods, which any sane woman might have done but which would have led to a chase. A person willing to run is a person who likely has something worth stealing. Grace held her ground, demanded that they let her pass, and told the lot of them that their mothers should be scolded for raising such ill-behaved boys. It was when she brought their mothers into it that the men finally decided to let her go.

Once they were well clear of the men, she pulled the horse to a stop in a grove of trees off the road where they were out of sight and allowed herself to drag in great gasping breaths.

"I can't believe you did that!" Arell said.

"I can't believe we're alive!" she responded before twisting in the saddle to look at him. "Well, one of us is alive anyway."

"I already told you—"

"I know. I know. I'm just teasing, trying to calm my heart from thumping right out of my chest and onto the dirt."

Understanding her reasoning, he let the joke pass. "You held yourself more firmly than any man I've seen in battle. I'm impressed."

"Don't be too impressed. I feel like fainting here and now."

But she didn't faint. She kept her seat, and after only a moment longer, she clucked her tongue and continued.

He watched her the second night as she slept as well and the third. By evening of the fourth night, they'd come to the outskirts of the king's city. He wanted to urge them farther, but the hour was late, and this close to the city, they were far more likely to run into trouble. He watched as she set up her camp and felt guilty that he couldn't physically handle anything enough to help her. He could move himself to various locations in the physical world but could not act upon the physical world. He'd become as useless as the ghost she accused him of being.

"Where did you get these quilts?" he asked once she was settled. "They're quite lovely."

Her hands stilled on the branch she'd been using to trace shapes in the dirt. "I made them when I was younger, in anticipation of starting my own family. I don't know why I keep them locked away in the trunk where they never receive any use. To save them means they're still meant for their original purpose, and they're not any longer." The crease in her brow deepened.

"Why not?"

"I'm too old to marry. Any of the men my own age in my town are already married and living their lives. Any older men looking for a wife are really looking to manage the affairs left to them by a deceased spouse. I'd be stepping into someone else's shoes, and I'm not interested in an arrangement where I'd be a live-in governess rather than a companion."

He didn't understand why it needled him to think of her marrying anyone at all, but he forced himself to say, "There are other towns than your own."

"We've already established that I've never before left Daven."

"But you have now," he said, not sure why he pressed forward with the conversation.

"True. I'll just stop by one of the shops and pick me up a husband on the way out of town when we're done saving your life."

He didn't respond, because what could he say? Tell her she need not bother with a shop? He was being absurd.

"You're brighter tonight," she said after a moment.

"Brighter?"

"More defined. I can see you. It's like you're made from moonlight, but I can see you." She shook her head. "We should sleep. Tomorrow, we'll put you back in your body."

He mumbled an agreement as she burrowed into her bedding and fell asleep. She didn't pretend to be sleeping, which meant she had to be truly exhausted. He felt sorry for his part in her exhaustion but not sorry to have enlisted her help, not sorry to have her with him. He watched her the entire night, watched and thought that if he died on this adventure, he wanted the last thing he saw to be her.

Grace

GETTING INTO TOWN WAS not as complicated as Grace had feared. With her ghost looking more like a liquid man than nothing at all, she was certain someone would see them and have her hanged for witchcraft, but they left early and were on the roads before most people had left their beds. In no time at all, they were at the mausoleum. She slid off her horse and tied it up. Inside the mausoleum, the ghost led her to the stone covering his crypt.

"So what do I do?" she asked him.

"Remove the stone."

She arched a brow at him. Was he joking? What kind of strength did he think she had? "Is that really the whole of your plan?" With a grunt, she wandered the building and the surrounding outbuildings until she found a shed with tools. She returned with a sturdy pry bar.

It took some effort, and she sweat profusely, but she managed to get the capstone off. With a breath for courage, she peered inside. "Well?" she said.

"Well what?"

"Get back inside your body so you can go warn the king."

He tried and failed.

"You certainly look dead," she said, trying not to shiver

at the task set before her. She tugged the body, which was quite heavy, out of the crypt into daylight. She hoped the sunshine would do him some good. That didn't work either. "At least you don't smell bad."

"I'm not dead."

She looked from the spirit to the body, both perfect in form. He was a handsome man, and now that she knew him, she really wanted him to live. "You look dead. But let's see what we can do to fix this. Think of what the man who did this to you said. Was there anything?"

"He called it a moonlight spell. He said, 'When the moon phases full, he'll expire, unless moonlight actually touches the body.' Do we wait until moonrise?"

"It's worth hoping for. I don't know what else we can do. I'm no magician."

"But moonrise is too late. Tonight is the night. The royal family could die while we wait."

"No. *We* won't wait. I might not be a magician, but I've been cooking for my family for years. I know my way around a kitchen. You stay and do what you have to do to be yourself again. I'll stop dinner."

Grace bent over his body and kissed his cold forehead. "For luck!" she called as she leaped to her feet and bounded off to the palace. She felt the ice of him in front of her, forcing her to a halt.

"You don't just kiss a man and run off like that," he said.

She felt the heat on her cheeks. "It was for luck." What had she been thinking? If he survived the night, she'd have to face him, and what would she have to say for herself? "And you shouldn't be here scolding me. You should be keeping watch over your body. You don't want to miss the chance to fix your situation."

"I'm not here to scold you. I'm here because you don't

know where the kitchens are. And I'd rather miss my own chances than take chances with the lives of others. I'll help you get in the palace."

He led her to seldom-used doors and coached her on what to say to anyone she might run into. He had to hide himself several times because he'd become more substantial as the evening deepened into night. By the time she found the kitchens, he looked solid enough to pass for a regular breathing man.

"Look at you," she said, aching to reach out to him, to offer comfort, to drag him back to his body so he didn't die. "You finally look whole." She touched his shoulder, but her hand felt as though she'd doused it in ice water. "It's enough," she said, forming an idea. "The king knows you, doesn't he? He trusts you?"

He understood immediately. "Yes, of course! I can go to him, but you'll need to open the doors. I still can't grasp anything."

Together, they stormed the dining hall where the family waited for the princess's birthday dinner.

A man jumped to his feet and said, "What mischief is this? Depart here, spirit!"

"He's not a spirit!" Grace cried out, assuming the man was Norton. "But how dare you cast a spell on him and then bury him for dead just so you could poison the royal family's dinner tonight!"

"What is this?" A man at the head of the table stood, his robes declaring his position as king. "Arell, is it really you?"

"Yes, sire." Arell bowed low to the king. Grace knew she should too, but she didn't want to take her eyes off of the betrayer in case he tried to run. "I came here tonight with the aid of this woman—Grace of Daven—to warn you that Norton is conspiring against you and your family. And he has done it with the help of Simmons and Simmons's lady friend who works the kitchens. They mean to poison you and your family. I had to warn you. You can verify my word by checking the food. It's poisoned, sire."

The king signaled other guards in the dining hall. Some of those men took hold of Norton while others went off to find Simmons and the kitchen girl.

"There will be an investigation." The king approached Arell. "Thank you. I'm glad you're alive and glad for the service you've rendered this night." The king placed a hand on Arell's shoulder and gasped as his hand went straight through.

Norton laughed. "You're not here! Which means," he looked to the tall windows and the rising moon coming up over the hills, "you're too late to save yourself. You may have caught me, but you caught yourself as well. A little self-preservation would have served you well."

"Shut up!" spat the king. "Get him out of my sight!" The guards dragged Norton away, but as they did, Grace cried out.

Arell had disappeared.

Norton's laughter rang through the stone halls.

Arell

GRACE'S CRY FILLED ARELL'S senses and cut off in abrupt silence. He saw nothing but the depths of black that went forever. Was this what death felt like? A painful, fiery, pricking that flowed from his feet to his fingers? He hadn't even told Grace thank you and goodbye. He hadn't told her how extraordinary she was.

The light exploded in his eyes. And he realized the light was the moon. He was on his back, in his body where he'd left it behind the mausoleum.

Am I alive?

He twitched his finger. That seemed to work. He wriggled his toes. Doing both of those things made his nerves prick and tingle with agony as the blood flowed to his extremities again.

"I'm alive!" His hoarse voice did little to magnify the awe he felt in that one statement. He tried to sit up, but the pain in his head forced him back down again.

And they'd done it! They'd really done it! They'd saved the king and the queen and the little ones. They'd saved him too. Tears leaked from his eyes even as he fell asleep, exhausted by all his body had been through.

When Arell woke again, he was in his room in the guard

house. His eyelids scratched open over his eyes. "Grace?" he asked for her before anything, before the water his throat so achingly required.

"I'm here."

"Course she's here. Fool woman hasn't left your side since we brought her to you. A week it's been, as you've come in and out of consciousness. And she's been here the whole time. She's as underfoot as the queen's awful dog."

Arell recognized the apothecary's voice. A gentle hand gripped his own as the bedsprings sagged under the weight of her warm body. He tightened his fingers around hers. "A whole week?"

"How could I leave until I knew for myself that you'd live? Are you all right?" she asked.

"I'm all right because you stayed. You could've gone back to your life, but you stayed."

"My family is well. The king sent a servant to Daven to help with my family when I refused to leave."

He brought her hand to his parched lips and kissed her soft skin. "I think you should not stop in any shops to find a husband when you return home. I think you should stay a while longer and see if you've already found one."

Grace gasped. The apothecary did as well.

Arell laughed.

Healing from his ordeal took several months. Grace stayed by his side reading to him things she found interesting and talking with him about everything. And when he offered a bride price to her mother that more than took care of Grace's family and Grace accepted him, he knew he could not find any greater happiness.

As a surprise to his newly betrothed, he decided to return

to Daven to see her family. They could bring her family back with them to the palace for a wedding fit for a member of the king's personal guard.

But first, Arell stopped on the outskirts of the town just across the bridge on the other side of the river from Daven. He wrapped a blindfold around Grace's eyes, hoping she didn't recognize where they were yet. "What is all this?" she asked, smiling.

"Something you deserve." He trotted the horse the rest of the way into town where he helped her down, blindfold and all, and walked her to the artisan's shop. He waited until the right moment and removed the blindfold.

"The glassblowers!" she breathed. She clapped her hands as she watched them spin the blue and green blobs into bottles. He smiled as he watched her. When she turned and looked up, she tilted her head toward his face. "I love you, my moonlit ghost," she said.

"And I love you." He met her mouth with his own and, for a moment, lost the sense of himself all over again as he held her warmth to him. But losing himself in everything Grace was, he realized he didn't want to be found.

Julie Wright started her first book when she was fifteen. She's written over a dozen books since then, is a Whitney Award winner, and feels she's finally getting the hang of this writing gig. She enjoys speaking to writing groups, youth groups, and schools. She loves reading, eating, writing, hiking, playing on the beach with her kids, and snuggling with her husband to watch movies. Julie's favorite thing to do is watch her husband make dinner. She hates mayonnaise but has a healthy respect for ice cream.

Visit Julie's website: www.juliewright.com
Twitter: @scatteredjules

The Truest Treasure

by Annette Lyon

One

RITVA, THE VILLAGE HEALER, finished her examination and turned from the bed, where Saara's sister lay sick and weak, getting worse all the time. Saara tried to read the healer's face, which age had lined so deeply that not a knitting needle's width existed without a furrow of some kind. The old woman's downturned mouth and pitying eyes gave no solace. "I am sorry," Ritva began. "But—"

"No," Saara cut in. "There must be something you can do."

Ever patient, the healer reached out and took her hands and cradled them in her own, as if Saara were her own grandchild. Saara looked at their hands: Ritva's nearly translucent, wrinkled skin with age spots, her hands always cool to the touch, and Saara's own—young and plump, pink and warm.

Saara's gaze slid to the shape of her little sister, who lay in fitful sleep, moaning and moving restlessly. *Oh, what I would give to know that Fia will one day have hands as old as those that hold mine now.*

The old woman shook her head sadly. Saara's middle tightened. She didn't pull her hands away; in some measure, having hers inside Ritva's was a comfort, as if the gods knew that Saara had been without a mother's touch and nurture for too long, and this was a sign that the gods were mindful of her, showing her in this small way that she hadn't been forgotten. Perhaps from Tuonela, land of the dead, her mother had sent Ritva to give this small act of kindness.

Yet if the gods could be so merciful as to send this drop of comfort to Saara, why wouldn't they heal Fia?

"What has made her sick?" Saara asked. "Isn't there anything we can do?"

Ritva patted one of Saara's hands and gave a tiny smile. "Come. Sit with me, and I'll tell you what I think is happening. My aching bones need a rest." She turned and half shuffled to the other side of the small cabin where Saara and Fia had lived their whole lives—now alone, orphaned since their mother's death.

Neither sister remembered much about their father. Two years Fia's senior, Saara remembered a bit more, but even her memories were little more than blurred images and fleeting wisps of emotion from when she was small—the feel of Father's rough brown beard against her cheek when he hugged her, the sound of pride in his voice when she caught her first fish, the image of his well-practiced hands showing her how to stack wood when building different kinds of fires. She still knew how to create a hot, fast-burning fire, a low-burning but long-lasting fire, and one that created almost no smoke—helpful if one needed to hide, though Saara never knew whom one would need to hide from. Animals, including the great bear, could find people with or without smoke, so her father had to mean hiding from people.

Saara didn't know precisely how their father had died, only that it had happened on a hunting trip in autumn, when he left to seek meat for their winter stores. She'd always wondered if a bear or wolf had caught him before he could fell it. But perhaps a human had hunted him. She'd never considered that option until this moment, as she walked from the bed she shared with Fia to the small rectangular table.

Out of respect for the elderly healer, Saara waited for Ritva to sit before she did. The elderly woman moved slowly and grunted with effort as she lowered herself to the wooden chair, rough-cut and made by the hands of Saara's father. Goodness, she hadn't thought of him in ages, and suddenly she couldn't get him out of her mind.

Folding her hands on the table, Ritva began. "As I'm sure you have guessed, Fia's condition is quite serious."

"Yes," Saara said, eager to hear more and sensing that asking questions would only slow down the flow of information. She held her breath, waiting to learn her sister's fate.

"Her fever hasn't broken in three weeks," Ritva said. "That alone is worrisome enough."

"Do you know what caused the fever?" Saara pressed.

"Not precisely. A week ago when I visited, I thought it was due to bad air or water, but . . . not anymore."

Saara sat up straighter, needing to know more at once, as if a sharp needle had pricked her between the shoulder blades. "*Now* what do you think the cause of the fever is?"

"I sense that Fia is very sad," the healer said, then shook her head. "No, what she is experiencing goes beyond sadness. I sense a deep well of sorrow pulling her down. She feels as though she's living in a dark cave in the middle of winter."

"A dark cave," Saara repeated. Fia felt this despite long summer days that stretched well into the night and despite the summer solstice about to occur—a night without darkness, when the sun circled the horizon but never dipped below it. Instinctively, Saara glanced out the window, as if she could spot the source of her sister's sadness.

Ritva took a deep breath and let it out with a sigh. "The

causes of the fever could be many things. Fia could have angered a *haltija*, who poisoned her food, or perhaps Ajatar walked a forest path and your sister went the same way later."

"Oh, please, not that," Saara said. *Haltijas* were spirits known to take care of certain areas, and they could play tricks on mortals who upset them. That would be bad enough. But the healer was suggesting that the evil goddess Ajatar might have entered their lives—the goddess who left disease and pestilence in her wake. If Fia had unwittingly walked the same path that Ajatar recently had, then yes, she would have fallen gravely ill.

"Well, it wasn't Mielikki," the healer said grimly, referring to the goddess of the forest, who was often prayed to by travelers and hunters before they left on their journeys.

"No, I suppose not. But it's not Ajatar, is it?" Saara said.

The kinds of diseases the evil goddess of the forest could spread were fast, painful, and quickly fatal. Though Fia's condition worsened by the hour, she'd been sick for weeks.

"There is another explanation," Ritva said, but she didn't seem happy about it. Why did she look so glum? Anything would be better than contracting a disease from Ajatar, wouldn't it? The healer pressed her lips together for a moment as if mustering the courage to speak her mind. Every second felt like a day as Saara waited. "Can you think of anything that might have greatly upset Fia? Something that might have broken her tender heart?"

Saara thought back. Fia had cried herself to sleep the night before she fell ill, but Saara hadn't considered her sister's tears to be related to her illness. "The day before the fever, Hannu rejected her and began courting Elsa instead. That can't have to do with her ailment... could it?"

Ritva's sad nod said otherwise. "That fits with the sadness inside her, a misery I believe was caused by heartbreak, one that left a hole behind."

A hole? Try as she might, Saara couldn't understand what Ritva meant by a hole or what Hannu's dancing with Elsa a fortnight ago had to do with Fia's illness. "I don't understand."

"Your sister is missing part of her soul."

"Oh." That indeed was serious—and something Saara had only heard tales of, never seen firsthand. But then, Pilvikoski was a small village. What did living here her whole life tell her about the world? She slumped against the back of her chair as dread spread over her. Her eyes watered, and she lifted trembling fingers to her lips. "This is because of Hannu?"

"We cannot lay the blame at his feet; not returning her love is not his fault."

"But he certainly could have handled the rejection in a kinder way than embarrassing her in the village square."

"He did?" Ritva pursed her lips. "Oh, that boy . . ."

Saara swiveled in her chair to look at Fia, as if doing so would reveal which of the three parts of the soul her sister lacked. "Can Hannu help return the missing part?"

"He doesn't have it," Ritva said, then she held up a hand. "Before you ask, no, I don't know where it might be. Only a shaman can find it and restore it to its proper place."

If Saara hadn't been looking at her sister, worrying over whether she would yet be breathing a day or a week hence, she mightn't have believed Ritva. But the evidence lay before her, and she could not deny it. She angled back to face the healer, hoping to learn and understand so she could find something to do that would help. "What part is missing? Surely not her *henki*."

"Of course not," Ritva said with a sad half smile. The *henki* could not leave a body without the body dying. Fia yet lived, yet breathed, so her *henki* was still with her. "But the loss of either *luonto* or *itse* creates sickness. In either case, that sickness gets worse the longer that part of the soul is missing."

"How do you tell which it is?"

"Often you can't, but in this case, I'm quite sure it's her *itse*. The darkness, the deep melancholy ... they indicate a heavy loss, a great cavern in the soul when even a sliver of *itse* is lost. An absence of *luonto* usually creates physical pain and often brings confusion, but not this level of dark despair."

Saara stood and began to pace the small cabin, determined to find a solution. "So we need to find her *itse* and get it back." She stopped and turned to face the healer. "How do we do that?"

"*We* do not. I am not trained in those arts, and this is something herbs cannot heal. As I said, only a shaman can help. They can enter the trance state required to find a missing *itse* and return it to the soul."

Panic threatened to grip Saara's chest. "But the nearest shaman is several days' travel away, and I have no money to pay one." The sharp prick between Saara's shoulder blades had disappeared; she now felt as if she'd been struck with a hammer in the same spot. Refusing to give up hope, she paced some more. Movement often helped her mind to work and puzzle out problems, though she'd never faced one like this. "We can go without eggs, and I can sell them. In a few weeks when the blueberries ripen, I can gather them—strawberries and mushrooms too—and sell them in the market. By autumn I could have saved—"

"Not enough," Ritva interjected. "And autumn will be too late." The healer's words sounded final, inescapable.

Their reality stopped Saara mid-step. She pictured what her life might be like soon. Surviving dark winters with snow as tall as the door—alone. She couldn't bear the prospect.

Hardly able to get in air, Saara whispered, "How much time do we have?"

Ritva lifted her lined face. "A week, perhaps." She raised

one finger and added with a flicker of hope in her eyes, "Your sister couldn't have fallen ill at a better time. It's almost Midsummer Eve, when the gods roam the land freely and the barriers between them and the mortal realm grow thin. If you are ever to find help—such as gold coins to pay a shaman—this is the time."

The decision took Saara only a moment to make. "I'll go," she said, though she had no idea where she would go or what she'd find or how to identify the help she needed. She hurried to Fia's side and dropped to her knees, cradling her sister's face between her hands.

"I'll care for your sister during your absence. Have no fear on that account. Do not concern yourself with paying me for my time. I will consider it an honor to care for her while you are away."

Tears of gratitude and sadness—she already missed her sister—streaked down Saara's cheeks. She took a few moments to look at Fia, memorizing every feature from her pale hair—matted by sweat and weeks in bed—to the perfect bows of her dark eyebrows and the thin line of her pink lips. Saara kissed Fia's cheek, then whispered in her ear, not knowing if her sister could hear.

"I'll be back soon, dear sister. And when I am, you'll be made well."

She stood, crossed to the old woman, and embraced her. "Thank you. For everything."

Ritva sniffed and gently pushed Saara away, hiding a quick swipe of tears. "Go on now. You need to pack a bag."

Two

For two weeks, Timo had traveled across miles of forest paths, stopping at swamps too numerous to count in hopes of catching sight of the elusive wisp of light that marked hidden fairy treasure. Thanks to the increase in magic across the land on Midsummer Eve, this was the best time to see the lights. But the brightest sign would do no good if one didn't already know which general area might have such a treasure buried beneath the muddy ground and where to look for the ethereal glow.

He trudged along a half-overgrown forest trail, glancing at the sky periodically out of habit, something useful in spring and autumn, when one could gauge the time of day by the rising or dropping sun. In the summer, when even nights had light, however, that skill was about as useful as casting a spell to make a lantern glow all night—useless. If you knew which direction was north, you could guess the time based on where the sun was in the circling horizon. For Timo, in an unfamiliar forest, that was impossible.

During the weeks leading up to and following the solstice, sunlight abounded, with each day growing longer by several minutes until finally the festival day arrived, and with it a night without darkness. After the festival, days were slightly shorter until the winter solstice, which was as dark as the Midsummer Eve was light.

Leading up to the festival, locals collected pieces of wood to be burned—leaky boats, broken fence slats, and more—which were then stacked until the celebration day. On Midsummer Eve, people across the land gathered for song and dance, food and drink. The old wood, stacked into a spire, was lit and set adrift in the lake, a bonfire that would burn all night long, a backdrop to the festivities.

Occasionally, a young woman would skip the festivities, going to bed and sleeping upon a pillow beneath which she left seventeen flowers from seventeen different plants. Supposedly, such a maid would dream of her future husband. Timo had no idea if the practice ever proved accurate, and he doubted whether many young women attempted it, seeing as how spending the night in the town square instead meant dancing and flirting with the very young men they likely hoped to make a match with. At least, that's what his elder sister did, and she had indeed met her husband while dancing at a Midsummer Eve festival.

Timo peered through a slight thinning in the trees, squinting to see if he could spot a swamp or other body of water off the path. For days, he'd peered and squinted, constantly searching, to the point that he'd given himself headaches. The pain would be more than worth the suffering if it meant finding the treasure required for securing his magical education. Learning the skills of a wizard took intense study, often as the sole apprentice to an experienced master. Masters were both rare and picky.

As for himself, Timo had a knack for magic. He'd worked on the skills he'd need, developing his singing voice and musical ear, both crucial to powerful magic. He could mimic tunes perfectly after hearing them once, and he'd invented a few small spells with songs of his own.

He also had a memory as quick and strong as a bear trap,

which he'd developed through memorizing poems and lists of words—another key skill required for the best of magicians. The strongest magic combined words with song, and therefore the most powerful wizards were also the best singers, often possessing coveted words and songs known only to them.

More than anything, Timo wanted to be such a singer. He wanted to help others, raise his station in life, and yes, be respected as one of the greatest to ever live, like the famed Ilmarinen and Väinö. He knew he could be one of the great masters, if only he could find a master who would teach him.

But he had a big disadvantage: his age. At four and twenty, he was several years past the age that most singers *completed* their training. Many believed that becoming powerful was impossible if one didn't receive proper training by the age of twenty. Timo had worked to save money and, in the last few years, had sought buried treasure so he could pay a master to train him.

He'd come close to laying claim to different fairy treasures hidden centuries ago, now buried in swamps and bogs. Such treasure buried by fairies could be identified only by an occasional landmark, except on Midsummer Eve, when a brief flash would appear from a *piru*, one of the mischievous spirits who guarded the treasures. The first time he couldn't find the treasure at all. Another time, someone else treasure hunting had followed the path of clues Timo had deciphered, then swooped in and taken the treasure before he could.

Last summer, he felt certain that treasure was buried in the valley by Karhunen, so he'd climbed a tree to find the *piru* flash—and he *had* seen its mesmerizing purple glow. But when he'd climbed down to the ground, he'd been unable to locate the spot.

This year was his final chance, and his odds were good:

he'd found specific details about where to look. He'd also found one master willing to take on an apprentice at his age, but no older. If he didn't get the money he'd need on this Midsummer Eve, he'd have another birthday, become five and twenty, and never get an education.

He'd sometimes wondered if the kingdom of *pirus* had decided to frustrate his efforts purely for their own enjoyment, like dangling a honey candy before a child and then pulling it away before the child could take it.

This Midsummer Eve was his turn. It *had* to be. He felt the urgency, the desperation, in his bones. As he walked, he couldn't help but picture returning home to Taivola and becoming a farmer like everyone else in town. He'd marry someone who'd care for a cow or two plus a coop of chickens. She'd make cheese from the milk and gather the eggs to cook with or to sell at the market. He'd grow rye and vegetables and try not to hate his life.

No, he would *not* fail. Mustering his determination, he continued to study the woods. The trees grew so thickly that a swamp or pond—even a massive lake—could be a hundred paces away but invisible from the trail. After spending a week in nearby Karhunen, he knew to look for three large boulders that made a triangle about the borders of a swamp. Somewhere in that triangle, or so said the tales in Karhunen—was a particularly valuable treasure. The people in the village didn't believe the tales, of course, or they would have sought the treasure themselves.

Timo, however, had studied all the lore he uncovered and had listened to any storyteller he found, knowing that such stories held far more truth than fiction. He'd read of the triad of boulders in an old rune found in a book he'd collected three years past. That poem said that a knife called Voimakas, made entirely of the rare stone spectrolite, lay hidden beneath the swamp. Spectrolite was dark blue until light fell on it, then it released a rainbow of color.

This valley just outside of the Karhunen village had three boulders: one that narrowed at the top like a spire, one with the profile of a man, and one with ancient carvings of a bear—where the village got its name. Yes, this valley and a nearby swamp must be the home of the knife Voimakas. He could feel it.

The knife, whose name meant *powerful* in the old tongue, was made of the single largest piece of spectrolite ever found. It had been fashioned into a blade by an unknown wizard from centuries before. The resulting artifact was far more than a knife for daily use in cutting cords or gutting fish. No, in a wizard's hands, Voimakas could magnify magical powers by a hundred.

In short, it was precisely the kind of treasure that would convince a master to train a grown man like Timo.

Gods willing, he would have the knife tonight. He paused in his step and closed his eyes, sending pleas to any of the gods he could think of who might be of help, which meant three goddesses: Mielikki of the forest, Ilmatar of the air, Luonnotar of spirits and nature.

He opened his eyes and carried on. He'd already found the spire boulder, and several minutes ago, he'd thought he'd spotted what he felt sure was the second. If he could confirm that one and find the third, he'd have located the right place. Crouched in a hiding place, he'd wait, never taking his eyes off the swamp inside the triangle of stones, waiting. He'd know the time was close when he heard the people of Karhunen cheering the approach of midnight in the distance.

That was the moment when a flash of light would appear from a *piru* right above the spot where the treasure was located. He'd heard *piru* flashes described in many colors—

green, blue, yellow—the length varying from so short that a single blink would mean missing it entirely to an ethereal, beautiful sign pulsing for several magnificent seconds.

He paused on the faint forest path, which once might have been commonly traversed but was now barely visible beneath the undergrowth of ferns, nettles, and moss.

He walked a hundred paces from the first boulder. The second should be nearby, but he couldn't see it. He turned in a slow circle, studying everything he could see, searching for a glimpse of gray and perhaps the bright-green lichen of another boulder. Nothing. Maybe he'd gone the wrong direction from the first boulder. He didn't think so, but perhaps he should return to the first boulder and head in a different direction.

After making a slow rotation in search of the boulder, he headed back toward the first one. After a hundred paces, though, something didn't feel right. His gut told him to stop and look about again, so he did. A bird flew above his head and whistled, drawing his attention. It seemed to swoosh and float until it alighted on . . . a boulder. The second boulder; he was sure of it.

With excitement, he ran to it. When he reached it, the bird whistled again and flew away. Timo walked around the stone, studying it to be sure it was the right one. Just as the stories said, from the side, it had the profile of a man who looked toward the third and final boulder. This was definitely the right place. He lined himself up with the stony profile, seeking the third and final stone, his stomach feeling as if something were bouncing around inside it, he was so giddy.

I'm so close. Soon, he'd have the knife Voimakas in his hands. He'd be able to pay the best living magician to teach him. And in a few years, he'd be a master singer of magic himself. He smiled so wide it stretched his cheeks.

He wanted to find the third boulder right away, but he could feel his mind and body growing weak with hunger. *I must keep my mind sharp.* He needed to eat. Midsummer was too early in the season for plump, red lingonberries and orange cloudberries, his favorites, but the forest could provide plenty else to eat.

If he didn't find any mushrooms off the path, he'd likely eat some cheese and rye bread from his bag, though he was loath to do so. He wanted those to last as long as possible. Right now, he didn't dare leave the path or the boulders in search of a lake to fish in. Not when he was this close. He wouldn't risk getting lost and not returning in time.

To his right, the path curved and then went up a steep incline. He could climb the hill in search of food and then go no farther. He went that direction, but as Timo was about to go up the hill, a glint of red caught his attention from the corner of his eye. Wild strawberries or red currants? Both of them could ripen this early. His stomach gurgled as he searched for the source of the color, trying to see through the thick green forest floor of ferns and nettles.

There. Next to a huge felled pine, a cluster of berries peeked out. Before he could act on the discovery, however, he heard a yelp and several thumps. No sooner had he glanced up the hill beside him at the source of the noises than a figure, slipping and tumbling down the path, knocked him off his feet.

He yelped too, and the two of them landed in a heap at the bottom of the hill.

Three

"Oh! I'm sorry!" Saara scrambled off the young man she'd knocked to the ground. Still on her knees, she looked him over, trying to ascertain whether he was hurt. She reached out but then pulled back, unsure whether to touch him.

He groaned. That meant he was alive, at least. He rolled over, his face a mask more of confusion than pain, which she took as a good sign. He sat up, shaking his head as if to clear his vision. That's when she got her first good look at him and realized that she'd knocked over a young man slightly her elder—and arguably the handsomest she'd ever laid eyes on.

"S-sorry," she said again, stammering as her face heated with embarrassment. Growing up in Pilvikoski, she'd only ever been around a few hundred people, and even fewer young men. She most certainly did not know how to talk to them, let alone one who looked like someone from one of the legends—handsome and broad-shouldered. Maybe as strong as the wizard Väinö, but young. "Are you injured?"

"No, I'm quite all right," the boy said, but the cautious way he got to his knees and then stood slowly belied his sunny tone.

"Are you sure?"

Though he seemed to be purposely not putting weight on his right foot, he waved away her concern. "I'll be fine. Got a few scratches is all. My fault for stopping in the middle of the path."

"Oh, yes. This was *your* fault." Saara managed a slight smile. "As we can both see, this trail is bustling with travelers. Mighty dangerous to stop in the middle of the forest the way you did."

He chuckled, conceding her point, but he went along with the joke. "I should have remembered. It's the first rule of travel: never stop, or you might get bowled over by a pretty young woman."

Saara's blush spread to the roots of her hair. She lowered her face, unsure what to say next, and found a big scrape along the toe of her boot and dirt all over her skirt.

"What about you?" he asked. "Are *you* hurt after tumbling down the hill?" All humor had vanished from his tone, replaced by genuine concern.

"A few scratches is all," she said, echoing him, then shrugging one shoulder. Halfway down the steep hill, she'd tripped on an exposed tree root, then found herself falling down, down, until she collided with him at the bottom. She had a feeling that come morning, she'd be covered in bruises, but that wasn't worth noting. She didn't seem to have any significant injuries.

"That scrape looks painful," he said, gesturing toward her left eyebrow.

Her hand came up to feel it, and her fingers came away with a few drops of blood. Not a big cut, then. Good thing, because she hadn't time to waste if she was to help Fia. Yet as soon as the thought crossed her mind, she could imagine Ritva's chastisement:

If you don't help yourself, you won't be able to help your sister.

"Doesn't hurt," she said, rubbing the drops of blood away

between her fingers. It didn't hurt much anyway. "I'm sorry again. The top of the hill overlooked so many pretty lakes. I'd never seen so many at once. Guess I wasn't paying attention to where I was stepping, and I tripped."

"Still my fault," he said, the humor back in his voice. "I never should have stopped, even if I spotted currants nearby."

"You did?" Her empty stomach ached for food, and Ritva's admonition to care for herself returned. Food in the woods meant it cost nothing. She stepped closer to him and looked into the trees on one side of the path. "Where?" She scanned the greenery, which was so thick that a bear could have been hiding there and she wouldn't have noticed it.

He turned and pointed. "Other side. There. By the felled tree."

"Oh, I'd love some currants."

He eyed her and tilted his head. "You sound as if you haven't eaten in three days."

"Just one." She meant it to sound light and humorous, but his eyebrows drew together. Either her tone was wrong or he'd guessed the truth—that she was running low on food and hadn't eaten in nearly two full days.

He squatted down by his sack, all soreness gone now. "I'm Timo, by the way," he said, digging through his supplies. He held out a piece of rye bread cut from a round loaf with a hole through the middle, the same kind that she and Fia strung onto a pole and hung in the cabin. Her middle made another gurgling sound, and she covered it with one hand as she reached for the bread with the other.

"Thank you. I'm Saara." She bit into the bread, which was dry and hard to chew, but at the moment, it tasted like a royal feast.

"Wait here and eat while I gather some of those currants," Timo said. "I won't be long."

She didn't have to be asked twice; her entire body ached from exhaustion and from the tumble down the hill. Now that she was eating, she didn't know if she'd have the strength to stop even if an angry wolf appeared.

As she chewed, she watched Timo's progress. He stepped over vegetation and rotting logs, picking his way through the brush. He no longer seemed to favor one foot, which was a relief. But then he flinched and caught his balance by grasping a branch. A few steps more, and he had to lean against a birch trunk.

His right foot *was* hurt, and it seemed to get worse with every step.

By the time he returned, carrying a sack filled with berries, she'd eaten enough bread to think clearly and gain a little strength. Her concern for him now outweighed her hunger.

"They're perfect," he said, popping a few currants into his mouth and chewing them blissfully. He put no weight on his right foot at all, relying on a nearby pine trunk to keep his balance as he lowered himself to the ground. When he settled into a spot, Saara realized his right foot was at an unnatural angle. Before she could react, he held out the sack of currants. "Here. Eat as many as you like."

She peered inside at the ruby-colored beads. Mouth watering, she reached in and took out a palmful. "Thank you," she said, trying to decide what to do about his foot. She didn't know Timo—she'd barely learned his name—but he was hurt, and it was her fault. She hadn't intended any harm. But an accident didn't make his twisted foot any less injured.

Helping him would be the right thing to do. *What if helping him means not finding treasure and a shaman for Fia before it's too late?* Death was already breathing too closely to Fia. Any delay, even for a good cause, might cost her life.

Saara put a few berries into her mouth and bit into them, but instead of bursting in her mouth with delicious tartness, they tasted bitter.

She could simply continue on her way for her sister's sake. If she explained the purpose of her journey, Timo would understand her need to go. He wouldn't expect her to stay behind to help him.

But I ought to.

If she left him here in the forest, would he be able to get to someplace safe on his own? She'd never know. Just thinking of abandoning him to wolves, badgers, bears, or thieves made her shudder. If she left, guilt would eat at her until she lost her *itse* or *luonto*.

"Saara?" His voice sounded distant as he called her back to the moment. "Are you sure you're well?"

Instead of answering his question, she posed one of her own: "Where are you traveling?"

"Why do you think I'm traveling? Maybe I live nearby."

She indicated his sack. "A stroll near home doesn't usually require a sack full of supplies."

"Clever observation," Timo said. "You're right. I'm not close to home." He bit his upper lip in thought, and she did the same to keep herself from prodding, hoping he'd tell her more on his own.

She needed to know *why* he was here in the forest. Without that information, how could she decide whether to leave him? What if he also had a sick little sister?

His next words fit her guess almost exactly. "I am on a journey in search of something of utmost importance to me."

Four

"As am I," Saara said, looking amazed. She eagerly dug into the sack of berries and withdrew a few, but before eating any she asked, "What are *you* looking for?"

Timo glanced at the bag, her palm holding the berries, and then her face, questioning. His eyes narrowed slightly. "What are *you* searching for?" he countered.

Saara tossed back the berries and chewed them with a smile. "I asked first."

How much to tell? Did she know much about how singing and magic worked? Had she ever encountered a wizard before—someone more powerful than a simple healer? Many people hadn't, especially if they'd stayed in their own villages and farms all their lives. He supposed he was lucky in that respect; he'd grown up near the wizard, and his influence had ignited Timo's own yearning to learn and master the same skills.

She might not appreciate why he needed to fund his training now, why the urgency. She might think his seeking an apprenticeship foolish. Not all people believed in the magical arts, though such people were generally those who hadn't come in contact with it and therefore assumed the stories were nothing more than that—fables and myths without very real truths.

Timo reached over to a clump of grasses and picked a few stalks, which he then smoothed and worried between his fingers, weaving the long green strands between to give himself something to do besides sit here next to Saara and talk.

"I'll answer," he said at last. "But I it may take some explaining, so I have a question for you first."

"Uh-uh. I asked you—"

He shook his head. "I promise I'll tell you my story."

"Very well," Saara said. She folded her hands on her lap. "What is your burning question?"

"Did you grow up with a village wizard?"

"That's your burning question?"

"I never called it that. Just tell me: did you grow up with a village wizard?"

Her brows rose; she clearly didn't know why he'd asked. "Not in Pilvikoski, no, but it's one of three nearby villages who once shared a singer among them. When I was just two years old, he left, so I never knew him, but I know plenty about what he did for the townsfolk—and about things he tried to do but failed at." A sadness crossed her face like a shadow, and her gaze dropped to her hands in her lap. "I understand he tried to save my father's life, and when he failed, he left. Some claim he went to seek his fortune in a more populous area, but others say he left in shame because he'd boasted about powers he clearly did not possess."

"I am so sorry," Timo said, sensing her sadness and her loss. "Did you grow up with your mother, then?"

She nodded, but a tear fell down one cheek—which she quickly wiped away, as if hoping he mightn't see it. "My mother and my little sister. Ever since Mother passed, I've wondered whether a skilled singer could have healed her fever and saved her."

The more she spoke, the sadder the feeling between them

grew. Timo could feel her grief like a cloak. He'd gotten the answer to his question, and he sensed that she would, in fact, understand the urgency of his quest. Yet he felt compelled to ask one more question, though he felt as if he'd regret it even as the words came out of his mouth. "And your sister?"

Saara, still not looking at him, squeezed her eyes closed, hard, sending more tears down her cheeks. He quickly reversed course. "I'm sorry. I shouldn't have asked." He'd wondered if her sister was traveling with her, though he hadn't seen any evidence of a companion. Those tears had to mean that Saara was alone in the world.

He took a deep breath as he braced himself to vocalize the words he'd thought a million times but never said to another soul so bluntly. "I'm seeking fairy treasure to pay for an apprenticeship with a master wizard."

That caught Saara's attention, and her face lifted to his. "You're a singer? Do you know healing spells?"

"I don't. Not yet anyway."

"Oh." Saara's shoulders slumped slightly.

"I don't know that I can claim the title of singer in any real sense," Timo admitted. "I'm self-taught, as much as I can be, but I lack any formal training."

Saara's head tilted to one side as she seemed to size him up. "Aren't you a little old to begin training? Unless you're extraordinarily tall for a sixteen-year-old. Then again, I did know a boy of twelve who was taller than anyone in the village, and anyone traveling through Pilvikoski assumed he was at least ten years older than he really was, so—"

"I'm twenty-four," Timo interjected. "So yes, rather old to begin training."

"Ooooh." Saara held out the single word as if she truly did understand that soon the door of opportunity would close—might have already—locking him out of the world of singing and magic forever.

Seeing her comprehend his situation, he shifted his position and went on, feeling more comfortable talking to her. "At first I tried to save up enough money, but I come from a small family farm, and—"

"Not enough money there," Saara filled in. "Not if you saved your whole life."

"Exactly." Timo was excited to see that she understood. "The last three years, I've searched for evidence of fairy treasure, always to no avail. This year will be different."

"How can you be so sure?" she asked, eyes looking interested rather than sad now.

"I've tracked down the source of a story I've heard told across many villages. There's a specific spot they all refer to, and I've nearly located it. Tonight, when the Midsummer celebrations are underway, I'll be waiting to see the *piru* flash—"

"Which tells you where the fairy treasure is hidden." Once more, Saara had finished his sentence.

"Yes," he said, trying to make sense of this young woman who was so different from others. "You know more about fairy treasure and singers and such than most people."

"My knowledge of fairy treasure is quite new. In fact, it's why I'm here. I need to find a treasure too." With her eyes shining with excitement, she leaned even closer and placed a hand on his knee. "Perhaps we can find the treasure together and each have a share."

As Timo looked into her face—so full of hope—opposing emotions warred inside him. He knew that the treasure hiding within the square of fairy stones was a single item: a knife made from a block of spectrolite, a gem found only in rare places, and almost always in small amounts—finding a gem any larger than a pea would be cause for celebration, because the finder would be rich for the rest of his life.

The spectrolite knife was the single largest piece of the stone ever found. It couldn't be cut into pieces without fairy magic. There was no way to split the treasure between them. It couldn't very well be split in half like a bunch of coins could be. Finding a buyer for Voimakas wasn't realistic either; the artifact was priceless. Bartering directly for his training with the blade would be far more likely to convince an aged master to take on an apprentice who'd passed his boyhood.

Fairy treasure was worth far more than coins or silver; wizards wouldn't have need for money, but they would certainly be tempted by a magical artifact they could use in practice.

Either he or Saara could have the knife, but not both.

Perhaps more than the knife is beneath the swamp, he thought hopefully. A second treasure, even a smaller one, would be enough to save her sister, surely.

"Timo?" She pulled her hand away from his knee and leaned back, worry etched across her face and her brows drawn together. "What's the matter? Is it your foot?"

"My—" He cleared his throat to win himself a few seconds before needing to answer. Apparently his dismay had shown on his face, but she'd attributed it to his injured foot. And here he thought he'd hidden the limp and the pain. Better for her to think that any uneasiness on his face could be explained by the very real throbbing in his foot rather than anything else.

Such as his own greed in wanting the treasure to himself. Was it so selfish to wish for an education, though? With training, he'd be able to help thousands of people with all kinds of problems, from leaky boats to serious illnesses. Would it be right to give up that future of doing so much good to save one girl's life now?

"My foot, yes," he said.

I am a despicable man.

"I must have twisted it and stepped on it funny." Now that they were focused on his foot, it did indeed throb and ache.

"Goodness, it's swelling," Saara said, scooting toward his right foot, which was outstretched. He'd purposely rested his leg extended when he sat to avoid putting any strain on it. She reached out and touched his foot. He sucked air between his teeth and winced. She'd done hardly more than tap the skin, yet pain had shot through his foot and ankle, up his leg, and then throughout his entire body. He was shaky and breathed shallowly.

No longer touching him or even coming close to doing so, Saara leaned over his foot to study it from all sides. "I think it's broken. Look." She pointed at one spot, and he braced himself for another stab of pain, but she didn't touch him. "The shape is all wrong . . . right . . . there." She indicated a spot on the outside of his foot.

"Broken?" he said, dismayed.

"I can't be sure, but I think so." She stood and held out both hands to help him up. "Here. Stand up."

He took her hands and was surprised when he had to lean against her so much; his foot couldn't bear even a little weight anymore. The one time he tried, he nearly collapsed.

"Good," she said, wrapping an arm around her shoulders. She reached down for his sack, tied it, and slung it over her free arm. "Now lean on me, and we'll walk back to Karhunen. They must have a healer." Saara moved toward the trail going up the hill, but Timo held back, making her stop and look at him, curious.

"I can't make it up that hill—not quickly, anyway. It would take hours."

"You can't stay down here forever. Come." Once more, Saara attempted to walk.

"I must stay until after the *piru* flash."

Saara backed up a step and looked at him, their faces much closer than before now. "The treasure is nearby?"

Now he'd done it. She'd stay with him, find the knife, and then leave with it. She was kind, so she wouldn't abandon him. He could picture it now: she'd stay until they found the knife, then help him to a healer in Karhunen. And then what? She'd leave to save her sister, taking the knife, and with it, his last hope of ever reaching his dream.

I can't condemn her sister to death, he thought. The fact that the idea had so much as flitted across his mind made him feel awash in shame.

"Down here," Timo confirmed, his mouth going dryer with each word. He sighed, then hopped on his good foot to rotate a bit, then pointed. "See that boulder?"

"Yes."

"That's the second of four fairy stones outlining a swamp that contains . . . fairy treasure." He was telling her so much as it was; she'd find out that he was looking for the spectrolite knife, but he couldn't get himself to reveal everything all at once.

"I understand," Saara said, and he knew she did. "We'll stay here, and with both of us watching, surely one of us will see the flash and know where to dig for the treasure." She craned her neck to peer around him, as if searching for the sun along the horizon. When she found it, her mouth pursed in thought. "Can you tell what time it is? I can't tell time by the sun for a week on either side of Midsummer Eve. I need a sun that rises and sets for that."

As if on cue, a cheer rang out in the distance, marking the hour before midnight. That was the moment when the bonfire was lit, made of broken boats and other stacked woods collected in the lake over the last month. Soon they'd hear music—flutes, drums, and a few stringed lyre-like instruments, *kanteles*, accompanied by sounds of dancing and laughter as both young and old celebrated.

Timo thought of home, of how his cousin Matti used to walk among the dancers on stilts he'd built himself, doing his own "dance" and impressing everybody so much that the gag had become a tradition in their town of Taivola. He sighed at the memory of having missed the last four Midsummer Eve celebrations. He'd missed seeing Matti dancing on stilts, missed the dancing and cheering, missed the bonfire going up in flames against the golden horizon, where the sun backlit the fire and never set.

He'd been so focused on his goal, on making his dream a reality, that he'd kept himself from thinking of home during the solstice. Not until now, when his foot ached and he heard another town's celebrations. He wasn't alone, as he had been every Midsummer Eve for years. This time, Saara was at his side, reminding him of home, friendship, and the days when he could enjoy life rather than yearn for what he did not have.

Saara's attention had been drawn by the village sounds too, and her gaze was still trained in the direction of the hill.

"Hey," Timo said, wanting to break the sadness. "Let's go find the best place to watch for the *piru* flash," Timo said.

"How do you know where to look for it?"

He tilted his head. "I assumed you knew."

"I'd heard that a treasure is in this valley, and that to find it, I had to watch for the flash, but I don't know much more than that."

"Ah. Well, in this case, three boulders mark the corners of a triangle, and somewhere inside it, a knife is buried. *Piru* fire will tell us where it's located."

"Tonight, right? But how do you know when?"

"At midnight." He pointed at the boulder. "I found the second stone right before we, um, ran into each other."

At that, she nudged his arm playfully. He pretended to flail and nearly fall, and she gasped out an apology.

"Teasing," Timo said, hopping to catch his balance. He'd nearly fallen over—not from her gentle bump but because the slightest weight on his foot nearly made him pass out.

Saara looked at him carefully and then licked her lips as if mustering her inner strength and grit. "So we're going to find the treasure together?"

Guilt threatened to knock Timo over. He should tell her the truth: that only one of them would leave this forest with the spectrolite knife. He could hardly stand; he wouldn't be able to wade through the mud of a swamp or dig about to seize Voimakas without her help.

He knew more about fairy treasure than she did, and she seemed to be relying on his knowledge to find the treasure required to save her sister.

Instead of explaining anything, he held out his free hand to shake hers. "Together."

Five

"THE BAKER IN KARHUNEN told me about the fairy treasure in this valley," Saara said as they picked their way from the second boulder toward where Timo believed the third to be. The overgrown path was narrow, not allowing them much space to maneuver. A squirrel skittered in front of them and then climbed a tree, circling the trunk as it went up. "I don't suppose the baker could have meant another treasure..."

"Just the one, if the stories are to be trusted, and I have no reason to think they can't be. Often it's the stories passed down in bedtime songs that are the truest, and Karhunen has at least six songs about this treasure, but none hinting about other nearby treasures."

When they came to a narrow spring, figuring out how to get him over it became a several-minute process. Once they'd gotten across—both somewhat wet—Timo checked his bearings and nodded to their left. "There. I think that's the boulder." Off they went in that direction.

"If the villagers in Karhunen know about the treasure," Saara said, "why hasn't anyone tried to claim it?"

"That's the best part," Timo said with a laugh. "Most people think that bedtime songs are nothing but fanciful stories. They don't believe that a magical relic could possibly be so near. And then there's the fact that I've done a bit more searching than anyone else up there."

"How so?"

"I've been looking for any magical relic, any fairy treasure, for years now. With each trip I've taken around Midsummer Eve, I've collected more songs and stories from all over. I heard about this treasure from other places too, including specific details about the three stones. The first two already match the lore. But most people think the stories are just that—stories."

She had another question. "What if someone else learned where it was last summer or a generation ago? What if it *was* here, but it's gone now?"

Timo stopped walking, which made Saara stop too, as they were practically attached, with her arm about his waist and his arm around her shoulders. She looked at him expectantly.

"It was here last summer," Timo said. "I saw the *piru* fire myself. It was . . . glorious." His voice sounded far away.

"Why didn't you claim the treasure?"

With a sigh, Timo hopped forward on his good foot, toward the third boulder. "I was too far away to know exactly where to look. I'd climbed a tree on the far side of Karhunen, looking for the flash. As it happens, when you're deep inside an unfamiliar forest, things look very different from how they did above the trees. I couldn't find it."

They lapsed into silence, both of them focusing their strength on reaching the boulder. When they finally got there, Timo rested his back against it with a groan. After a moment, he straightened and looked all around the boulder. His hand ran over some weathered carvings, and he smiled. "This is it."

"It is?" The prospect of finding treasure so soon made her feel as if she could fly with the birds, so much of the weight of dread had lifted from her.

"The other two boulders are there"—Timo pointed where they'd come from—"and there."

"We know where to look for the flash," Saara said with amazement. Fia would be saved after all. Until that moment, she hadn't let herself consider how near to impossible her quest had been, and only since meeting Timo did she comprehend that her quest had nearly been doomed to fail. If someone with the skills of Timo had needed years to locate one treasure, how could she possibly have done so in a matter of days?

She leaned against the boulder too, feeling its steadiness and welcome coolness seep through her blouse. Their arms brushed each other, and a tingle shot through her body. When this was all over, when Fia was well and Timo was under the tutelage of a master, she wanted to get to know him better. She'd had friends who were boys, especially when she was young, but she'd never looked on any of them as anything other than brotherly neighbors.

Timo was different. His kindness, humor, and tenacity drew her to him. His hair, which flopped to one side like a dog's ear, and his broad shoulders only added to her attraction.

As they rested in silence, she let herself release the worry over her sister for a moment and enjoy being with Timo.

"Saara, there's something you should know."

"Oh?" She said the single word with curiosity, but when she looked at Timo, who had an unexplained heaviness in his expression, her stomach dropped.

"It's about the treasure buried here." He licked his lips, then looked away, across the swamp before them.

"Is it not valuable enough to get enough money for both of us?"

He let out a heavy breath as if each word was a stone he had to push to get out. "It's beyond valuable enough. It's priceless."

"Then what's the problem?"

"The treasure is a relic—a knife made entirely of spectrolite."

"I didn't know spectrolite could be found in large pieces."

"Usually it can't. This is the biggest piece ever found. The knife is very old and *very* valuable." His tone didn't ease her worry.

"But?" she said, wanting to hear everything all at once.

"To secure an apprenticeship at my age, I'll need something besides money. The best singers have no need of it, and no sum would be enough to convince any of them to train me."

A flicker of understanding, and worry, began at the corners of her mind. "So . . . what *would* be enough?"

"A magical relic, intact. Something a singer could use to focus and magnify his power."

Full comprehension fell onto her so hard that she practically heard a thud. "Then we can't sell the treasure and split the profits."

"Not if I'm to be a singer, no."

Either Timo would be able to attain his dream at the last possible opportunity he had, or Fia would live. They couldn't both have what they needed. She looked out over the swampland too, the weight of her sister's life weighing on her even heavier than before.

"Mightn't something else be buried with the knife?"

"We can't know for sure until we find it, but relics were generally hidden alone."

Saara clenched her teeth, trying to keep her tears from falling. She had to think, to figure out what to do. With his injured foot, Timo was in no condition to wade into a swamp and dig up treasure. He'd need her help if he was to find the knife.

But *she* didn't necessarily need *him*. She knew where to look for the *piru* fire. She could watch for the flash, dig up the treasure for herself, and pay a shaman to save her sister.

Stealing Timo's treasure and abandoning him in the woods? What a horrible thing to consider, even for a moment.

And yet.

She didn't know Timo, not really. They'd met by accident—quite literally—only an hour before. She owed him nothing. She would be perfectly justified in saving her sister—her blood, a life—before helping a stranger hobble to a healer and become a singer.

He's a good person, her heart argued. *I'd be robbing him of the only thing he cares about, the only thing he's devoted his life to. And what if he couldn't crawl to the village to get help? He might die in the woods, eaten by bears.*

Aside from those things, she'd begun to care for Timo. She still wanted to see if their friendship could continue and maybe become something more one day.

She folded her arms and lowered her head, trying to muddle through the problem. No matter what angle she used, she couldn't find a way that would give both of them what they needed. If she took the knife and he survived, he'd end up old and miserable, cursing the girl who stole his future from him. If he took the knife, Fia would die, and Saara would always know that he'd taken not just a relic, but her sister's life.

As she stared at her feet, thinking, Timo shifted his weight, bringing his bad foot into view. Her eyes widened, and she gaped at his foot, now swollen three times its original size. The skin was streaked with angry lines of black and purple that thickened before her eyes.

"Timo," she said under her breath, as if speaking too loudly would increase the pace of whatever evil was attacking him. "Look."

He didn't look, instead nodding with a mask of pain. He had the same pinched eyes as Fia when her pains first hit her. "I must have been scratched by . . . something."

The way he said the last word made Saara's skin break out in gooseflesh. "By something evil?"

He closed his eyes and gave two quick nods.

Saara looked around frantically, as if she could somehow spot what had scratched him, though whatever it had been was surely out of sight and had been for some time. "Do you think it was when I landed on you, or was it on the way to this boulder?" As if the answer would help heal him.

"No, when I fell, it twisted a little, but this is different. When I was gathering the berries just now, I felt . . . something . . . pierce it. Magically." He pushed against the boulder, beads of sweat breaking across his hairline.

"We have to stop it from spreading." Saara heard her voice rising in pitch as her panic increased. She tried to sound calmer. "It's moving quickly. It's past your ankle already. How do we stop it? And what will happen if we can't?" She was thinking aloud as much as asking him for an opinion.

"If it continues, I'll die." Timo grimaced.

She watched his lower calf expand, growing like bread dough. The angry streaks of black and purple wound upward with the swelling, leaving his skin black and purple. His foot looked more like a gnarled branch burned through.

Horror erupted inside Saara, but something else filled her chest too: a glint of hope that she could claim the knife without guilt. That drop of hope was quickly followed by a flood of shame.

The glimmer of hope was for her sister, and the shame was for wishing, even for a moment, that her new friend—this man with the face of a god and the heart of one too—might actually die.

Six

TIMO'S PAIN HAD GROWN gradually at first, but it increased faster after that, mounting until he nearly vomited from the pain on the last few paces to the third boulder. Now as he leaned against the stone, his whole body felt clammy and shaky.

"I don't know how it happened," he said between his teeth. His voice was barely more than a whisper. At least, it sounded like one to him, but he couldn't be sure; pain was roaring through him, making it hard to clearly make out other sounds. "But it didn't happen when we fell." The more he thought back—the little he could think—the more certain he was that he hadn't been injured then. Not beyond a slight scrape or two on his hands, anyway.

He meant to explain more, that whatever had pricked or cut his skin wasn't a nettle or an insect or a snake. He had no clear explanation for why his foot—now his lower leg—swelled ever larger, purple and black except for the sudden pain that felt like being pierced by magic. That was the best way he could describe it. He felt such agony that he could barely speak anyway. Pressing his back against the rock for support, he slowly lowered himself to the ground.

Saara realized what he was doing and quickly grabbed his arm, helping to ease him onto the grass pushing through the soil from under the boulder.

Timo couldn't stay in a sitting position for long, though; weakness spread throughout his body, up his leg, into his trunk, extending through his arms and back down the other leg. Leaning to one side, he slid down with Saara's help so he could lie on the ground. She stroked his hair back with a gentle touch that wiped away some of the sweat.

The gesture was a comfort. What if he'd hurt himself on his own in the forest? *Please stay close,* he wanted to say, but he couldn't. He could scarcely breathe.

Saara took one of his hands between hers. Whatever coursed through his veins reacted to her touch. The thick darkness dimmed in his hand ever so slightly. With a worried brow, Saara shook her head. "If Ritva were here, she'd know what to do."

He must have made some kind of expression of confusion, because she added, "She's our village healer." Saara bit the corner of her lower lip; Timo could almost see the tracks she was making in her mind, puzzling out the situation.

"Ritva never taught me much," Saara said, more to herself than to Timo. "The most I know about sickness is from our last conversation about what caused Fia's illness. Ritva explained a little—that she knew it wasn't from an angry *haltija*, and Fia had no obvious wounds from Ajatar . . ." She gasped, and she pointed to his foot. "Wait. *This* is the work of Ajatar. The black and purple are her mark."

Timo closed his eyes with a grimace, knowing in his gut that Saara spoke the truth. If he had to describe what his injury felt like, it would indeed be that evil had attacked him and was trying to take over his entire body. Turning his head to the side, he hoped Saara wouldn't see a tear leaking out.

Would there were a way to block out the world and the reality that he'd somehow stumbled onto a spot where the evil goddess had recently walked and likely left a trap. Once he'd stumbled upon her evil taint, it had spread throughout his body with excruciating pain. He wished the end would come soon. Let him die so he wouldn't have to endure such torture any longer.

Abruptly, Saara released his hand and jumped to her feet, suddenly scurrying around, looking around the carpet of the forest floor like a mad woman, grabbing one plant, looking at the back of the leaves of another, poking at a mushroom with a stick. He couldn't watch her for long; his neck grew tired, and he let his head fall to the ground.

The evil was spreading into his arm, and this time it made his muscles spasm and contort. He tried to call to Saara. He needed her to hold his hand again, ease the agony if for but a moment. Though he couldn't speak, he must have made some kind of noise, because Saara turned to him suddenly.

"I'm looking for herbs that might help, but Ritva didn't teach me much, and I don't remember most of what I saw her do." She covered her mouth with one hand, and when she spoke next, her voice cracked. "I don't know how to help you. I'm so sorry, Timo."

This wasn't her fault, and even Ritva the healer couldn't have helped him, he felt quite sure. He held out his hand, palm up, and Saara rushed back. She dropped to her knees and wrapped both hands around his, then tried to make contact with as much of his arm as she could. Her touch lessened the agony. Not by much but a little, making it not exactly bearable but less heinous.

"You ... can't ... fight ... Ajatar's ... power," he managed.

"You're right. Of course you're right." Saara's voice held unshed tears behind it. "Only another god can fight her. And look at us: a boy and a girl from small villages. Pilvikoski is hardly a village. We're no match."

He tried to stroke the side of her hand with his thumb—the only comfort he could try to give her—but even that proved too much.

"Wait." Saara lifted her face to the woods as if an idea had just called out to her. "Who's to say we can't ask one of the other gods to help?"

He could barely make out her words as he drifted into unconsciousness and a blessed blackness without pain.

Seven

WHICH GOD TO PRAY to? Saara's childhood lessons and bedtime stories all fled her mind, and the harder she tried to remember any of the old tales and songs about the creation of the world, life in the underworld, or anything from the ancient days, the blanker her mind went.

Think, she ordered herself. *Think.*

Yet she had to force out unwelcome thoughts: that Timo was fated to die, that she could do nothing to stop it, and that his death would be a blessing to Fia.

No. Timo's death would never be a blessing, but a tragedy. Saara would do everything in her small—oh, so small—power to prevent that very thing. She wouldn't let Fia die either. She'd figure out how to help her sister after saving Timo. Even if succeeding at either one of those tasks bordered on the impossible.

The thwack and swish of bushes moving one way and then bouncing back into place came from somewhere beyond the second boulder. Like someone walking through the brush. Someone who might help them? She nearly called to get the figure's attention, though her mouth went dry at the thought that it might be Ajatar.

When she saw the source of the noise, she choked on her words and gasped, but it wasn't the purple and black of the evil goddess she saw. Instead, plainly visible even through the thick trees, a huge bear lumbered along. Saara had seen bears, but never one this large and never so close—at least, not alive. Bears were sacred, yes, but also huge and powerful and capable of snapping a person in half with a single bite. There would be no outrunning a bear, no matter how fast you ran. Timo couldn't even crawl.

Trying not to move a muscle or make any sound at all, she whispered, "Bear."

Timo looked to be unconscious, but his good leg had been shifting restlessly. At her voice, it stopped at once, and his eyes opened wide with worry. She squeezed his hand, regretting to have awakened him to this. She kept an eye on the bear as it moved through the wood. For a moment, the animal seemed to be heading toward them. Saara's grip tightened, and she held her breath.

The bear sat back on its haunches, then stood at its full height, front paws high. One paw dripped blood, and when she looked closer, Saara spotted the cause: an animal trap had closed on it. The creature's roars no longer sounded threatening but like a bellow of pain. It seemed to be looking right at Saara when it groaned again, so deep it made the earth rumble beneath her.

The trap opened, seemingly of its own accord, and dropped to the ground. The bear lowered to all fours and continued walking, with what she recognized as a limp. The bear's path gradually curved away from them, and after a minute or two—which felt like a *lifetime* or two—she couldn't see it anymore.

"It's gone," she said.

She and Timo both breathed out shakily, and his body returned to uneasy movements that surely helped the pain, at least a little.

Saara gazed through the trees where the bear had disappeared. Could seeing it now have been a coincidence? No, a bear of that size appearing out of nowhere, near a village? That seemed unlikely at best.

Maybe a god was aware of them and had sent the bear as a sign. The trap on its paw returned to Saara's mind. She clung to the image, knowing that it was significant—especially that the trap had simply fallen off the bear.

At last, the answer came to her: Mielikki, goddess of the woods. She was known for helping hunters find prey as well as for healing animals that had been injured just like the bear's paw. More, Mielikki had created the bear, giving the animal claws and teeth for hunting and protection. She'd also been known, or so the stories said, to help humans find healing herbs, if only they asked her. Mielikki had rescued the bear. She'd heard the bear's plea. Perhaps she would hear another.

"Timo, I'm going to try something."

Ashen, he gave no response, not even a flutter of an eyelid, to indicate that he'd heard her. She could barely make out a rise and fall of breath. She didn't have much time.

Face lifted to the sky, Saara clasped her hands and prayed. "I pray to Mielikki, goddess of wisdom and the woods. I seek guidance in herbs and healing. My friend has been cursed with the taint of Ajatar. I fear for his life. Please bestow upon me a small portion of your wisdom so that I may save him."

Tears slipped down her cheeks and dripped off her chin. Was she praying correctly? She had no idea.

"Oh, wise and good Mielikki, help me find the herbs to heal Timo. Teach me how to prepare them." Not knowing how to properly end a prayer, she finished with a simple, "Please help me."

Now what, wait? What if she had prayed incorrectly and became cursed too? She and Timo would both die here on the forest floor, and no one would know what became of them.

Another swishing sound caught her ear, similar to the one that had alerted her to the bear's presence. Careful to move nothing but her head, Saara looked to see the source of the noise. Another bear? This time one ready to attack?

A gleam of sunlight caught something silver, then something gold, both so bright that Saara had to blink to clear her vision. When she looked again, she could scarcely believe her eyes.

Before them stood a woman with fiery red hair, wearing a long gown of deep green. A ring of silver keys hung at her waist from a shining golden belt.

Mielikki had heard. Mielikki had come.

Eight

A GOLDEN-COLORED FOG swirled around the goddess's feet, slowly dissipating as she stood before Saara and Timo. The woman's face was raised, and she looked about the forest, as if not seeing them at all. She wore a deep-green gown and a coronet of gold strands braided into her hair with pine cones and berries. Gleaming red hair spilled down her shoulders, contrasting with the emerald green of her gown.

Struck mute from awe and fear, Saara could hardly remember her own name, let alone her sister as the reason for her journey.

Mielikki's head slowly came to center. Her face lowered until she looked upon the two travelers and pierced them with her gaze. Saara sucked in a breath, and Timo, brought back to consciousness from fear, grabbed her hand. They clung to each other, waiting for . . . the goddess to speak? To punish them?

Was she a good deity after all, or were the stories wrong?

The prayers of hunters gave her the reputation of a goodly deity. What if her support of hunters meant that Mielikki was bloodthirsty, that she sought to aid those who committed to violence? That she preferred those who killed and destroyed? That she wasn't a kind goddess who healed and oversaw safe travel within her wooded home?

When Saara began praying, she'd hoped for some kind of communication from Mielikki—a hare leading the way to the proper plants with which to make a poultice to draw out the poison, perhaps. Certainly not a visit by the goddess herself.

She stood before them in majesty, power radiating from her so strongly that Saara could barely stand to remain seated. She couldn't manage more than the tiniest glance at her face before needing to look away.

Was Mielikki angry? Saara couldn't tell; she could only feel the magic flowing through the woman before them. What if she felt that they'd trespassed? What if she saw them as thieves for trying to take the spectrolite knife?

She was taller than any woman Saara had ever seen. She appeared to be hovering above the ground, high enough for a dog to fit under her emerald slippers, which had the same gold braid and berries as her coronet.

Saara couldn't think past her fear of Mielikki. Silence stretched before them and grew heavier. Saara nudged Timo, hoping he was yet conscious and would say something. He made no sound, not even a moan of pain. He was as mesmerized and terrified as she was.

The goddess tilted her head, sending a dusting of gold and silver to the ground from her coronet. "Why have you summoned me?"

Saara struggled to think, struggled even harder to speak. She'd vocalized their needs and reasons for praying; should she repeat them? Would Mielikki think that impudent? On the other hand, if she didn't repeat her needs, would *that* be considered rude?

A small grunt of pain escaped Timo's clenched teeth—enough to break Saara's paralysis. With a shaky hand, she pointed at Timo's leg. "My friend is wounded. I lack the skills of a healer, but you, oh wise hostess of the wood, know how to make him well. I beg you to guide me, help me know the herbs to use so he may live." Saara lowered her head subserviently, hoping the goddess would recognize the respect she tried to convey, would sense her utter helplessness.

"Hmm." It was a thoughtful sound coming from the goddess, one Saara couldn't interpret. Was she curious? Annoyed?

Despite herself, Saara lifted her face very slowly, enough to peer at the goddess the tiniest bit. Mielikki had her head cocked to the side, and she seemed to be analyzing Timo's foot, which was even bigger and blacker than before.

He tried to speak. "Is—is this—" Timo gritted his teeth, then managed, "the work of Ajatar?"

"Yes," Mielikki said simply. She clasped her hands behind her and began to walk around them, gliding on air and leaving a trail of gold and silver dust in her wake, which drew a circle. "Why should I help?"

"Why?" The word popped out of Saara's mouth, and she immediately wanted to call it back. She hadn't meant any offense; Mielikki's question had merely taken her off guard. "Wise Mielikki, I apologize. I mean no disrespect. Please forgive me. My friend will die. That is why you should help."

The goddess sniffed and kept walking around them. "That is what you wish, certainly. But what is that to me? Why should *I* decide to help you?"

Preventing the death of an innocent man apparently wasn't reason enough to intervene. Mielikki needed to benefit in some way. What could two young travelers possibly offer a goddess?

Timo took a shaky breath and then another before saying, "The woods are your home, but my wound is proof that some of the beautiful paths of your kingdom have been tainted by Ajatar."

At his statement, Mielikki pulled back slightly—not

precisely a flinch, but her expression was one of distaste, and she didn't seem to be fully aware of how plainly her thoughts played out on her face.

Good thinking, Saara thought. He'd found a way to sway Mielikki—convince her to remove Ajatar's stain from her domain. To do so, she'd need to help Timo. The goddess folded her arms and eyed the travelers, first him, then her, and then dropped her eyes to his disfigured limb. With a sniff of disdain, she lifted her head and looked about as if searching for something—other traces of Ajatar.

After scanning the landscape, she faced them again suddenly, making her skirts ripple with the movement and sending more gold and silver flecks into the air. "Where are you journeying from and to?" She gestured to their sacks. "You don't appear to be hunters."

Saara glanced at Timo to see if he planned to answer again, but the pain must have intensified again, because he'd gone whiter than fresh snow and seemed ready to faint away once more. "We are not traveling together," she said, "but we are both looking for fairy treasure. For important purposes. Noble purposes."

"Hmm." The goddess sounded skeptical.

"I have nothing to hide," Saara said, head bowed. "I speak the truth. Timo and I met just today, and we both seek fairy treasure." Perhaps volunteering information and revealing so much was foolish, but Saara daren't toy with a goddess. Deceit and hiding facts were as liable to make Mielikki turn her ire on them than not.

"You seek fairy treasure." Mielikki stretched out an arm and pointed toward the swamp. "Looking for the knife Voimakas, I presume?"

"Y-yes." Saara said, momentarily surprised.

Of course Mielikki would know of any buried treasures. Did she rule over the swamps, too? Did *pirus* answer to her?

Saara couldn't remember. If only she'd paid more attention to the town's rune-teller—and realized that his stories were more history than fable.

Another thought dawned on Saara, and she summoned her *sisu* to be brave enough to propose it. "Oh wise Mielikki," she began, "Timo and I each have great need for treasure, but only one is buried within this swamp."

Mielikki folded her arms, giving no indication of her thoughts, instead waiting for Saara to finish, so she did. "Surely you must know of other fairy treasures. Could you help us find another so Timo and I can each have one?"

The goddess sighed. "I could, but again, why should I? Everything I do must build and strengthen my realm, or it is a waste of power." She held up a finger before Saara could voice a protest. "I know what you must be thinking: that I help hunters find animals to kill. Yes, I do. But that is precisely why they must pray to me. I know which animals should die to keep my kingdom healthy and balanced."

Everything Mielikki did strengthened her kingdom. Saara's hopes wilted.

"I will heal your foot," the goddess said to Timo. She wrinkled her nose as it as if it were already decaying. Saara turned to see it again and nearly vomited; it *did* seem to be rotting already, and now that she'd noticed a stench, she couldn't help but smell it. "I will heal it," Mielikki repeated, "but only, as you said, to erase the trace of Ajatar from these woods."

"Oh, thank you!" Saara cried with outright relief. Throwing her arms around Timo's neck, she said, "She'll heal you!"

But he slumped, lifeless into her arms, and he chest remained still.

"Timo! Timo, no. Breathe. Breathe!"

Nine

"Timo, stay!" Saara took his limp hand in hers—so cold—and pressed it to her heart, hoping against hope that her touch would have an effect on the taint. "Don't go."

His face, lifeless and translucent, suddenly tightened. His eyes shot open. His mouth did too, and he screamed louder than Saara knew was possible. He clawed her hands, gripping them painfully under his nails. She winced but knew he was in far more pain than she was.

"He's dying," Saara said. "Can't you see?" She lifted her face to the goddess, only to see strands of gold and silver flowing from her fingers into Timo's toes. The chastisement dried up on Saara's lips, replaced by awe at the power before her eyes.

Timo's foot glowed, and she watched it changing shape, slowly returning its original form, the parts that had looked like burned wood smoothing out and growing paler, as if Mielikki's magic was polishing his foot like a stone, removing the evil Ajatar had left upon it. Though he was clearly being healed, Timo continued to writhe in pain, screaming, veins in his neck thick and pulsing as the magic did its work. Saara held him, tears falling from her face onto his, hoping Mielikki's "help" wouldn't kill him before she was through.

Gradually, almost imperceptibly, Timo's cries softened,

and his body went from stiff and tense to trembling from exhaustion. The glowing strands of magic faded, and then all went still.

Timo breathed in ragged gasps—but he was breathing, taking in deep gulps of air.

Saara laughed with relief through her tears. "Oh wise Mielikki, thank—"

But she was gone. Saara looked about, but there was no sign that the goddess had ever been there, not even the circle of dust.

"Thank you," Saara whispered to the forest. "Thank you."

Timo was shivering now as if it were the winter solstice. She scooted him to a spot of grass warmed by the sun. He lay on his side, looking out at the swamp. She lay beside him, facing the same way and wrapping his arm about her waist, hoping her body heat might help warm him.

After a moment, he raised his hand, pointed, and, in barely a whisper, rasped, "There."

Saara looked toward a fallen juniper and saw, beside it, a purple dancing flame. "Is that—"

His arm dropped to the grass, and he nodded, smiling.

"I'll go find the knife, and then we'll get you to a healer. You can come home with me. Ritva can help you grow strong. You'll see."

He shook his head.

"No?" Saara sat up and turned to face him. "But someone must care for you until you're strong enough to . . ." Her voice trailed off before she could mention his search for an apprenticeship. Her insides tightened. "You needn't worry; the knife is rightfully yours. I'll get it for you. You have my word."

Timo slowly pushed himself up to a sit position, regaining some strength already. "It's not right for your sister to die so I can be a singer."

"But—"

"You could have let me die. You could have taken the knife for your sister, and no one, not even the gods themselves, would have blamed you." With every word, the color seemed to be returning to his cheeks. "You saved my life, though you knew it might cost your sister hers."

"I could *not* let you die," Saara said. "I wasn't trading her life for yours. I'll keep looking for a way to pay a shaman to find her *itse*. I don't know how, but I'll find a way."

"I want to help your sister."

"Why? You don't even know her."

"My situation is not so dire; I won't die if I don't become a singer." Timo slowly got to his knees, then to his feet, with Saara watching him carefully to be sure he wouldn't fall.

They stood facing each other, and for a moment, nothing existed save the two of them. Instinctively, she stepped close and wrapped her arms around his neck, relieved that he was well and strong. His warm arms enveloped her, and they stood there in the wood, embracing, their hearts beating in tandem. They seemed to fit together as if they'd been made that way. Holding him and being held by him seemed entirely natural.

He pulled back slightly, and she looked up at him, gazing into the warmth she saw in the depth of his eyes. For a breath, her heart seemed to stop beating, turning her insides into pure molasses.

He took her hand and led her through the knee-deep swamp toward the juniper. The spot looked different from its surroundings: the spot where the flash had been was almost dry, and this close, it seemed to pulse with purple light.

"This *is* it," Saara said in awe.

"Let's find Voimakas," Timo said.

They reached down in unison. They wrapped their fingers around the hilt and drew the stone knife from the swamp. Water and mud dripped off their hands, but the deep-blue knife emerged clean and spotless.

"It's beautiful," Saara said. Sun glinted off the blade, creating a stunning rainbow effect.

"Put it in your pocket, and we'll get back to the trail," Timo said.

She did, and they headed back for the trail. With each step, she wondered what would happen when they reached it. She and Timo would say goodbye, and who would leave with the knife? He'd handed it to her, had said she should have it, but that didn't seem right.

She climbed out of the mud, helped Timo do the same, then walked to the boulder they'd sat by before, dreading whatever would come next. She wiped the worst of the mud from the hem of her skirts, then rubbed her hands together to clean them a bit. Not turning around, she smoothed back some wisps that had escaped her long braid.

"Saara," Timo said from behind.

"Mm?" She was unwilling to reach the inevitable crossroad that turning about to face him would bring. She'd have to say goodbye, then try to figure out what to do with the knife. Suddenly finding the treasure didn't feel victorious.

"Saara," he said again. He touched her shoulder, and at the warmth of his fingers, she turned about against her will. She couldn't bear to look at him. "In less than a day, I've learned more about you than anyone, including those I've known all my life."

"Timo, don't—"

"I know that Fia has a sister who is remarkable and brave. I know she has more *sisu* than most shamans and singers ever reveal."

Her head slowly came up, as much from wanting to know what he was going to say next as wanting to see his beautiful face one more time.

He took a step closer. "I've long known that my chances of becoming a singer are slim. I'd rather have a life with a much greater chance of happiness, one where I spend my days with *you*. A life where I know that your sister is well. I'd much rather that than spend the rest of my days seeking for something I cannot have, living my life in misery, thinking about what might have been. Spending my life alone."

"You'd be happy even without your dreams realized? After you've tried for so long?" She felt tears prick her eyes, this time for Timo and the thought of what such a sacrifice would mean.

"Even without that particular dream, yes, I'll have a much greater chance at happiness with you." He squeezed her hand. "If nearly dying and being saved by a beautiful woman taught me anything, it's that such a woman is even more beautiful when she is willing to risk everything to save a stranger. Also that I shouldn't base my happiness on one thing that is out of my control."

"You're . . . sure?" Saara could hear the hesitance she felt in her voice.

"I'm sure. Happiness comes in many forms, but a life of solitude is almost certain misery." The longer he spoke, the taller and stronger he seemed, the more life he had in his face and hands. He might have become even stronger after Mielikki's healing touch. "I've spent so long chasing a dream, only to realize that life is fragile. I'd hate to die without having ever *lived*. Let's go seek out a shaman and save your sister."

"On one condition," Saara said.

"Oh?"

"That after Fia is healed, you and I find a way to secure your apprenticeship."

"But—"

She placed her fingers over his lips. "You've returned

from the brink of death after a wound from Ajatar. You found a knife of legend. Don't you think a wizard master might take on such a pupil?"

A slow smile began to spread across his face. "Perhaps."

"So you'll go with me to Pilvikoski, and then we'll find a way for you to be trained?"

He held out a hand and said, "Only if we do it together."

A flurry of emotions tumbled through Saara. Through it, she knew one thing: she'd never felt such joy and relief and, yes, even excitement and *rightness* at the thought of Timo being part of her life for years to come.

I might be able to look on that face every day, she thought with a thrill.

One day's adventure, no matter how intense and unbelievable to others, wasn't enough to guarantee anything, but she felt in her heart that she knew Timo better in one day than nearly anyone she'd known her whole life.

And she could scarcely wait to get to know every little thing about him. It would take a lifetime, years she was happy to spend learning more about him day by day.

She stepped past his extended hand, went onto her toes, and kissed his lips. She lowered her heels and said, "Together."

Annette Lyon is a *USA Today* bestselling author, a four-time recipient of Utah's Best of State medal for fiction, a Whitney Award winner, and a five-time publication award winner from the League of Utah Writers. She's the author of more than a dozen novels, even more novellas, and several nonfiction books. When she's not writing, knitting, or eating chocolate, she can be found mothering and avoiding housework. Annette is a member of the Women's Fiction Writers Association and is represented by Heather Karpas at ICM Partners.

Find Annette online:
Blog: http://blog.AnnetteLyon.com
Twitter: @AnnetteLyon
Facebook: Annette Lyon
Instagram: @annette.lyon
Pinterest: Annette Lyon
Newsletter: http://bit.ly/1n3I87y

The Isle of Rose

by Jane Redd

One

CORNELIA TEA ROSE READ the note a second time, then a third time. Her sister, her beautiful, perfect sister, Felicia Damask Rose, was gone. Eloped. With the stable boy—now a man, of course, but a boy whom both sisters had grown up with.

Tell no one, the note read in Felicia's flawless cursive script. She'd always been praised for her penmanship by their tutors. *Until the sun has reached its zenith, and I am long gone.*

Cornelia's gaze flitted to the long, narrow window opening, colored orange with the early hues of dawn. How was it possible to keep such a secret? Especially when today, Midsummer Night, was Felicia's wedding day?

As the younger sister of a genteel family, Cornelia had been raised to serve the elder sister—the sister with prospects. And for Felicia, having prospects turned out to be true. Twelve months ago, her father received an official letter from the government center on the Isle of Rose, requesting Felicia's hand in marriage to Lord Moss Rose. Lord Moss was next in line to inherit the title of Lord and Master of the Isle of Rose.

Cornelia knew there had been a chance for her sister to receive such an honor. Not only was Felicia's beauty known far and wide, but their father was second cousins to Lord Moss. They shared the same last name, and that only seemed to strengthen Felicia's claim to a life of beauty, luxury, and honor.

But now ... she was gone. Off to marry, or perhaps she was *already* married to Louis Phillipe.

Cornelia sank onto the bed of silk sheets and satin quilts and gazed about Felicia's abandoned room. Cornelia's bed was not so fine, but covered with mere cotton blankets, as befitted a second daughter of the house. Felicia's room was also gorgeously decorated with a sculpted fountain in one corner, the water creating its own musical melody, and tapestries that were said to be woven by women with silver fingers and golden hair.

But now the room was abandoned, and despite all the privilege that Felicia had grown up with, she left it all behind. She'd left her family behind. Her future position as the Lady of the Isle of Rose. And she'd left Cornelia behind.

Cornelia stood and crossed the room, then stopped in front of the cold hearth. She'd come early this morning, as was her usual duty, to light the fire in her sister's room. By the time Felicia awoke each morning, Cornelia had already lit the fire and brought in a steaming tea kettle with a dainty porcelain cup, along with fresh biscuits and cream from the kitchen.

Each morning, Felicia would awake to warmth, sweet smells, and a smiling sister as a companion.

Now, Cornelia stared at the words on the note, fragments swimming together, then separating as tears gathered in her eyes.

Tell no one.
I am sorry.
I am in love with Louis Phillipe.
We will begin our lives anew, together.
Away from the castle.
Away from the Isle of Rose.

Our love deserves its own future.
It is my destiny.
Someday I hope to see you again.
My dear sister.
Until then, blessings.
And love.

Cornelia crumpled the note, then began to shred it piece by piece, tossing each sliver into the black ash of the fireplace. Maybe this was a dream. If she got rid of the note and went about her usual morning routine, she'd discover that Felicia hadn't left at all. Cornelia knelt before the still hearth and picked up the kindling. She struck a long match against the flagstones and set the bits of paper to light.

The edges of the ripped pieces blackened and curled, then burst into orange flame. Cornelia added two small logs and watched, mesmerized by the advance of flames until the logs were engulfed. The warmth reached Cornelia, but she hardly noticed. Nothing could penetrate the cold that her hands had become.

Because she heard voices coming along the corridor.

Her father's voice, and another man's, whom she knew to be the emissary from the Isle of Rose. Cornelia straightened from the hearth and brushed her hands off, then took a step back. The men wouldn't knock on her sister's bedroom door, but Cornelia wanted to be closer in order to hear their thoughts. Spoken words were never the best indicator of what a person was truly thinking.

Only Felicia knew of Cornelia's gift of mind reading. There had been tales of their grandmother, now long gone, being a mind reader. Cornelia had never told anyone else because mind reading might be considered witchcraft. And witches didn't fare too well in their lands, as indicated by frequent stake burnings of suspected witches.

Cornelia was not sure how her grandmother's gift had worked, but Cornelia could only hear men's thoughts, not women's. It was why she hadn't known of her sister's plans until she found the note. And since she didn't spend time in the stables or around Louis Phillipe, she hadn't heard his thoughts either.

But now, the voices of her father and Portland grew closer, and Cornelia listened ... hearing her father's desire that her mother hadn't spent so much money on the wedding gown and Portland's desire for a smooth trip across the inlet to the Isle with the wedding party. Apparently, he was hoping for a promotion, up from emissary for Lord Moss to commander of his personal guard. Portland was worried about the repeated attempts on the lord's life.

Cornelia had heard about the assassination attempts. But men in power were always in danger. That fact never seemed to bother Felicia, and now Cornelia knew why.

The men passed the bedroom door, and their voices and thoughts faded with their clipped footsteps.

Cornelia looked toward the window; the orange hue had brightened to yellow. The sun had fully risen, yet there were hours until it reached its zenith, when everyone's life would shift toward an unknown future. Hours until she could make the announcement.

Two

A MAN'S WEDDING DAY should at least bring some happiness, right?

Lord Moss had been wrong before. And he must be wrong on this account because even though his marriage to Felicia Rose had been planned for well over a year, he was still dreading it.

He currently stood in the banquet room in his castle on the Isle of Rose. Felicia's portrait hung above the large hearth, her crystal-blue eyes gazing at the opposite side of the room. Her gold-yellow hair hung in heavy waves about her shoulders, and her long, slender fingers were tightly clasped in her lap. Her lips were pink and prim, as if she were holding back her true thoughts. Thoughts that Lord Moss would soon be privy to, whether he wanted to be or not.

Felicia was beautiful, yes. Accomplished, yes. And marrying her would fulfill his duty to the Isle of Rose and secure his posterity, yes.

But, it was just another step in holding onto the thin reins of the Isle in his hands.

Upon his father's deathbed, Moss had promised to secure a wife, and his father had immediately said that it must be a woman from the Rose family to keep the bloodline pure. Well, that had certainly narrowed things down a bit since his father's second cousin Crest Rose was the only living relative who had grown daughters. Two of them, in fact.

When Moss had written to Crest, the immediate response was favorable, and a miniature painting of Felicia had been sent. Along with a contract.

Moss signed the betrothal contract under the watchful eye of his mother. Then his mother had commissioned the miniature to be made into a full-sized portrait, which was the current portrait Moss now stood before. Tonight, as the sun set over the Isle, Moss would be making marriage vows with this woman. For better or worse. In sickness and in health. For richer or for poorer.

"Why so melancholy?" a woman's voice said.

Moss stiffened as his mother walked into the room, her heeled shoes *click, click, clicking*.

She stopped next to him, lifting her chin to gaze at the portrait of his bride-to-be.

"Just think," his mother breathed in her sing-song voice. "Tomorrow morning at this time, you'll be a married man."

Moss said nothing.

"No one can take the Isle from you then," his mother continued as if his silence didn't bother her. "Your title will be secured forever and ever."

He wanted to laugh. His title would never be truly secured. Since the betrothal was announced, three attempts had been made on his life. Two of the assassins had been caught and put to death after refusing to confess who'd hired them. One had gotten away.

Moss swallowed back his bitterness.

"Your Lordship, Your Ladyship," a smooth voice spoke from the far entrance to the banquet room.

Moss didn't need to turn to know that Bourbon had just arrived. His smooth tones and pretty words might have his mother approving of their every interaction, but Moss was convinced that Bourbon was about as shallow as a puddle after a spring rainstorm.

His mother spun on her heel. "Bourbon, you must cheer up my son. Today, after all, is his wedding day."

"So it is," Bourbon said, striding easily across the marbled floor. *Slap, slap, slap* went his leather boots.

Bourbon stopped a pace away from Moss and gave an extravagantly deep bow, which made his mother's green eyes light up with delight.

At least someone was happy today.

"And how are you today, Lady Alba?" Bourbon said, displaying a second, deep bow.

Moss barely held in a scoff. The pomp of the elite members of society had always bothered him. Why all the pretention? A genuine conversation was so much more interesting.

"I am only as happy as my son," his mother cooed, holding out her hand, which Bourbon promptly kissed.

Bourbon straightened and turned toward the portrait of the blond beauty Felicia. "What do we have here, now?"

Moss's mother tittered. "The bride, of course. I heard that her gown will be adorned with fresh white roses."

How his mother had heard that news, Moss had no idea.

"Sounds absolutely enchanting," Bourbon said, ever the man to flatter the most powerful woman on the Isle. That was, until that power transferred to her new daughter-in-law tonight.

"I never thought this day would come," his mother continued. "Imagine, my own son will be a husband."

"You have raised him well, my lady," Bourbon said, his voice as smooth as dark liquor.

"You flatter me."

Bourbon chuckled. "If the truth is flattery, then so be it."

Leave, Moss wanted to tell the pair. *Let me brood in silence.*

"I know." His mother snapped her fingers. "We shall find a rose to adorn his jacket. One that will complement his bride's beautiful wedding gown."

Moss didn't need to look over to know that Bourbon's smile was as wide as his face.

"Allow me to escort you into the gardens in search of such a rose," Bourbon said.

At last, the pair of them left, with promises of finding the perfect rose and with talk of the wedding banquet and all the dignitaries who'd be in attendance.

Moss found himself in grateful silence.

Indeed, his mother was right. Tomorrow at this time, he'd be a wedded man. But he'd received another death threat upon parchment this morning, which promised that he'd not live to see the sun rise again.

Three

IT WAS TIME, THIS Cornelia knew. She could not delay any longer. Slowly, she stood from the chair in her small, bare-walled room. The note from her sister had long since burned, and the ashes had cooled. So there was no real proof in what she was about to tell her parents. But it didn't matter. Whether they believed her or not, Felicia was long gone.

Cornelia left her hovel of a room and walked sedately along the wide corridors to where she knew her parents would be in the library. Her father with his drink and his books of science. Her mother with her needlepoint. As far as parents went, Cornelia had few complaints. Unless she counted the disproportionate treatment between her and her sister.

But Felicia was the eldest, born into her birthright, meant for greater things than living in a country manor, the daughter of a modest landowner.

That had all changed now.

Sure enough, Cornelia's parents were exactly as she guessed them to be.

Her father looked up first. She'd been directed the evening before to come and fetch them both when Felicia was packed and ready to begin the journey across the bay to the Isle of Rose.

So her father's expectant gaze was no surprise. Both her

parents were blond and blue-eyed like Felicia. Cornelia, apparently, took after her grandmother and her crow-black hair and deep-brown eyes.

Cornelia had never been good at hiding the emotions on her face, which was why she'd stayed sequestered in her room until now.

"What is it?" Her father's voice was sharp, which meant that her mother was on alert too.

Cornelia exhaled and stepped farther into the room. "Felicia has eloped with Louis Phillipe." Getting it all out at once was the best method.

Her parents said nothing for a moment, although the shocked looks on their faces were enough to make Cornelia want to return to her room.

Her father snapped first. "What do you mean? *Eloped?*" His face deepened another shade of red with each word.

"Louis Phillipe is the *groom*," her mother said in a querulous voice.

Cornelia answered her parents' rapid questions while her own heart pounded and her stomach plunged.

Her father took to pacing, barking out angry retorts mixed with cursing, and her mother fled the room, determined to see for herself if Felicia was truly gone.

When her mother returned, her face was streaked with tears, and she rushed to her husband. "She's truly gone, Crest. I questioned everyone and discovered there are two horses missing, and all of Louis Phillippe's things are cleared out."

Her father stared at his wife, his red face looking as if it were about to boil over.

"How long?" he asked, his gaze cutting to Cornelia.

She wanted to disappear. Instead she said, "The note begged me to wait until high noon to tell anyone." Her words faltered. "So that it would be too late to change her course of action."

Her father blinked, and her mother gasped.

"So it is done, then," her father said, his tone steely. "Even if she returns and begs for our forgiveness, she is no longer our daughter."

Her mother whimpered.

"And you," her father ground out, pointing a finger at Cornelia. "You kept Felicia's secret, which makes you *equally* guilty."

Her father had never spoken truer words, although unfair. Yet the weight of that guilt pressed upon Cornelia even now.

"*You* will fix this, Cornelia," her father continued, his blue eyes turning to ice. "You will wear a blond wig and a veil and marry the Lord of the Isle of Rose tonight."

"No." Cornelia could hardly breathe. "I cannot replace my sister and marry . . . What happens when I am discovered? Surely, I cannot—"

Her mother had been stunned into silence, but now she rallied. "You must!" She rushed to Cornelia and grasped her hands. "You must become your sister right away! With a veil, no one will know the difference. They will see the blond hair, the wedding gown, and they will never suspect."

Cornelia's stomach twisted. "What about . . . *tonight*?" Her voice dropped to a whisper. "In the marriage bed." Her knees felt like water.

"Blow out the candles." Her mother's blue eyes glittered with what could only be insanity. "Bed your husband, and in the morning when he realizes the switch, it will be too late. The marriage will be finalized with consummation. He *cannot* back out then."

Cornelia pulled away from her mother's hot grip.

"He could condemn me as a traitor," Cornelia said, desperation flooding through her. "The very worst kind. Would you send your own daughter to the guillotine?"

Her parents' calculating stares were answer enough.

"Why should he find out?" Her father stepped closer, his gaze moving down her body. "Keep the blond wig on. He has only seen a miniature portrait of Felicia. Never in person. There's no reason that he should find out. Bear him a son or two, and I can guarantee that Lord Moss won't care if his wife is a gentleman's daughter or a scullery maid. Just be sure, when you sign your name on the marriage certificate, that you write *Cornelia*. And we will pray that Lord Moss does not inspect your signature. Yet."

Four

Moss stood on the ramparts of the castle and watched the skiff bob in the sea as the wedding party crossed the sea from the mainland to the Isle of Rose. He could make out his emissary, Portland, the parents of the bride, and the bride herself. Were there no other family members or siblings, or even a lady's maid in attendance? No matter; his mother would see to it that his new wife had a lady's maid.

From this distance, he could not see much of the bride beneath her veil. It was a curious thing to wear, but perhaps she'd remove it for the wedding ceremony. Was it some tradition he did not know about? It wasn't like he attended weddings on a regular basis to know all the ins and outs of them.

But he could no longer gaze upon the wedding party because he needed to greet them at the castle entrance. Surely his mother was now wondering where he was. Moss made his way down the winding staircase in the tower, feeling as if each lowered step only brought him closer to his fate.

Before opening the heavy oak door that would lead him into the castle, he straightened his shoulders and cleared his mind of all regret. Then he placed his hand on the latch and pulled.

"There you are," his mother said as soon as she saw him.

She was dressed in her wedding finery, befitting her station on the Isle. From glittering jewels at her throat to the fine silk of her mauve dress, his mother's elegance rivaled that of any lady on the Isle.

"Your boots need another polish," she continued.

Ah. Her elegance did not always extend to her tongue.

"They've been polished," Moss said, not wanting to have an inane discussion about the state of his boots just now.

The skiff had landed, and through the open doorway, he saw the wedding party approaching. Led by Portland, then the man who must be Crest Rose, father of the bride.

"She will do, will she not?" His mother's voice was soft now, reflective.

Moss knew she was speaking of whether he was pleased with the woman picked to be his bride. That had never been a consideration though. Not with the title at stake, and the Isle's future to secure.

Moss gave a brief nod, but kept his gaze on the group. Felicia Rose was indeed wearing a veil that covered her cascade of blond hair. She was taller than he thought she might be, and she was also more . . . curvy. The woman in the portrait had been quite slender, but perhaps a woman changed over a year's time?

His gaze shifted to Crest, who was beaming a wide smile. He was also blond, although his hair had thinned, and gray threaded a good portion of it. His wife, China Rose, had a narrow face and bright-blue eyes and was an older version of her daughter in the portrait. She too was slender and dainty, to the point of reminding Moss of a fairy in a children's fable.

Oh, please let this man be happy with my daughter.

Moss frowned as the woman's thoughts infiltrated his own mind as if he were overhearing a whispered conversation. What a wish. Perhaps it was the worry of all mothers-of-the-bride. He expected the mother's thoughts to be mixed in with Miss Felicia's, but there was nothing from the veiled woman.

"Greetings, my lord," Portland said, stopping before Moss and bowing.

Moss nodded. "Welcome. I trust your journey was safe."

"Perfectly safe." Portland turned. "Let me formally introduce you to the Rose family. Sir Crest, Lady China, and their daughter, Miss Felicia."

Crest bowed low, and the women curtsied.

When Felicia straightened, Moss listened. But he heard nothing from her thoughts. It was possible that she was able to keep her mind blank, but highly unusual. The other possibility was . . . she could read minds too.

Moss wished she'd remove that veil so that he could look into her blue eyes. He couldn't even see the color through her veil, but surely eye color didn't change, did it?

His mother greeted their guests, and soon-to-be family; the conversation continued between his mother and Felicia's parents. All the while, Felicia said nothing, thought nothing.

And unease settled over him. If Felicia could read minds, then she already knew that he could read minds as well. Because as amazing as the gift was, a male could only read the minds of females who did not have the gift. And a female could only read the minds of males who did not have the gift. So it was highly possible that Felicia already knew his greatest secret.

He had to speak to her. Alone. Before the marriage took place. He had to know if she would betray him. Or if she would, as his wife, be loyal.

But the mothers were already speaking of the chamber that Felicia would take over to prepare for the wedding. Before Moss could get any word in, the women had left in a fluttery group.

His almost father-in-law placed a firm hand on Moss's shoulder. "A tour, then?"

Moss blinked. Had he offered a tour? So be it.

"Of course," Moss said, keeping his tone placid, when in truth, he wanted to call after the women. Find a way to separate Felicia from the rest. Lift that veil of hers and question her.

Instead, Moss led the way along the marbled hallways, passing slender columns, intricate tapestries of hunting scenes, and low-hanging candle chandeliers, and walking beneath ornate arches. He showed Crest the main rooms of the castle, and they came to a stop in the banquet room. Moss paused to look at the portrait of Felicia again.

Crest said something about moving on, as he was interested in seeing the trophy room, but Moss held up a hand.

"Wait a moment, sir," he said, gazing at the blond woman in the painting.

Something wasn't right. The portrait might be a bit off because it had been expanded from a miniature, but surely even a miniaturist would craft a more exact replica.

The tightness in his throat multiplied, and Moss realized something in that instant. The woman beneath the veil, the one he was about to marry, was not the same woman in the portrait. He couldn't pinpoint how he could be so sure, but he knew. To the depths of his soul, he knew.

But instead of confronting that man who was trying to entice him out of the room, likely for good reason, Moss wanted to confront Felicia . . . or whoever she was.

Five

CORNELIA SPUN SLOWLY UNTIL she faced the gilded mirror. The woman in the white wedding gown staring out from the mirror could not be her. She looked a dream, a vision, like a fairy at a Midsummer Night's party. Felicia's wedding gown had been frantically altered by their mother, since they could let no one know of the deception. And it fit perfectly.

The white silk curved with her body, scalloped at the neckline, then formed soft sleeves that reached just below her elbows. The length edged the floor, then billowed behind in an elegant train. Her mother had pinned roses at the V-waistline and threaded more tea roses throughout Cornelia's blond wig.

She did not look herself, yet she looked like she'd always imagined she might look if she had a wedding day. Her hair was a different color now, but the makeup her mother had applied made Cornelia's brown eyes look like vast pools. Her lips were shaded a dusty pink, and the dangling pearl earrings made her cheekbones seem higher and more pronounced.

"It will do," her mother said simply, and the satisfaction in her voice would have to be enough for Cornelia.

If this had been Felicia, their mother would have dumped out a bucket full of praise.

"Now, let's get that veil back on," her mother said in a hushed voice. "Before Lady Alba returns."

Cornelia dutifully bent her head as her mother placed the veil once again over her head, then adjusted the folds. Sure, there were similarities between the two sisters, but in body size and eye color, the differences wouldn't fool any at their estate. Here, on the Isle of Rose, they had the advantage.

"Goodness," a voice said from the doorway, where Lady Alba had just entered. "What a lovely bride. Moss will be enchanted."

Cornelia's first instinct was to smile, but that was quickly covered up by the heaviness in her chest at the betrayal. She also didn't miss the slightest edge she'd heard in Alba's voice. Could it be that the woman wasn't completely satisfied with the marriage arrangement?

A page came to the doorway and announced that the guests had assembled. The officiator would be Lord Moss himself since he held the highest authority on the Isle, and her father would present the marriage contract to be signed as a legally binding contract. The one hundred guests would serve as witnesses.

Cornelia's heart fluttered as she walked out of the dressing room. Her mother was on one side of her, and Lady Alba on the other. They escorted her directly to the grand ballroom. Cornelia couldn't have changed her mind if she wanted to, not with these two matrons matching her every step.

The page arrived ahead of them, and upon his announcement of the bride, music swelled from somewhere in the ballroom. Cornelia swallowed against the dryness of her throat as she reached the entrance.

More than a hundred pairs of eyes turned toward her. The room was resplendent in candle light, which wasn't needed, because the glow of the setting sun coming through the tall windows had turned the room into a fiery glow. Women added to the glow with their glittering dresses of gold, silver, and blue. The men were equally glorious in tailored suits of dark colors and moon-white shirts beneath.

Cornelia's father stepped forward, his chin lifted in pride, shoulders erect, back straight. He held out his arm, and she gratefully clasped onto it. The guests parted, and then Cornelia saw *him*. Lord Moss. The man who would be her husband. The man she'd already deceived and was about to deeply betray.

Her breath felt shallow and her feet heavy. But she could not look away from the man standing on the dais waiting for her. His long sable-colored jacket cut away from his torso, emphasizing his broad shoulders and narrow waist. Beneath the jacket, he wore a white linen shirt and sable-colored trousers. His black boots nearly reached his knees, and their high polish gleamed along with everything else in the room.

But it was his eyes she could not look away from. Despite her veil, she felt his gaze penetrating to her very mind. His green-gold eyes were the only thing he had in common with his mother's looks. And his hair was a thick wave of deep brown, reminding her of the shadowed trunks of the deep forest on a summer day. His jaw was set firm, and she could just make out the barest stubble.

She had thought it impossible for her pulse to pound any harder, but at the quirk of his lips as she approached, her pulse rocketed. Because she was thinking of the wedding night and how it might be to kiss her new husband. And what might happen when he discovered her deceit. Surely she couldn't hide the truth forever.

That beautiful mouth of his would turn cruel. His green eyes would narrow to slits. Would he strike her? Would he order her out of his sight, to be locked up in the dungeon until her date of execution could be set?

Cornelia wanted to turn, to run back through the parting

of the guests, until she was outside the castle. Perhaps she could man the skiff herself and return to the mainland. She'd live out her days as an outcast, that she knew, but perhaps it meant she would live.

But her legs kept moving forward, her feet walking, her heart beating, her words staying silent. Phrases and words bombarded her mind as the thoughts of the men competed inside her mind. Some thoughts were dull, some tired, some worried, others leering, about her or about other women. Other thoughts were more sinister. One planning a rendezvous with someone named Musk. The thought felt very dark, but Cornelia didn't have time to search out the man in the crowd. She tried to block all the competing thought streams and focus on what was going through Lord Moss's mind. So far, she'd heard nothing. Not upon their first meeting and not now.

Once they reached the dais, her father released her arm, and for a moment, it was like being stripped of all clothing and adornment. She'd have to ascend the five steps by herself. She'd have to stand across from Lord Moss and make her vows in front of one hundred witnesses.

Her father murmured something, but Cornelia had no idea what he'd said. It was time to do this. She grasped the sides of her gown and put one foot on the first step. Then another. And another.

Before she took the final step, Lord Moss held out his hand. Gloved, of course.

She swallowed down the surfacing panic and placed her hand in his. Warm and strong. Steady. And he did not let go as she stepped onto the dais and faced him.

"Hello," he said in a quiet voice that she could just hear over the rustle and murmuring of the wedding guests.

She opened her mouth to return the greeting, but her

voice stuck. She frantically tried to read his thoughts, anything, a single phrase, a lone impression, yet there was nothing. She could see in his green-gold eyes that he *knew*. He knew she was not Felicia. But he was going to marry her anyway.

Six

Despite the wedding veil doing its job of concealing the brown eyes of the woman standing across from him, Moss could see the shift in her gaze. Although he couldn't read her mind, it was possible she could read his. But he didn't think so. How he knew this, he couldn't explain.

"What is your name?" he asked, keeping his voice quiet.

Her lips parted, then closed. She had pretty lips. Full and pert. The lips of the woman in the portrait were thinner.

"Please, give your attention to our esteemed Lord Moss," the page said, commanding the attention of the guests so that even the barest whisper went silent.

The page continued, but Moss wasn't listening. "Who are you?" he tried again, quiet enough that only she could hear.

"The daughter of Sir Crest and Lady China," she said.

Moss stared, willing the veil to disintegrate beneath his gaze, but it remained firmly in place. Then he realized the page had stopped talking and had turned toward the dais expectantly. In fact, the entire room full of guests was watching him in silence.

Moss had a decision to make. This very instant. But the questions tumbled through his mind, urgent and unanswered. What had happened to Felicia, the sister he'd been betrothed to for a year? And how in the history of the Isle did Crest Rose think that he could get away with marrying off a different daughter?

The pieces of the puzzle clicked into place. What if Crest was behind the assassination attempts? Perhaps he'd switched out his eldest daughter for this younger one—this mind reader—so that she could be the perfect spy.

The plan was rather brilliant, if Moss were to admit to it.

He had two choices. Expose the trembling woman in front of him for the fraud that she was. Or. Marry her and thwart their plan, bring down Crest and his loyal followers. Let it be a warning to all who dared infiltrate the Isle. And by weeding out any dissenters or followers of Crest, Moss would then strengthen his power.

"Miss Rose," he said in a strong, clear voice, still holding the woman's hand in his. "With the authority that I hold, I vow to take you as my wife."

Her fingers tightened on his ever so slightly, and he thought he heard her exhale.

"Lord Moss," she said, her voice not as timid as he expected it to be. "Under your authority, I vow to take you as my husband."

Two simple vows spoken, and it was done.

Except for their signatures on the marriage contract.

Her father walked up the stairs and joined them on the dais. With a bowed head, he offered the contract first to his daughter.

The woman took it in hand, and Moss kept his gaze on the quill as she penned her name. Her writing was small and curvy and not entirely legible at first glance. But Felicia was not the name she'd written, of that he was certain.

Next, Moss signed his name to the contract, and he sensed his new wife was holding her breath as he did so. It was going to be inconvenient that he couldn't read his wife's mind, so he'd have to pay even closer attention.

As he handed the contract to Bourbon, the guests cheered.

Moss smiled indulgently at his guests, then turned to the woman he'd just married. He did not lift her veil and place a kiss on those dusky lips of hers. Instead, he took her hand and pressed his lips to the top of her hand.

Her trembling had subsided, but it was still evident.

He lifted their hands together, and the guests cheered again. Then, Moss led his new bride off the dais, where they began to accept the congratulations of their guests, one by one. As the men and women approached, Moss clearly heard the thoughts of the women, and he shouldn't have been too surprised to learn that not everyone truly wished his new wife well.

Jealousy was something he'd dealt with his whole life, but now that he knew his wife was not the one he'd been betrothed to, he wondered why he hadn't suspected a woman before. Women could be just as deceitful as men, and perhaps he'd been naïve in not considering them.

As Moss accepted congratulations, along with a single glass of wine, he kept Crest in his line of sight. And his wife. Moss was finding that one could never be too careful, and it appeared that the entire Rose family was involved.

The banquet tables had been set up and platters of food brought in. An unending stream of marinated meat, poached fruit, steamed vegetables, delicate desserts, and of course unlimited wine. But Moss stuck to one glass. He could not let his guard down. Not ever.

Moss escorted his new bride to their place at the head of the main banquet table. She ate sparingly, never lifting her veil, and he wondered how long she'd wear the veil. All night? Until tomorrow? Surely she didn't think she could stay hidden from him forever?

The banquet continued, with the guests eating, drinking, and offering toasts, and all the while Moss watched the men and listened to the women. Their thoughts were inane, full of speculation, jealousy, and some of boredom. Nothing about a plot against him or the castle. And all the while, his wife's thoughts stayed absolutely silent.

An hour passed, then two, and during the third hour, when Moss couldn't stand one more minute, he stood. A hush rippled across the tables as people noticed him. "Thank you all for attending this joyous occasion," Moss said. "I hope you will continue to enjoy yourselves."

Glasses were raised, and Moss took a sip of his water.

He turned to his veiled bride and held out his hand. "Shall we?"

Her hesitation might be minute, but he'd seen it. Soon, she placed her gloved hand in his and stood. As they walked out of the banquet room, multiple guests, including his mother and the bride's parents, bade them farewell and good wishes.

The thoughts of the female guests intensified and grew more bold, mixing in marriage-bed predictions and guesses on whether the bride would conceive that very night.

Moss kept his posture erect, his face expressionless. A skill he'd perfected over the years so that people would never know when he could hear their thoughts.

Stepping out of the banquet was a relief. Not only to escape the stifling air and cacophony of constant noise, but because he needed to discover the truth about the woman he'd just married.

Seven

LORD MOSS STRODE AT a brisk pace, but the last thing Cornelia dared ask him to do was slow down. She had no doubt that he was fuming, and he was about to get her alone somewhere to berate her, or worse. Would he give her a chance to explain before he accused her of treason?

His grip was quite tight on her upper arm, and it had likely been seen as a gesture of affection and possession by the wedding guests. But Cornelia knew better. His fingers were like fire, and even through the silk of her wedding gown, she felt like she'd been branded.

Lord Moss did not lead her up the grand staircase like she'd expected him to, where she supposed his bedchamber suites were. No, he led her down a long corridor that seemed to grow damper by the moment. The lighting was scant too, the oil lamps few and far between, and an involuntary shiver ran through her.

But Lord Moss seemed oblivious to her quickened breathing and shivering limbs. She probably should have been warned when she'd first realized she couldn't read his thoughts. It wasn't completely unusual to come up against a small barrier when meeting a man for the first time. Sometimes it took careful concentration and focus to break into the man's mind. And reading another person's thoughts was harder when she was upset about something.

Her emotions had certainly been all over today. But she'd spent nearly three hours trying to break into the mind of Lord Moss, and *nothing*. It also didn't help that he intimidated her in every possible way. From his height, to the breadth of his shoulders, to his strong and capable hands, to what he'd said to her just before they'd spoken their vows of marriage. *What's your name?* he asked.

He *knew* she was not Felicia.

Lord Moss came to a heavy wood door at the end of whichever corridor they'd now turned into. Without releasing her arm, he lifted the latch and tugged it open. The door opened with a groan as if it hadn't been used in years.

Cool, damp, musty air rushed to meet them, and they stepped into a sort of garden. Lord Moss finally slowed his stride as he steered her along a winding path. They passed trees and high bushes, flowering plants, and prickly plants. The sun had long since set, and there were no outdoor lamps or torches, so the only light was the half-moon above.

Again, she wanted to question her new husband, but her heart was now racing with fear. Would he do away with her on his own? Bury her in the rich soil beneath one of these overhanging trees? Cornelia concentrated as hard as she could, hoping to read his thoughts. His intentions. Yet what good would it do her? She couldn't escape a man who had more strength in his one hand than she had in her entire body.

She was so focused on her own self-pity that when Lord Moss stopped in front of a small building, she was startled she hadn't seen the building until now.

With his free hand, he unlatched the door and drew her into the dark building.

"Don't move," Lord Moss said. The first words he'd spoken directly to her since their marriage vows.

He released her arm, and blood rushed through her

limbs, fiery and tingly. She folded her arms, if only to keep herself in one place and draw a bit of warmth. She heard a soft scrape, then smelled sulfur. Lord Moss had lit a lamp, and the feeble light flickered to reveal a room about the size of her bedroom back home. He crossed to the door they'd come through and locked it.

Her pulse stuttered.

When Lord Moss turned around, he didn't look at her, but moved about the small room, lighting more oil lamps. As the shadows retreated, then disappeared, Cornelia realized the room was cozy and quite lovely. Wall hangings of garden scenes covered the walls. The jewel-colored rugs were thick and soft, and two chaise lounges faced each other before a stone hearth.

A table sat off to one side, and it looked as if a game of chess was currently underway. Next to the chess board was a large basket covered with a linen cloth. One wall teemed with bookcases, and another table was covered in open books and sheaves of paper.

Still, Lord Moss hadn't looked at her. He moved to the hearth and knelt before it, where he lit kindling, then started a fire.

Cornelia swallowed. Where were they? And why had Lord Moss brought her here? "What is this place?" she ventured to ask, her voice trembling.

He didn't answer at first; he merely straightened, keeping his gaze on the young flames. Finally, he said, "It's my work room. Where I design the gardens and research cross-bred plants."

Cornelia waited for him to say something else, but he didn't. She looked to the table of books and papers. After another moment of silence, she took a step toward the table, then another when Lord Moss still didn't turn around. When she reached the table, she didn't touch anything, but gazed down at an elaborate diagram of a rose garden. They hadn't passed a rose garden on the way to this building, so maybe it was somewhere else on the grounds.

A shuffle sound from Lord Moss's direction told her that he'd turned to look at her. Slowly, she lifted her chin and met his green eyes. In the warm glow of the multiple oil lamps, his eyes seemed dark. And penetrating.

Heat stole along her chest, moving to her neck.

"Take off the veil," he said.

Of course he'd ask that, but the words caused her to flinch anyway. She raised her hands, and she was quite sure he could see them trembling from his place by the hearth. Slowly, she lifted the veil from her face.

She kept her gaze lowered even as she felt his on hers. Then she pulled out the pins that held the headpiece in place and slipped the entire thing off.

Lord Moss walked toward her, and she hardly dared to breathe. When he stopped in front of her, he didn't say anything for a moment, but then he touched her chin and lifted her face.

She had to look at him then. Instead of anger or disgust in his gaze, she saw intense curiosity. The pressure of his fingers on her chin made the heat in her chest multiply. Surely she was blushing like a simpering girl now.

"Tell me your name," he said, his tone authoritative, yet more gentle than she deserved.

She swallowed against the dryness of her throat. "Cornelia."

His green-gold eyes moved over her face, and this close, she caught his scent of earth and spice. "Cornelia," he said in a low voice. "You are the younger sister."

It wasn't a question, but a statement. "Yes," she whispered. "My sister Felicia . . . She eloped with her lover last night . . . And my father . . ."

Lord Moss released her chin, but he didn't move back, didn't shift his gaze, as he waited for her to continue.

"My father . . . and my mother . . . wanted to honor the betrothal contract," she said, her voice faint. "So they sent me in place of my sister."

Eight

IT COULDN'T REALLY BE that simple, Moss knew. One sister to replace another sister? Why not just send him a letter explaining the errant Felicia. Instead the family had been deceitful, so of course their intentions had to be more than honoring a marriage alliance.

Yet he only sensed truth coming from this woman's lips. No, he could not read her thoughts, no matter how much he concentrated. Was she some sort of witch, then? A seductress? Skilled in keeping her thoughts hidden and wooing the hearts of men? Because she was beautiful. Not in the extravagant way of the women of elite society, but in a way that intrigued him and made him want believe in what she'd told him.

"How old are you, Cornelia?" he asked.

She didn't hesitate. "Nineteen last month."

So she'd just reached the legal age of marriage. Fortunate, or unfortunate, for her. Her brown eyes were studying him just as frankly as he was studying her. He noticed how her thick lashes fluttered with each breath she took. This close to her, he could see the faint freckles on her nose and another freckle on the side of her mouth, as if it had escaped the rest.

Fine ladies didn't have freckles, but if she was the second daughter, it meant she'd been made to serve the elder daughter, and likely that included less structure on her activities. For an inane moment, he wanted to touch her face again because her skin had been so soft. And the way she smelled of the strawberry she'd eaten at the banquet wasn't making it any easier to keep his focus where it should be.

"How old are you, Lord Moss?" she asked, her voice trembling.

She was nervous around him, that was clear. Of course, she should be, the deceitful woman. Yet he sensed she was just as much a pawn as he was in this game of lords and ladies marrying for convenience and political agendas.

But that didn't mean he should trust her with much. "Twenty-six. And call me Moss. I am your husband now."

Her gaze flickered away, and she released a slow breath. The rise and fall of her chest was a bit of a distraction as she did so. Moss re-anchored his gaze on her face. "When did you plan on telling me of your deceit?"

A dusty pink stole over her cheeks, and her gaze shifted back to him. "I had . . . My parents told me to keep the veil on until you blew out the lamps tonight. And then, tomorrow, to continue wearing it—"

He chuckled. He couldn't help it. This young woman was certainly naïve, and her parents fools.

"Cornelia," he said, placing his hands on her arms. The silk of her wedding gown was smooth, and the warmth of her skin headed the palms of his hands. Her eyes widened at his touch, but she didn't flinch, didn't draw away, and strangely, this made him pleased.

"I knew the moment I saw you approach the castle doors that something was different about you," he said. "Do you really think you could pass for your petite, blue-eyed sister, even with a veil?"

Her faint blush now bloomed to red, which darkened the color of her lips as well. Fascinating. She took a heaving breath, which only emphasized her curves. No. She could not have fooled any man who'd spent any amount of time staring at the portrait of her older sister.

The pulse at her neck seemed to be racing as fast as his heart.

"Yet you married me anyway," she said, her voice less timid now. "Why?"

He inhaled her strawberry scent, mixed with something else. Roses. Of course.

"I believe in keeping my friends close but keeping my enemies closer," he said, holding back a smile as her lips parted in surprise. "I have yet to determine whether you, Cornelia, are a friend or enemy."

He watched for a subtle shift in her gaze, a narrowing of her eyes, a lift of her chin. Anything that might create a barrier between them and indicate that she was indeed taking her sister's place in order to do him harm. But she did none of that. She simply gazed at him, both confusion and innocence in those deep-brown eyes of hers.

"I am no enemy," she whispered.

If she was a witch, she was the best one he'd ever come across, because the purity in her gaze and words had him convinced of her innocence.

"I wish I could read your thoughts," he said. "How am I to trust a woman who married me under false pretenses?"

She did look away then, but he still had his hands on her arms, so he could also feel the tension in her body.

"Yet you married me, knowing I was not Felicia," she said in a barely-there voice. "And I signed the marriage contract with my true name."

Moss stared at her. She'd been a pawn. He'd been a pawn. "Why did you do it? Why did you agree? Your sister ran away and started a new life. You could have done the same."

"I have a gift," she said.

This admission shouldn't have surprised him, but it did.

She turned from him then, and he dropped his hands, yet she didn't move away. "I can hear the thoughts of men. Not all men, but most men. I cannot hear your thoughts, but—"

He grasped her hand and spun her toward him. "You cannot hear my thoughts?"

"No." She tugged her hand away from his and folded her arms. "I've been trying, but your mind is closed to me for some reason. And I've heard that your life is in danger. That there have been assassination attempts on your life. So I thought, if you didn't have me beheaded for treason, that I might help you. Listen to the thoughts of the men on the Isle. And uncover who wants you dead."

Could he believe that this woman, this new bride of his, had married him to *save* him and not to kill him?

Nine

LORD MOSS'S FACE HAD changed colors three times, and still he hadn't responded to her statement about reading men's thoughts. Would he accuse her of witchcraft, so instead of hanging for treason, she'd burn at the stake?

"You can hear a man's thoughts?" he said, his voice sounding incredulous.

She'd hoped that by telling him her greatest secret he would see that she had not set out to deceive him, but rather that she was willing to help him. "I am not a witch," she said.

Lord Moss's green eyes skated over her face as if he was trying to decide if she was telling the truth.

"I am not a witch," she repeated, desperation creeping into her voice. Would he take pity on her and spare her life? "My grandmother had the same gift, but not my mother or sister."

Lord Moss stepped away from her then, but instead of leaving her side, he walked around her, openly studying her as he walked. Finally, he stopped behind her, and she felt his fingers tug at her hair.

"Hearing another person's thoughts is a gift," he said in a murmur.

Was he sincere? She could not see him to be sure.

She waited for him to continue, her pulse wild.

"I can also read another's thoughts," he said. "Females, to be specific, except for yours."

She drew in a breath. Could it be possible? Was that why she could not hear *his* thoughts? She turned slowly to face him, and he let go of the lock of hair that he'd grasped.

"That's it, then," she said. "You have the gift too, and that is why we cannot read each other's minds."

His nod was slight. "That might be a problem."

"Problem?" Why did this send a rush of panic through her?

"I am used to knowing what a woman thinks at all times," he said. "But you are a mystery."

His gaze was open, almost vulnerable, and definitely curious.

Strangely, she felt like smiling. "You are a mystery too, my lord," she said.

"Moss."

She nodded. "Moss."

His features relaxed then, more than she'd seen thus far. But he was still carefully studying her, as if he weren't completely sure she was trustworthy, although she'd just told him her greatest secret.

She reached up and tugged off her blond wig. Moss's eyes widened, but he didn't look completely shocked.

"Your hair is as black as night," he said.

"Yes." She couldn't help the heat that rose to her face because of the way he was looking at her . . . as if he liked what he saw.

"It suits you," he said.

"You are not . . . disappointed that I'm not my sister?"

One of his brows rose. "I did not know Felicia. Marriages of convenience are just that . . . convenient."

Cornelia nodded. "I understand." But her voice sounded

breathy, unsure. She could not deny he was a handsome man with his dark hair, his green eyes, broad shoulders, and strong hands . . . but there was something more that drew her to him. When he looked at her, it was like he was really seeing her. It wasn't something she was used to. She'd always been the second daughter, the second best, the sister who served the eldest. The sister who made sure the eldest was happy and had everything she desired.

Cornelia had never considered her own desires. There had never been an opportunity to think of a life outside her home or lands. A life that was beyond her small bedroom or her parents' estate. No, Cornelia had never imagined that she might marry the Lord of the Isle of Rose and that he might stand before her, as her lawful husband, with appreciation in his eyes. Perhaps it was only a physical attraction on his part, and that was flattering enough, but it was more attention than she'd ever had in all her nineteen years.

"What now, my lord?" she asked, then quickly corrected. "Moss."

The edges of his mouth lifted, and although it was still far from a smile, it was also far from the soberness of before.

"I need to find out if I can really trust you," he said, his voice quiet. "And if I can, then we put a plan together. You and I. To find those who want me dead."

What a feat. How was she to prove to this man that she was sincere in her desire to help him and that she was trustworthy? Hadn't she followed her sister's wishes and delayed telling their parents the news of Felicia's departure?

"I am the second daughter, you see," Cornelia said, not sure where she was going with this but hoping it would have a good ending point. "I have spent my days in repairing my sister's gowns, keeping her hearth warm, bringing her meals in when she was ill, telling her stories to keep her smiling, and doing my duty by her in every way possible. For, you see, she was to become a great lady. All her life, and all my life, we believed that. And I wanted to help her achieve this greatness."

She paused and found that Lord Moss was listening intently.

After swallowing, Cornelia continued. "This morning when I found the note in my sister's room, she asked me to wait until high noon to break the news to my parents. And that is what I did." She released a slow breath. "I am loyal to my sister, always and forever. And if that means taking a man for a husband that was originally betrothed to her so that she can be happy with Louis Phillipe, then I will do so."

"You married me for your sister?"

"Like you said, I could have fled. But I did not," she said. "I hope you can believe that my intentions are honest and true."

"You make a pretty speech, Cornelia," Lord Moss said.

Her name on his tongue rolled off and sent a shiver through her.

"I know only the life of a veritable servant, my lord," she said. "And I plan to continue that life, although now I will serve *you*."

Lord Moss blinked, and his expression tightened. "I have servants aplenty. What I am in need of is a wife—a woman who will bear my children."

No amount of willpower could slow down the rushing heat through her body. But she kept her chin lifted, her gaze on him. "Is that another, higher form of servitude?"

His mouth twitched, but his eyes remained grave. "I believe it can be entirely different." He rested his hand on her shoulder, and Cornelia was too startled to react. It was like she'd been anchored to the plush rug beneath her feet.

When his thumb brushed against the bare skin of her

collar bone, Cornelia was pretty sure her heart had skipped several beats.

"How would it be different?" she asked, hating that her voice was breathless, because he would know how much he affected her.

He smiled then, and it was as if Cornelia were standing on a rocking skiff as the vibrant orange and pink of a sunset bloomed all around her.

Ten

"Being my wife will be entirely different than being a servant," Moss told Cornelia. "I can assure you that."

She puffed out a breath. "How so?"

Should he *answer* her, or should he *show* her?

Moss had wanted to kiss Cornelia the moment she removed her veil, and once the wig came off, the feeling had only intensified. This woman might have the gift of hearing, but she was no witch. Moss had heard the thoughts of evil women, and even though Cornelia's were silent to him, he could still ascertain much from a person's eyes.

Not only did he see the truth in them, he also saw her curiosity, mixed with her desire. *For him.* The feeling was heady, to say the least. Whatever events of misfortune had brought a different bride to him this day, he was grateful for the soft, supple woman who stood across from him now. Perhaps her pink-colored lips and her scent of strawberries had messed with his logic, but she was his wife . . . and kissing her would be perfectly acceptable.

Moss lifted his hand from her shoulder and touched her raven locks. Her hair was long, nearly to her waist, and it must have been uncomfortable keeping such a mass secured beneath the blond wig. The softness of her hair only drew him in, and he stepped closer. The only sound in the room beyond the crackle of the fire he'd built was their shared breathing.

He leaned down, and he almost gave in, almost kissed her, but as her eyes fluttered shut, he stilled. He'd heard a soft thud coming from the other side of the room. The closet, to be exact.

Cornelia opened her eyes, and by her expression, he knew she'd heard it too.

Someone else was in the room with them.

Moss brought a finger to his lips, indicating for Cornelia to be quiet. Her face had drained of color, but she nodded. Would she look so fearful if she was in on a plan to break into this place?

Whatever was going on, Moss wasn't going to delay. He reached for the dagger he kept secured on the inside of his boot. Cornelia moved away from him, and when he realized she was going to pick up the fire poker, he nodded his approval.

He walked toward the closet, where the sound had come from. There was a chance that once he opened the closet door, his new wife might also attack him, and Moss would be surrounded on both sides. But there was only one way to find out.

Moss reached for the latch, then in one swift motion, he lifted it and tugged open the door.

A boy of about nine years old tumbled out with a cry.

The little imp leapt to his feet, his blue eyes huge with fright.

Before the kid could flee, Moss grasped the boy's collar and twisted it tight. "Who are you? And what are you doing here?"

The boy yelped again and tried to escape Moss's grasp. But the kid was a skinny thing, and Moss didn't even need to use two hands.

"Identify yourself, right now," Moss said, bringing the dagger to the imp's throat.

The boy finally stilled, his eyes darting from Moss to Cornelia.

"He's only a child," Cornelia said, setting down the fire poker and joining them by the closet. She knelt before the miscreant and placed a hand on his shoulder.

"Don't touch him," Moss said. "He might bite, or worse."

Cornelia simply huffed out a breath. "Who sent you?" she asked in a gentle tone one might use for a non-criminal child.

The boy's lip jutted out, but he said nothing.

"Musk?" Cornelia asked.

Moss frowned. Who was she talking about? And then he realized that she was reading the boy's thoughts, and by the sudden paleness of his face, Moss could tell the boy wasn't pleased.

"Who is Musk?" Cornelia continued. "A man or a woman?"

The boy tried to shrink away from Cornelia, but Moss kept his grip firm on the boy's collar.

"A man . . ." Cornelia paused and looked up at Moss. "Do you know a man named Musk?"

"No," Moss said. "This boy needs to speak up and stop playing games."

Cornelia refocused on the boy. "We won't hurt you," she said in a soothing tone. "Are you hungry?"

The boy's eyebrow shot up, and Moss could almost feel the kid's hunger in his own stomach.

"Come," Cornelia said with a gentle smile. "Let's get you something to eat, and then you can tell us more about Musk."

Although Moss was still holding the boy captive, Moss felt the young body relent. Now that Moss thought about it, the skinny kid looked near starving. His clothing was worn and stained, and his hair needed a good washing.

Cornelia rose, then she gave Moss a look as if to say, *Release him.*

How dare she?

Moss released the kid, but not before giving Cornelia his own look of warning.

"Do we have food here, Moss?" she asked in a perfectly sweet tone. "Or should we send for it?"

"The covered basket on the table has food in it," Moss said.

Cornelia led the boy to the table with the basket.

Moss watched in wonder as she handed bread, cheese, and fruit to the boy, which he ate like he hadn't tasted food for days. The color slowly returned to the boy's cheeks, and when his eating finally slowed, Cornelia began to tell him stories of her childhood.

Moss wasn't sure where she was going with these tales, but he found himself listening with interest. He also discovered that Cornelia loved dogs and books and experimenting with baking in the kitchen. She'd also spent a great deal of time taking care of what sounded like a rather spoiled older sister.

When she had the boy's rapt attention and growing trust, she said, "I'll bet a clever boy like you has a clever name."

The boy's face flushed, and he must have thought his name because Cornelia said, "Swany?"

By the expression on the boy's face, Moss knew she'd guessed right.

"So unique," Cornelia continued with an unaffected smile. "Are you named after someone?"

"No," the boy said. "I have no family."

"Musk is not your father?" she asked.

Swany shook his head adamantly.

"I'll tell you what." Cornelia removed one of the bracelets from her wrist. "I'll give you my bracelet to do with what you'd like if you tell me why Musk sent you here tonight."

The boy looked from Cornelia to the bracelet and swallowed.

Moss watched in fascination as the boy reached for the gold band. His thin fingers wrapped around the luster, and he turned the bracelet over. The gold gleamed in the light of the nearby oil lamp.

"He wants me to listen to everything Lord Moss says to his new bride." Swany looked up. "You."

Cornelia nodded her encouragement.

The boy continued, "He wants to know where Lord Moss will take you for your . . . honey . . ."

"Honeymoon?" Cornelia cast a glance at Moss, her own face flushed.

Swany nodded, looking nervous again.

"And once you report back to Musk," she said, "what is he going to give you?"

"A loaf of bread," Swany said.

Cornelia didn't say anything for a moment, then she spoke in a soft tone. "If you report back what I tell you to say, then I will give you bread *every* day. Isn't that right, Lord Moss?" Her gaze was back on him.

"Of—of course," Moss said, clearing his throat. He crouched to look the boy in the eyes. "Do you know what a counterspy is?"

A wrinkle appeared between Swany's eyebrows.

"It means that you keep Musk believing you're a spy for *him*, but truly, you're a spy for *me*."

Eleven

"Do you think this will truly work?" Moss asked Cornelia.

"It has to," she whispered, scanning the looming trees beyond them. They were currently hiding behind a hedgerow as they waited for Swany to return from reporting to Musk.

They'd followed the boy through the garden to the forest beyond. Cornelia had donned her wig again and brought her veil in case they should come across any of the wedding guests. Swany had informed Moss of the agreed-upon meeting place with Musk, yet Cornelia didn't want to get too close. The boy would report to Musk where she and Lord Moss would honeymoon, and then they'd be ready for whatever attack was about to take place. Lord Moss had already dispatched his most trusted guards to the location, where they'd wait in hiding.

There wasn't much to see, since the forest was dark with the night, and when the form of a small boy emerged from the trees, Cornelia grasped Moss's arm. Swany wasn't alone.

He walked with a tall man, dressed in dark colors.

"Do you know him?" Cornelia whispered to her husband.

Moss tone was gruff when he replied. "Yes. His name is Bourbon, and he's my mother's lover."

Cornelia had been introduced to many people throughout the day, and she wasn't sure who the man was, but she'd met Lady Alba. "Are you sure?" she whispered.

Moss put his hand over hers; his fingers were cool in the night air. "Can you hear his thoughts?"

"I will try," she murmured. Then she closed her eyes, the touch of Moss's hand on hers propelling her on. First, she heard Swany's thoughts. He was nervous and scared, yet he was looking forward to eating more food at the garden lodge, which made Cornelia want to smile.

She steadied her breathing and moved her mind beyond the young boy's thoughts of food and focused on the man next to him. She heard a low rumbling, discontented words, and dissatisfaction directed toward Swany.

Cornelia snapped her eyes open. The man named Bourbon didn't trust Swany. Something had happened, or perhaps the boy had somehow revealed his deceit. Whatever it was, Bourbon was not planning on letting Swany get away with anything.

"Moss," Cornelia whispered. "Bourbon knows that Swany has tricked him. Whatever trap we lay for him, he will be ready to counteract."

Moss reached for the dagger he'd strapped to his thigh. "We will end this now."

"Wait," Cornelia said. She had no doubt that Lord Moss was an able fighter, but Bourbon's thoughts were now tumbling into her mind. "There's someone else. A mastermind. Bourbon is only part of the game."

Moss darted a glance at her, and she held up a hand as she listened. "He has a rendezvous with *her* tonight."

"A *woman*?" Moss said. "Are you sure?"

"I am sure." Cornelia met his gaze beneath the moonlight. He still gripped her hand, and although she couldn't read his mind, she felt the tension radiating from him.

The two of them watched as Bourbon and Swany separated in the forest, Swany hurrying back to the garden lodge. Bourbon continued on whatever path he was following, which brought him a few paces closer to the hedgerow, then away again.

After his form had disappeared into the night again, Moss said, "What woman would be powerful enough to command a man such as Bourbon?"

By the way his eyes widened, Cornelia knew that he'd made the deduction at the same moment as her. But surely his own mother wouldn't plot against Moss.

"I could be mistaken," she said in a stilted whisper.

"You were sure a moment ago."

She blinked. "Yes."

Moss held her gaze for a moment, then he lifted his hands and placed them on either side of her face. In the garden lodge, Cornelia had wondered if Moss was about to kiss her, but now that they were completely alone, and he was so earnestly gazing at her, she sensed his thoughts were far from anything romantic.

"Can I trust you, Cornelia Rose?" Moss whispered in a fierce tone.

And in his gaze, she saw his desire to trust her and the hope he clung to. She'd only met this man, this husband of hers, this morning, but already, her heart was becoming involved. He had been nothing but open and honest with her. And now, his very life was threatened by his own mother.

Somehow, some way, Cornelia wanted to protect this man from more heartache.

"You can trust me, husband," she said, hoping that he would know she spoke the absolute truth.

He gazed at her for a long moment, his hands still cradling her face, as if he wanted to dispel all of his doubts.

She slowly raised her hands and placed them over his.

His gaze intensified, and the only sound was their shared breathing.

"What do you want me to do?" she whispered.

After a small pause, Moss said, "Go to my mother's chambers. Listen in as long as you can. If you are discovered, say that you've lost your way. Discover Bourbon's thoughts. Find out if the woman he speaks of is my mother."

Cornelia gave the smallest nod. "And if it is?"

The edges of his mouth tightened. "Then I will put her on trial for treason."

The breath hissed out of Cornelia, and she nodded.

He lowered his hands.

"I will go now." Cornelia rose to her feet and straightened the cloak she wore over her wedding gown. "There's no telling how long Bourbon will wait before putting his plans into action against Swany."

Moss stood, his expression mixed with anger and determination. "I'll take you to one of the back entrances." As they walked toward the castle, they didn't speak.

By the time they reached the door that connected the castle to the gardens, Cornelia's pulse was drumming with nerves.

Moss pulled on the latch, then turned to her. "Take my dagger with you." He pressed the hilt of the knife into her palm. "Be careful."

She knew the action meant he wholly trusted her. At last. He'd just given her a weapon, making him an unarmed man now. She looked up at him, meeting his dark gaze.

"I will," she whispered.

Then he stepped closer, so that his tall form loomed over hers, and before she could think of what he meant by it, he pulled her against him.

He leaned down and pressed his lips upon hers, softly.

Cornelia had never been kissed, and as his mouth moved against hers, fire raced through her body. And she wanted more. With her free hand, she grasped the lapel of his jacket, pulling him even closer, tasting him as he was tasting her. The night was no longer cool, the danger seemed far away, and any reservations about becoming this man's wife were forgotten. Her heart raced, her skin buzzed, and her thoughts swirled.

All too soon, Moss released her. "You must go now," he rasped. "I will be waiting at the garden lodge with Swany."

He stepped back as if he was trying to keep distance between them.

Cornelia's mind had not quite floated back to reality yet. She took a couple of deep breaths. "I will be swift."

She turned from him then, because the urgency in his eyes made her want to hurry, though the desire in them made her want to stay.

Cornelia hurried inside, leaving him behind and following the directions he'd given her. She passed by a couple of servants who looked surprised to see her, but no one tried to stop her. Surely they recognized her as the blond woman who'd married Lord Moss.

Once she reached the corridor of Lady Alba's chambers, Cornelia breathed more freely. This plan would work; it had to. She stopped outside the blue door that Moss had described, then quieted her breathing so she could hear what was going on inside. The moments passed slowly, but there were no sounds from within. Was she too late?

"Well, well, what do we have here?" a deep voice said.

Twelve

TEN MINUTES PASSED, THEN ten more. When Cornelia had been gone for an entire half hour, Moss decided he'd waited long enough. He'd stayed at the door that led to the garden, but there had been no sign of her return.

Was he being unreasonable? What if she was in the middle of a heart-to-heart with his mother? It didn't matter. Because the possibility of his mother being behind the assassination attempts infuriated him. Disgusted him.

Moss opened the garden door and stepped into the dank hallway. The dimness was brighter than it had been outside, so he had no trouble navigating the hallways. He took the steps of the back stairway two at a time until he reached the floor where his mother's chambers were.

The corridor was silent, and perhaps that should have been a warning, but Moss pressed on.

He wanted to see his wife. He wanted to assure himself that she was all right.

When he neared the set of blue doors, a form stepped out of the shadows.

"Bourbon," Moss said. Maybe he should have been surprised to see that man lurking, but nothing surprised him now.

"Lord Moss," Bourbon said in his deep voice. "To what

do I owe this pleasure?" His tone was a scraping sound against stone, and Moss involuntarily shivered.

"I am seeking my bride," Moss said. "Have you seen her?" He tried to keep his words calm, bored even, but he could tell Bourbon wasn't fooled for a minute.

"You've come to the right place." Bourbon nodded toward the door. "Step inside. Your mother is waiting for her loyal son, and your wife is waiting for her devoted husband."

A chill crept along Moss's spine. This was surely a trap. One he'd already stepped into. He had no dagger, no way to defend himself, save the strength of his own body. Yet he opened the door and walked into his mother's chambers.

The sight of what he found nearly took his breath away.

Cornelia was bound and gagged. Her blond wig had been discarded, her cloak removed. Her eyes widened as their gazes connected.

Behind her stood his mother, the dagger in her hand—the one he'd given Cornelia.

"What's going on?" he said, tone seething.

His mother laughed. "You're cleverer than I gave you credit for, my dear. Bringing in this minx to fool us all."

The door shut behind Moss, and Bourbon latched it.

Moss looked from his mother to Bourbon, then to Cornelia. "She is no minx," Moss said. "She signed her true name on the wedding contract, and she is my wife. So tell me why you are treating her like chattel and why you want me dead."

His mother's green eyes flashed. "You are direct."

He scoffed. "What other course is there?"

Bourbon folded his arms, keeping his defiant stance by the door.

"Is my very existence so abhorrent to you?" Moss asked his mother.

"Your existence has been tolerable," his mother said. "Until I met Bourbon."

The man had the audacity to grin.

"We have plans for the Isle that don't include you," his mother continued.

He should have felt like he'd been punched, but instead he felt the numbness of disbelief.

"If I die," he said, "then my cousin will inherit."

"If you die," his mother said in a smooth tone, "the people will side with the grieving mother and widow. The people will stand with us, and we'll win against any army or resistance brought against us."

Moss stared at the woman who'd borne him. "You seem so sure. How long have you been planning this?"

"Two years," his mother said in a triumphant voice. "Once I built a tolerance to nightroot, it was just a matter of getting your father to take the draft that I'd prepared for him."

This revelation jolted through Moss. "You poisoned Father?"

His mother didn't even look remorseful.

Moss's mind reeled. Lies. So many things had been lies.

Bourbon stepped closer, and Moss stiffened. He might not be able to read the man's mind, but there was no doubt the man was ready to follow any command of Moss's mother.

"What do you want from me, Mother?" Moss ground out.

"I want you gone," she said in a steady tone. "Whether you go into exile or fall at the hands of one of my assassins, it doesn't matter to me."

It took Moss only a moment to decide. "Release my wife, and we will disappear."

Out of the corner of his eye, he saw Cornelia strain against her bindings. She didn't agree, but Moss could see no other way right now. He was outnumbered, and—

The door burst open, and Moss spun to see Swany, Portland, and several men step into the room. And they were armed.

But Moss didn't have time to feel relieved, because Bourbon was already charging the men with his dagger raised. His mother moved behind Cornelia and pressed another dagger at her neck.

The time for discussion had ended, and Moss could only hope that Providence would be with him and that his mother wouldn't harm Cornelia while he enacted his desperate plan. Leaving Portland, Swany, and the others to fend off Bourbon, he slipped behind his mother and grasped the hand with the dagger.

She whirled on him and plunged the dagger toward him. Her strength was greater than he could have anticipated, so the dagger scraped along his arm before he was able to wrest it away.

She screamed for Bourbon, calling him Musk, but Moss captured her arms behind her back.

"Swany!" Moss called out, and in a moment, the boy was by his side. "Untie Cornelia, and I will use the bands."

The boy made quick work of untying the bands, then he handed them to Moss.

Once his mother was secured, both wrists and ankles bound, Moss looked toward the other skirmish. Portland overpowered Bourbon, and more guards had arrived.

"Put him in the dungeon," Moss commanded. Then he looked down at his mother. Her mouth trembled, but her gaze was fiery. He took a deep breath and said the words he'd never thought he'd say. "Take my mother to the dungeons too. She is a traitor to the Isle of Rose."

Thirteen

CORNELIA HAD BEEN LIKE a prisoner herself. No, not in the dungeon beneath the castle, but confined to the luxurious chambers that belonged to her new husband. She had not seen him the rest of the night as he met with his council.

She had not seen him all the next day, not when she bade farewell to her parents and tried to answer their questions. Cornelia hadn't seen Moss when meals were brought to her. She'd tried to read, she'd tried to write, but she couldn't focus on anything. So she'd paced, eaten a little, and slept intermittently. And now as evening fell once again, Cornelia was still alone. Still without word from Moss.

So when the door to the chamber cracked open, she looked over, expecting a servant.

"Moss," she said as he strode toward her.

The darkness beneath his eyes was proof of his exhaustion, but there was also triumph in his green gaze. He'd shed his jacket at some point, and he wore his sleeves rolled up.

Cornelia rose from the chair by the window, unsure what to say to him first. She had so many questions.

He continued to walk toward her, his gaze moving over her face.

"You are well?" he asked, stopping in front of her.

He was asking *her*? "I am well," she said. "What about you? What has happened?"

Moss exhaled and ran a hand through his hair. He looked toward the window and the darkening landscape beyond. "The trial is over, and my mother and her co-conspirator have been exiled to separate principalities." His gaze found hers again. "If you hadn't heard Bourbon's thoughts the other night, I don't know what would have happened. We certainly wouldn't be standing here, free from threats."

Cornelia could only hope. She took a step toward him and touched his arm. "*Are* we truly free?"

"As free as we can expect to be," Moss said, his other hand folding over hers. "Cornelia," he continued in a quiet voice. "We will always have to be on our guard. There will always be those who want our power and wish us ill. Are you ready to live such a life with me? Or have you packed your bags already?"

"No," she whispered. "I've sent my parents home, and I've done nothing but wait for you because I wanted to know you were safe."

His lips curved into a smile, but his gaze was sober. "I am pleased to hear that, and perhaps we could forget the outside world and its dangers for a short time."

She nodded, feeling numb, but also allowing some relief and joy to creep in.

Her husband clasped her hand and brought it to his lips. After pressing a kiss there, he said, "I am grateful for *you*, dear Cornelia. Providence has brought us together, and I intend to keep it that way."

Cornelia's pulse drummed as Moss released her hand, then cradled her face with his hands. A slow heat began where he was touching her, spreading throughout the rest of her body, and she remembered how he'd kissed her in the garden.

Looking into his eyes now, she knew that she too was grateful that he was *here,* wanting her to be his wife.

Cornelia placed her hands on his chest, feeling the thump of his heart. She was nervous, yet she also wanted to be closer to him.

"I am pleased to be your wife, Moss," she said.

He smiled then, and his eyes glittered as he gazed at her. "Truly?"

"Truly."

Moss slid his hands behind her neck, and bits of fire danced along her skin at his touch as he leaned down. His mouth touched hers. Warm and soft and urgent. The scruff of his whiskers from not shaving for the past couple of days both tickled and exhilarated her.

Cornelia wound her arms about his neck, and he moved his hands down her back, drawing her ever closer until she was sure every part of her was encompassed by every part of him.

"Cornelia," he whispered moments later when he broke off his kissing.

But she didn't have a chance to answer, because he kissed the length of her neck, and she couldn't be sure if her feet were touching the ground any longer. The stars that were beginning to appear in the night sky on the other side of the window were nothing like the stars bursting inside of her.

This man was her husband now, and she looked forward to the months and years ahead. Getting to know him. Learning all she could. Appreciating all that he had to offer.

He drew her by the hand to the window, and in the fading light, the gardens of the Isle spread below. "How far can you see?" he asked, sliding his arms around her from behind.

She leaned against him, and he rested his chin on her shoulder.

"I can see past the forest and to the bay."

His breath was warm against her neck. "As far as you can see is yours now. *Ours.* We will protect our land and each other always. Together."

She let the warmth of his body surround her, and his breathing sang to her heart. Now, in this man's arms, she knew that her true life was finally beginning.

Check out Jane Redd's next fantasy!
Visit Jane's [Amazon author page](#):

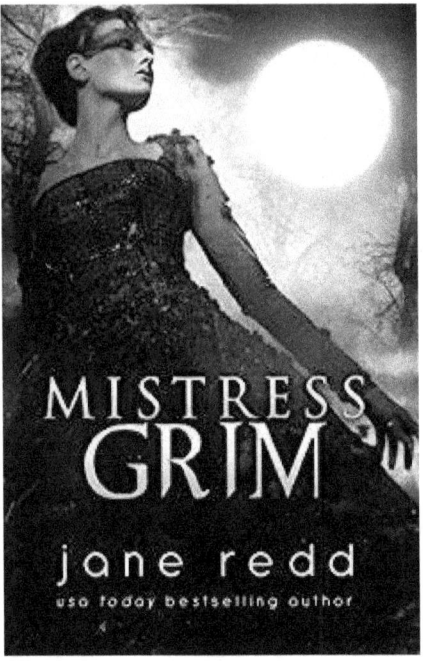

Writing under Jane Redd, Heather B. Moore is a *USA Today* bestselling author. She writes Young Adult speculative under Jane Redd. Recent titles include *Solstice, Lake Town,* and *Mistress Grim*. She writes historical thrillers under the pen name H.B. Moore. Her latest thrillers include *Slave Queen* and *The Killing Curse*. Under the name Heather B. Moore, she writes romance and women's fiction; her newest releases include the historical romance *Love is Come*. She's also one of the coauthors of the *USA Today* bestselling series: A Timeless Romance Anthology.

For book updates, sign up for Heather's email list:
hbmoore.com/contact
Website: HBMoore.com
Facebook: Fans of H.B. Moore
Facebook: Jane Redd Books
Blog: MyWritersLair.blogspot.com
Instagram: @authorhbmoore
Twitter: @HeatherBMoore

Lady of Shadows

by Amber Argyle

For Stacy Jacobson, who taught me when no one else would.

One

Hollow

CAELIA STOOD BEFORE HER family table in the back of the manor house. She pushed the heels of her hands into the warm, sticky dough. Too sticky. Her fingers dipped into the sack beside her. She sprinkled flour across the top and folded it in. The dough clung to her skin before coming clean away.

Her family's servant, Joy, stepped up beside her. Her hair was tightly curled and black as night. Her skin was a cool brown. The woman was like her bread, warm and soft and filling. She tested the dough's release. "Perfect."

Caelia smiled to herself, proud of the simple task she had mastered. The fire was warm behind her, pleasant in the cool, predawn morning. Joy and her kitchen were like splashes of rain to Caelia's parched soul, each drop thrumming into the hollow emptiness inside her.

Wearing his most elaborate leather vest, her father stepped into the room. They had the same pale skin and black hair, though his was turning gray at the temples and beard. Caelia's smattering of freckles and her winter-blue eyes came from her mother.

Her mother. Dead of the putrid throat three years past. The pain in Caelia's heart was still sharp and poisoned.

Papa frowned when he saw Caelia's dress, the lines

bracketing his mouth severe. "I buy you a wardrobe of the finest dresses from Landra, and you wear a peasant's attire."

Caelia brushed her hands down the apron, aware of the baggy shirt and plain brown skirt she'd bought in town yesterday—the shopkeeper had assumed she was buying it for Joy, and Caelia let her think it.

She couldn't bend in her fine dresses—not with their blasted corsets and tight bodices. Not to mention that it was impossible to brush the dirt from the fine velvet skirts. "I need to work in the garden."

Her father pulled out a chair and sat at the table. "That's why we have Joy and the hired hands. You're a lord's daughter. Not a maid."

Caelia's head dropped. She was trapped in this house. Trapped by the disgusted looks and the buzzing gossip that followed her like angry wasps—never to her face. Not yet. After all, she was still the lord's daughter. Expected to manage the household, plan parties, and keep correspondence with their family throughout the United Cities of the Idelmarch. Not hoe the garden barefoot, the sun-warmed earth soothing the hurt inside her.

Joy pulled the skillet of dala bread off the hearth stones, and plopped it down hard on the table. "Taking nothing and making it into something can be its own kind of healing, Lord Daydon." She was obviously angry, but smart enough to keep her tone civil.

Papa clearly wanted to argue—the servant shouldn't talk back. But Joy wasn't just any servant. Her breads and jams were enough to keep any man silent. And there was the matter of Caelia and her father's secret. Joy couldn't know anything. Not for certain. But she had to suspect.

"Fine," Papa grumbled. "But you will not wear that attire beyond the yard."

Caelia bowed her head. "Yes, Papa."

Grumbling, Papa looked around the spacious kitchen. "Has that boy not come down yet?" He cupped his hands around his mouth. "Bane! Breakfast! Now! Or you'll have nothing until lunch."

Caelia shot Joy a thankful look as pounding footsteps traced Bane's progress from the side of his bed on the second story down the narrow stairs—where he skipped the last four to jump to the bottom—and rounding in through the kitchen.

Still half asleep, he raked thick, black hair out of his eyes. It promptly fell back. He had the same pale skin and hooked nose as Caelia, though his eyes were bright gold surrounded by brown. He instantly zeroed in on the dala bread. "Is there honey?"

Joy chuckled. "Honey, yes, but only if you agree to a haircut."

He glared at them from under said hair. "I hate haircuts." Stuck between a child and a man, his voice warbled.

"I'm afraid that will have to wait." Papa laid a slice of ham onto his plate beside his dala bread. "We've a full docket of rulings today. The magistrate will be waiting."

Gleeful at his triumph, Bane wolfed his meal down like he hadn't eaten in days, though Caelia had heard him sneaking food from the cellar in the middle of the night.

Joy packed them eggs, bread, cheese, and an apple for lunch. "Speaking of which, I need permission to attend today."

He eyed her as he drank his tea. "You're a complainant?"

This surprised Caelia. Joy and her husband and daughter got along well with everyone in their small town.

Joy didn't meet his gaze. "Yes, sir."

"Why not tell me now?"

Joy shuffled uncomfortably. "Harben agreed to pay us ten bags of wheat and two chickens for our goat when his harvest came in."

Papa's teacup froze halfway to its saucer. Caelia's heart echoed frantically through her hollow chest. Harben's wife, Pennice, knew their secret. If the woman told anyone, rumor would be confirmed as fact and Caelia was through.

"If Harben can afford to keep the pub in business all on his own," Joy went on, "he can afford to pay us for our goat."

Harben had a bloated sense of self-importance and poor money-managing skills. Papa couldn't offer the man leniency. And if Papa started favoring Harben now, when would it ever end?

Papa studiously avoided Caelia's panicked gaze as he pushed to his feet. "Maybe you'd better come after all, Joy." He stiffened as he noticed Bane watching them from underneath his unruly hair. "The forest take you, boy, get dressed! I'm ready to leave."

Bane shot to his feet and out of sight beyond the kitchen.

Joy untied her apron. "Make sure you grease the corners and mind you don't burn the bottom." Caelia didn't understand what the woman was talking about until Joy nodded to the bread pans.

All at once, Caelia became aware of the dough drying under her nails and around her cuticles. "Yes. I mean, no. I'll watch it." She turned away before Joy could note the desperation on her face. Their family servant already suspected more than she should.

"Fetch your cloak, Joy," Papa said. "And wait for me outside. It's chilly this morning."

"Yes, of course." Joy took her cloak from the peg and slipped outside, where the light had turned more silver than gray. Sunrise would be coming soon.

"I'll take care of it," Papa said softly to Caelia.

"How?" Caelia's voice broke.

"I'll tell Pennice we owe her one favor—anything she wants. But she can ask once."

"What makes you think she'll honor that agreement?"

Papa spread his hands on the table and leaned forward. "If she doesn't, she gets nothing."

Their secret lay heavy and dark between them. Caelia could feel the tears building.

"No one has any proof. Just stay by me until the storm passes."

Clearly, the town didn't need proof. "And if it doesn't?"

"I'll make sure it does," he said firmly.

Wanting desperately to believe him, she hastily wiped her eyes and nodded.

Her father went for his own cloak when a distant shout sounded from the town. Then another. And another. Each closer than the last. The bell tolled, the peal resonating through the hollow of Caelia's chest. A girl had been taken in the night. Stolen by the beast of the Forbidden Forest. A fist of dread reached up from Caelia's middle, choking her.

Papa was already out the door. Caelia hurried after him, her boots leaving dark prints in the rime. Spread out below them, the town glittered white with early-morning frost. Chimney smoke rose from the split-shingle roofs of a few hundred homes surrounded by dead fields.

Past the low stone wall, a man rode a black horse bareback up the hill toward them. Steam burst from the animal's flared, pink nostrils. Its coat was dark with sweat.

Caelia recognized the rider and froze, everything inside her going blank.

Chickens scattered as Kenjin reined the animal in and looked down at them, his face ashen and his feet bare. "Atara is gone."

A dozen memories assaulted Caelia. When they were children, she and Atara had caught frogs by the river. Later, they had giggled over boys at the town fair. Later still, as Caelia lay sick with fever, Atara had come to visit nearly every day, the smell of wind in her dark hair.

No. Not Atara. Not the one friend who hadn't deserted Caelia. Her legs trembled, threatening to buckle beneath her.

"The beast took her in the night." Kenjin's voice was wooden, as if he were speaking of someone else's firstborn. Someone else's daughter. His haunted, hollow eyes met Caelia's. The emptiness there mirrored her own. She looked away first.

Papa exhaled and passed his hand down his face. More townspeople rushed up the hill as the sun crested the horizon. The harsh morning light robbed the world of color and set the frost to glittering. Everyone was silent. There was nothing to say. Nothing to be done. They all knew the pain of losing a girl to the beast.

The town parted before the town druid, Rimoth. With his pale, pointed face and sparse mustache, he looked like a dead rat. His silent daughter trailed after her father like a ghost.

"We must have a sacrifice," Rimoth proclaimed. "Tonight."

Girls tended to disappear in clusters. Two or three. Sometimes as many as five. As town lord, Papa would offer an animal for the beast to take to its lair and devour instead of one of their daughters. Caelia couldn't see the point, as Rimoth always cut them down for himself come morning.

"We must go after her!" Kenjin cried. "Her prints are still fresh. If we hurry, we can find her before—" He choked, breaking off.

Before the beast tore her apart.

Ancestors, Atara. Why hadn't she screamed? But none of them ever did. No one knew how the beast lured them into his forest. No one even knew what the beast looked like. All they really knew was that any girl who went into the forest never came out again.

"Papa," Caelia murmured, a note of pleading in her voice. Papa worked his jaw, his hands balling into fists.

"I'll go after her."

Everything inside Caelia stopped as Mal pushed to the front of the crowd. He was handsome as a midsummer day—eyes like a bright blue sky, hair straight and bright gold as a wasp's stripes.

Caelia was not beautiful, and she'd been flattered by the attention of the best-looking boy in town. But he'd never loved her. He didn't care about Atara either, not really. What he wanted was to prove something. All this time, and Caelia still wasn't sure what that something was.

A half dozen other boys shouted their agreement, forming up behind him.

The townspeople's gazes shifted between Caelia and the boy she had loved. In the excitement, the gossips had forgotten her. But now their heads ducked together, whispers a warning drone that made Caelia squirm.

"You go in," Rimoth said in his high, rat voice, "and you'll come back mad or dead." As the town druid, he was their intermediary with the forest. And he wasn't wrong. Less than a quarter of a mile inside the forest lay the stirring—the vile part of the forest that attacked anyone who dared breech her borders.

The village erupted in debate—some calling for sacrifice, others for action. As the town lord, it was up to Papa to decide.

"We will offer sacrifice," her father shouted over the din. "Gather at the bridge at twilight. Now go home."

Mal glared at her father. His gaze never once strayed to her. "We have a right to go after them."

Papa squared off in front of Mal. "The forest take you, you will obey me, or you will spend your day in the stocks."

The confrontation between her father and Mal had been building for months. More heads ducked together, more whispers buzzed. Caelia couldn't appear to have a stake in this fight. She locked her hands together to keep from wringing them, every part of her so tense she felt certain she would tremble apart.

The magistrate stepped closer. Clearly sensing the man, Mal let out a long breath. He turned on his heel and pushed through the crowd, his cronies close behind.

Knowing he'd lost, Kenjin pushed his horse closer. "And what will you do, Lord Daydon, when the beast comes after your own daughter?"

Papa didn't flinch. "We will honor Atara tonight, Kenjin. And I will mourn with you."

The loss in Kenjin's gaze shifted to fury that ran swift and cold as the heart of the river. "They disappear in clusters, Daydon. Keep an eye on your own child."

Caelia wasn't sure if the words were a threat or a warning. Kenjin turned his mount and rode away. A shudder shook Caelia hard.

"Caelia," her father said with a start. "Get inside! You'll catch your death."

Only then did she feel the cold and realize she'd forgotten her cloak. She folded her arms tight over her chest. Shame crept up her skin, making her shiver. Her father would never face his daughter's empty, cold bed. His daughter was safe. The beast never took broken girls. And Caelia was most definitely broken.

Two

Drum

SITUATED BEHIND HER FATHER and next to her brother, Caelia joined the long procession of people moving to the river. Each held a small homemade lantern. Caelia had made her family's this afternoon by pounding a nail to the center of a board, pushing a small candle into the sharp end, and tying a small paper dome over it.

West of the narrow bridge that spanned the river, Caelia came to a stop at the riverbank, the mud seeping into the leather of her boots and making her feet damp. Her father stood on her left, her brother on her right. The wind picked up, flaring her cloak behind her. Shivering, she gripped the collar tight.

Druid Rimoth took his place at the head of the bridge. Behind him, Kenjin stood dead-eyed with his family, his wife and children weeping. Rimoth began his tribute to Atara's life by illuminating her beauty. Her grace. Her goodness. He obviously didn't know her. Atara made an art out of cuss words and stomped everywhere she went. She laughed long and loud, her head tipped back with abandon.

How could it be that Caelia would never see her friend again? They would never sneak sips of brandy from her father's liquor cabinet. Never slip out of their houses in the dead of night to meet their friends by the river, where they would take turns scaring each other witless with stories of the beast. Never plot Mal's gruesome death while Caelia lay on her sickbed.

Bane's chilly fingers found Caelia's. He hadn't held her hand in months. Not since he'd decided he was too old to be coddled. At that tender touch, all Caelia's walls came down and she wept softly.

When the man finally stopped talking, Caelia handed the lantern to Bane. He bent down, carefully set it in the river, and gave it a gentle push. It bobbled in the shallows until it caught in the main current.

A river of lanterns passed before Caelia. She watched until the last disappeared into the Forbidden Forest. Her eyes slipped closed.

Last week, Caelia had sat with her friend in the garden, the smell of rotten pumpkins lending a spice to the air as they took a break from harvesting potatoes. Caelia's eyes were swollen and puffy from crying. She stroked the kitten in her lap as it purred fiercely.

"Do you really want to live in a place where you have to pretend it never happened?" Atara asked.

Caelia froze. She'd suspected that Atara had guessed, but she'd never dared ask.

Sighing, Atara sat beside her. "Those old gossips don't like me either. I'm not demure enough for them. This is a small town with small people. We're meant for more, Caelia."

"They'll never let me have more."

"Then we'll leave. Start fresh somewhere else. I have an aunt and uncle in Cordova. We could stay with them over the winter. Skate on the lake and flirt with pretty boys at the dances."

"I'll speak with my father." But Caelia hadn't worked up

the courage. And now, the drum of her friend's heart was silenced forever. *If I could, I would avenge you, Atara. I would kill the beast.*

A hand on her arm startled her. Papa's gaze was concerned. Rimoth was already passing them by, Atara's family directly behind him. Wiping the tears freezing her cheeks, Caelia hurried to slip into her place behind them, the townspeople following.

They passed the base of the hill that Caelia's home was built upon, the town temporarily shifting out of sight on the other side. They passed Joy and Vyder's home and the furrows of their fields. Until they came to the Forbidden Forest's border, the trees black against the pockmarked sky.

Standing boldly before the rest was the Curse Tree, the thorns as big as Caelia's smallest finger. "Nothing good comes from the Forbidden Forest" went the old saying. So the villagers paid Rimoth to write curses on ribbons and tie them to the branches. "May the forest take my daughter" when they really meant "pass over her in peace," or "let my harvest be full of worms" when they really meant "let the harvest feed my family through the winter."

Blessings from curses.

Caelia found her own curse—bright yellow ribbon that had faded to the color of rotten egg yolks. Her blessing had come exactly as she'd wanted. She hated herself for it.

They paused beside a large pile of branches gathered from the outer edges of the forest. Beside it was tethered the spring kid that Bane had tended through the summer. It nibbled at the sticks in the pile, oblivious to its coming death as much as Atara had been.

Her father took his place beside the druid. Rimoth took a torch from a man and pressed it into the nest of kindling at the base. It caught quickly, the fire devouring the small bits of pine needles and shredded bark. Startled, the kid bleated and backed away.

When the flame had started into the smaller branches, Rimoth turned his attention to the Forbidden Forest. "Beast of the forest, we offer sacrifice—a tender spring kid—in the hopes that you will pass over our daughters in peace."

The kid didn't struggle as Rimoth took hold of its neck and flank—it was used to being handled by Bane. Rimoth rolled the creature up on his knees and pinned it to the ground. Only then did the creature struggle, bleating pitifully. Rimoth held out his hand. His pale, silent daughter, Maisy, pressed the knife into it.

Bane buried his head in Caelia's side. She pulled him close, pressing her forearm and body into his ears so he wouldn't hear. Rimoth sawed across the creature's throat. It struggled in vain, its mouth open and silent, as it could no longer draw breath with which to make sound. Maisy shoved a bowl under its neck, catching the blood as it gushed in ever weakening pumps.

It was over in seconds.

Rimoth poured a little wine into the blood to keep it from congealing. He held the bowl out to the forest and intoned some more. Caelia no longer listened, no longer watched. The night was full of death and blood. Maybe it always had been; she'd just never realized before.

The bonfire grew by leaps and bounds, the heat surging against her bare skin, leaving her hot in front and cold in back. Rimoth threw the blood onto the fire. The flames sputtered and smoked, the burned-meat smell acrid and choking. The flames rose as the moisture sizzled away.

Rimoth tied the kid to a branch of the curse tree by its back hooves. They would leave it there all night. And in the morning, he would return for the carcass—the meat serving his own home. Caelia watched the dead kid sway on the breeze.

Had the beast cut Atara's throat? Had she tried to scream, but couldn't because she could no longer draw breath? Had she still been alive when he'd begun to devour her?

A cup was pressed into Caelia's hand. She gasped in a breath, coming around as if she'd been caught in a nightmare.

Her father peered into her eyes. "Drink, Caelia. It will make you feel better." He gave another one to Bane, who wiped the tears from his face before his friends could see, his back to his dead goat. He drank it all at once and then darted away.

Caelia lifted the wine to her mouth. It tasted of bitter earth—terrible wine, but she swallowed anyway. She stayed safely a step behind her father as he spoke with city officials about ensuring no one went into the forest and brought the beast's ire upon the town.

Shortly after, the musicians started. Atara had been grieved. The beast had been satisfied. Now, it was time to get drunk and forget.

There had been a time when the drums throbbed beneath Caelia's skin, beating in time to her thundering heart, the light from the bonfire crimson behind her closed eyes. Sweat had beaded her skin and her feet had pounded out a rhythm. Her skirts flared then tightened around her legs like a second skin. She hadn't cared about anything but the thrum, thrum, thrum pulsing through her until she *was* the drum. She had given into that call, dancing with Mal until the fire burned to embers.

Now, the beat that had lived within Caelia had gone silent and cold, leaving her with resounding, hollow silence. Silence so vast she threatened to crumble inward in an implosion of ash. She gulped the wine, wishing for the numbness to take away the pain, even if for only a moment.

Movement behind her. Bane stomped over to a log laid out around the perimeter and sat down with a huff. A spat with his friends? Or was this about the goat still? Bane knew better than to make a pet out of a wether. The wethers were always slaughtered.

She sat down next to him. "Aren't you going to play with your friends?"

He glared at his food. "They're not my friends."

She went very still. "Why?"

He wouldn't look at her. "Why did they call you a murderer?"

Humiliation and shame flushed hot through her. "I'm not." Deny, deny, deny.

"Then why are they saying it?"

She pressed her fist to her lips, eyes tightly closed.

"I hit him," Bane said softly.

She didn't bother to ask which friend. It didn't really matter. "It will only make it worse."

"I'll protect you, Caelia." He didn't look like a little boy in that moment. He looked like the man he would one day become. One who would protect their townspeople, down to the meanest, most pitiful of them.

She pulled him into her arms. "I know you will." She kissed his messy hair and released him. "Go home. I'll be along as soon as I say goodnight to Papa."

He nodded and slipped away. She watched him go, hating that her sins had hurt him. But instead of going to their father, she slipped away from the safety of his influence. Pulling her cloak's hood up, she stuck to the crowd's edge. To the shadows.

The townsfolk drank and wept and ate from the communal table. Caelia could make out the nearly empty plate of rolls she and Joy had made together that afternoon.

She'd reached the far side of the fire when she caught sight of him. Mal had his arm around a farmer's daughter—a lovely girl from the far side of the village. He reached down, whispering something into her ear. She tipped her head back and laughed, exposing the long lines of her throat. Mal eyed her skin like it was covered in honey.

He used to look at me like that.

Caelia hugged herself, shoulders high around her ears. Mal's gaze flicked her way, his expression falling. Her father had told her that Mal had a new girl. But a part of her hadn't believed. What a fool she was. She turned on her heel, fleeing the fire. Fleeing Mal.

Three

Forbidden

"Caelia," Mal called after her.

She plunged into the darkness, leaving the path to weave through an orchard. The air smelled faintly of rotten apples.

A hand closed on her arm. "Caelia, wait."

Protest hummed deep in her throat. She tried to jerk free, but he was too strong. "Let me go!"

He released her, hands lifted palms out, like she was one of his spooked horses he needed to calm. His features were lost to the shadows. All she could make out was his figure silhouetted against the firelight. She took a breath to say something, anything, but her mouth was as empty as her soul.

"I've missed you."

All the breath left her. "The forest take you, Mal. You do not get to say that to me." Ancestors, she hated him so much.

For two months, she'd laid in her bed, the fever so high she'd seen nightmare shadows oozing along the ceiling before darting toward her to gnaw on her bones.

It had been her father, brother, Joy, and Pennice whose faces had faded in and out of her consciousness. Her father had fed her and switched out the cool compress. Joy had bathed and changed her. Pennice had kept her alive. Her brother had read her every book they had. Twice.

Mal had only come once. She knew, because she had asked. Every day, she had asked. Her father's answer had always been the same: a tight shake of his head.

"Why didn't you come, Mal? I was dying . . ." She could still feel the looming hand of death. Feel it fisting around her body—an instinct she hadn't known she possessed until then.

And while she'd lay dying, he'd been falling in love with someone else. While she didn't dare go into the village for fear of ridicule, he lived among them—free while she bore the burden alone.

"What did you expect after your father turned me away?" Mal said bitterly.

Her father's disapproval had never stopped Mal before. "Won't that farmer's daughter be jealous?" she bit out.

"We're only friends."

Caelia huffed. He was the same selfish, feckless boy, while for her, everything had changed. She had changed. Her father had been right about Mal all along.

"Caelia—" Mal made to draw her into his arms.

The empty place inside her overflowed with hate that vibrated into her hands. She shoved him hard in the chest. Her body wasn't strong. Not like it used to be. But he took a step back. "Don't you ever touch me again. Don't even speak to me." She called him the most insulting name she could think of.

She didn't wait for his response. She marched out from under the orchard's shadows toward home. Instead of a steady thrum, her heart beat heavy and ponderous in her chest, the weight of it stifling the breath from her.

The sorrow, the heaviness was back. She shifted, heading toward the river, stumbling across the furrows of her father's and then Vyder's fields.

With each step, her body sank heavier and heavier into

her heels until it was an effort to take even one more step. Until she collapsed to her knees beneath the weeping willow. She leaned forward. Her palm rested on the bare patch of soil. A single, small river stone marked the place where her infant son lay.

She curled up beside him so the crook of her arm rested above him. She imagined him nestled against her. The wind teased her hair across her face, making her think of the yellow ribbon and the curse she'd written: let me keep him. She'd really meant for the forest to take her baby. Let her lose the thing that would ruin her life.

And she had. And in that losing, her life had been utterly destroyed. She sobbed silently. She would only ever be able to sob silently. No one could know. Not if she ever wanted any sort of life. So she held her pain close. Until it ate her from the inside out. How long until there was nothing left but bones and ashes?

"Do you really want to live as if it never happened?" Atara's words echoed through her.

Caelia lay until the last of her tears had dried. Until she was chilled to the bone. But she couldn't bear to leave him. Above her, the willow shifted. Out of sight, the river rushed, frogs called out to each other.

The night's peace was interrupted by heated voices. Too far away to make out. She could not be caught here, lying beside a bare patch of earth after two months of convalescence.

She rose to her feet, her body stiff and aching. She brushed away the dirt and grass and smoothed back her hair. Even at this distance, the drums felt like a distant heartbeat. She sifted through the swaying branches. The bonfire still blazed in the distance—the townspeople would keep it going long into the night. It illuminated the forest, making her shiver.

Pulling her cloak close, she found the path that would take her home. The further she traveled, the louder the voices became. She took a step off the path, determined to go around them, when she recognized a voice. Joy.

Which made sense, as Caelia was on the woman's land. But the man's voice... He wasn't her husband.

Worried now, Caelia moved toward the voices. Two dozen more steps, and she could see them—shadowy forms indistinguishable from one another in the distant firelight.

"You don't understand," the man said. "I don't have the money."

"That's not true," Joy said.

"Papa," said a small voice, "let's go home."

Harben. And the child would be one of the man's too-thin daughters—Larkin or Nesha.

A smack. "You shut your mouth, you little—"

"That is enough!" Joy said.

Had Harben hit his daughter? Joy? Caelia broke into a trot.

"Larkin, hurry home to your Mama now," Joy said, her voice gentle.

One shadow detached from the others and bolted down the path.

"Don't tell me how to deal with my child!" Harben snapped.

"You will pay me," Joy's voice shook with anger. "And if you were any kind of father, you would stop drinking and start taking care of your family." She pivoted and walked up the hill.

Caelia was close enough to make out the woman's profile in the distant firelight. And then Harben moved, shoving her hard from behind. Joy pitched forward, slamming into the ground with a wet thud.

"You will give me my money!" Harben shouted. "And

you will apologize for interfering with my disciplining of my own—"

Caelia pushed past him. Joy's body trembled and shook, her limbs kicking violently.

Afraid she would hurt her, Caelia picked up her head, cradling it on her thighs. Sticky, warm blood cooled on her hands—Joy had hit her head on something when she'd fallen.

"Joy?"

Joy went suddenly still. Caelia waited for the woman's intake of breath. The moment stretched—like counting for thunder after a lightning strike. No sound.

"I barely touched her," Harben said in a high, panicked voice. "She fell."

"Joy?" Caelia bent over, holding her ear over the woman's mouth. No stirring of air against the shell of her ear. No ragged inhalation. Even Harben was silent.

No. Caelia couldn't lose Joy too. Not the woman who had been there after her mother's death. Not the woman who had bathed her and helped her to the bed pan. Not the woman who had taught her the secrets of warm earth and hot bread.

"No, Joy, please." Setting her head down gently, Caelia scrambled to her side and pressed her ear to Joy's chest. The thump gave her hope. But it was too long before the second. And the third. And then . . . nothing.

"No. No. No. No." Caelia clutched Joy as a wail rose in her throat.

"She can't be dead," Harben said. Even five steps away, Caelia could smell the liquor on his breath. "She can't have died that easily."

Caelia keened, the sound resonating through the hollow places inside her. It wailed out into the night, an inhuman sound.

Harben staggered forward and gripped her shoulders. "I

didn't mean to. She shouldn't have died so easily. Not from simply tripping."

"You pushed her! You killed her, and I will see you hang for it!" She screamed for help, the sound ripping through her throat.

Harben stumbled back. He looked fearfully toward the bonfire, the light catching the terror on his face. But the music didn't stop. Didn't so much as pause. No one had heard her.

Harben gripped fistfuls of his hair. "You can't tell anyone. You won't."

Something in the man's voice—something cold and hard and dark . . .

Harben took a step toward her. "You will tell no one!"

When her son had breathed his last, Caelia had ached to go with him. But now, every trembling breath seemed precious. She did not want to die. So she remained silent, fury and devastation giving way to fear.

Harben paced. "You have no idea who I am. I am the son of a queen. One word to the right ear, and I will have money and power you could never dream of in this filthy, insignificant town."

The man was mad. Truly and completely mad.

He took a step toward her. "You will remain silent or I'll kill you. I swear I will. And your brother and your father."

Keeping her movements even—hidden in the dark—Caelia rolled her weight to the balls of her feet.

He took a step toward her. "Do you hear me, you vapid—"

She bolted, running hard for the bonfire. She cried out for help. Called for her father. Arms around her, wrenching her to the side. She fell on her stomach, Harben's body on top of her. She clawed at the soft earth, trying to get out from under him, screaming for help. He forced her face into the ground. Dirt pushed into her mouth, choking her, caking between her teeth.

He grabbed for her hands. She rolled onto her back and thrust the heel of her hand into his chin. He reeled back, enough for her to wiggle out from under him. He was between the bonfire and her home, cornering her between the river and the forest.

The Forbidden Forest meant death. But so did he. She sprinted, saving her breath for each gasping inhalation. His steps sounded behind her. She concentrated on each stride, on the uneven ground. The forest loomed before her, a wall of black death. She punched into it without hesitation.

Two steps later, she tripped over something and landed, her palms scraped and bloody, her wrists jarring hard.

She was up again in a second, her arms out and her steps placed with a little more care. The second time she fell, she stifled her gasp of pain as something banged into her side. She rolled away from it until she fetched up against something solid.

She went utterly still, forcing her breath to come evenly, her head spinning. Ancestors, she was in the Forbidden Forest. She had to get out. Get out! Get out!

A shadow shifted. Stumbled. Cursed. A dozen steps directly behind her. "I'm going to find you," he whispered into the darkness. "And when I do . . ."

Swallowing her whimper, she crawled on her hands and knees, easing her weight down to make sure she didn't make a sound. A sudden pulling of her dress as it caught on something. A rip sounded loud in the night. She froze, waiting. Harben's steps rushed toward her. She bolted, keeping low to the ground, her steps wide.

A vibration punched through her, sending her reeling. She staggered forward. All around her, faces loomed out of the shadows. Faces with black, empty eyes and mouths gaped wide enough to swallow her whole. The stirring—the forest attacking her.

A hand buried itself in her hair and jerked her back. She buried her elbow in Harben's gut. His grip loosed. She turned and kneed him in the groin. She tore free, leaving bits of her hair behind. Ahead of her loomed the largest face yet, a tortured moan slipping through its torn mouth.

She leaped straight into it.

Four

Gilgad

TRYING TO KEEP HER breathing even, Caelia stumbled through the forest, her ears keen to any sounds of pursuit. The faces continued to swallow her, and a horrible cold washed over her each time.

She knew the stories of the stirring. It didn't go on forever. If she could reach the other side, it would stop. She banged her shin against something, a throb of pain shooting up her leg. She was going to break a bone if she didn't stop. But stopping meant death.

So she crawled. Through brambles and sharp sticks and leaves. Bumping into trees. Until the lunging mouths suddenly ceased. She collapsed, breath sawing in and out of her throat. Ancestors, she was inside the Forbidden Forest. No girl who went into the forest came out again.

She stiffened, waiting for the beast's teeth to crack through her ribs. His claws to shred the muscles of her back.

Nothing.

She dared lift her head, turning her ears this way and that for the sound of claws through dirt. The sound of Harben's heavy footfalls. No sounds of pursuit, but she did hear something else.

Music. She tipped her ear toward the distant strains of a

heartbreakingly beautiful song. It wound around her, touching the hollow place inside her, skimming along its surface like a rock skipping across a pond.

There weren't any drums, but it had to be the bonfire. What else could it be?

She hadn't been in the forest long—maybe twenty minutes? She could still escape before the beast found her. Or Harben.

Caelia pushed up on shaking arms, searching for the glow of fire. All she could make out was shadow upon shadow, jagged shapes of trees against the pitted night sky.

She moved toward the strains, ear tipped toward them. The melody was lost to the wind. She shifted back, catching it again. Her reaching hands brushed up against bark. She cringed away, expecting something to grab her, teeth sinking into her neck.

She wanted to call out, but she feared making any sound might draw the beast. The threads wove together into a tapestry that tasted like a deep, cold well. It was like nothing she'd ever heard before. Like magic.

Suddenly, where solid earth should be, there was nothing. She threw her weight back, arms cartwheeling. The earth beneath her left foot crumbled. She slid, plummeting. A wild scream burst from her like a pot boiling over—it was out before she could draw it back. Her hands scrambled for something to hold onto, toes and fingers digging into the loose dirt.

She fell into hot, shallow water and gasped in shock. Had she fallen into the beast's cookpot? Terror robbed her of breath and movement. But no, there was mud beneath her hands. A hot spring? Had to be. In that in-between moment, she heard something. The intake of breath like a bellows. The shifting of a heavy body. A splash. Her whole body froze in terror. Because whatever this was, it was huge, and it was coming closer.

She'd stumbled into the beast's lair.

All her brave promises to kill the beast evaporated. She wasn't a warrior. She was nothing more than a shadow.

Instinct took over. She scrambled, feet churning into the slope she'd slid down. Mud and loose soil crumbled beneath her. And something else. Something solid and fibrous. A root or vine. Fear gave her extra strength. She caught hold, braced her feet, and hauled herself up. One handhold. Two. Three.

Something hit her from below, sending her swinging. It had a hold of her dress. Whatever it was bumped against her leg. Her dress tore. The thing slid down, and pain erupted from her leg.

Teeth or claws, she wasn't sure.

Spinning, she got her feet under her again and managed two more handholds. Whatever was below her hissed and snapped and writhed. But it did not climb after her. Another handhold. Another. She was going to make it. She was going to reach the end.

But her left leg wasn't working right. It slipped and dangled, useless and heavy. Weakness spread upward, moving toward her hip. Her arms trembled with her weight. She tried to take another handhold, but her arms were exhausted. Her muddy grip slipped.

No. She couldn't die. Couldn't leave her family to place lanterns in the river, never knowing what had happened to her.

At some point, the music had stopped. Maybe they could hear her now? "Help!" she screamed. Her hands trembled. Her father would come. He would hear her, and he would come. "Please! I don't want to die! Please!"

"Where are you?" a masculine voice called.

Hope surged bright and hot. "Here! I'm here!"

Wavering light appeared above her, illuminating a tree, the roots dangling bare over a sudden drop. It was one of those roots she held onto.

"Keep talking," the voice called.

"I'm down here! I fell down the embankment!"

A face suddenly appeared above. A man peered down at her and then past her, his eyes widening.

"Don't look!" he cried.

She looked. She'd always pictured the beast as a single creature, something between a man and a wolf. This was a nest of writhing lizards in a muddy pool, the biggest twice the size of a man. She'd fallen down an eroded embankment a story and a half high. She screamed again, clutching the root, her eyes closed tight.

"Easy," the man said. "They're not good climbers. You'll be all right. Get your feet under you and pull yourself up."

She looked up at him, tears streaming down her cheeks. "My leg won't work." Her right leg felt numb too. And her left side to her ribs.

He gritted his teeth and looked around desperately.

Her hands were growing tired. She commanded them to grip the root, but they weren't obeying like they should. "I don't know how much longer I can hold on."

"You will hold on!"

He pulled out a strange opalescent sword from his back, stripped off his baldric, and dangled one of the loops over a knot of wood where a branch had been broken off. Pushing his arm through the other loop, he eased down toward her. Loose soil rained down on her head, dirt stinging her eyes.

Dangling by one arm, his legs horizontal, he stretched a hand toward her. "Keep one hand on the root. Give me the other."

She couldn't catch her breath. "It's not going to hold." Those thin straps wouldn't bear both their weight.

"It'll hold."

Below, a lizard climbed over the backs of its fellows and pushed off its tail. Snapping teeth came within a hand's breadth of her foot. Panic wrapped its fingers around her throat and squeezed.

"What's your name?" the man said softly.

"Caelia," she panted.

"My name is Gendrin."

She looked up into warm brown eyes. Eyes that reminded her of her father.

"Caelia, take my hand."

The fist around her throat eased its stranglehold. Keeping her left hand on the root, she hauled herself up with her remaining strength. Her palm slapped against his, the mud making it slip. She fell back and dangled, dirt raining down on the lizards, which lunged and snapped. Above her, Gendrin swore.

She sobbed, her fingers fraying loose one at a time. The weakness had moved above her breasts now. She slipped, knowing it was the end. A shower of earth even as she fell, then a hand snatched her by the wrist. The same lizard as before—the biggest one, gathered for another lunge.

Gendrin pulled her up. "Grab on!"

She turned away from the lizard, not knowing if it would reach her, her weak fingers grasping his forearms. One hand on the root, his legs braced on the slippery slope, Gendrin strained to haul her up. The veins on his face stood out, a strangled groan slipping from his lips.

With her other hand, she pulled herself on top of his leg. His foot slipped, then held, muscles straining beneath her. She felt the lizard near, heard its jaws snapping over the place she'd just vacated. It fell back with a splash.

Gendrin let out an explosion of breath. "All right if I let go of you for a second?"

Balanced on his one leg, she nodded. He reached down, gripping her under her arm and hauling her up so her chest was even with his. She wrapped her arms around his neck, locking her hands at her elbows.

"Hold on." He climbed up the embankment, setting each foot with care. His tunic was damp with sweat, his arms shaking, the vibrations shifting through his chest.

The numbness spread to her shoulders. "I can't hold on."

He stretched for his baldric. "You can."

"My body—something's wrong."

He lunged, feet finding a foothold on roots. His left arm came around her, cinching her tight to him. Pulling and lunging, he hauled them up and over. She hit solid ground, her legs dangling.

He dragged her a few steps and then braced himself on his knees, panting. She tried to move, pull herself up, but her shoulders weren't working anymore. Somehow, she could still breathe. Her heart still beat.

Covered in mud, a lizard appeared on her right, its forked tongue flaring. Another came up behind it. And another. The creatures couldn't climb the embankment, but apparently there was another way up.

"Gendrin!" she cried.

Instead of reaching for his axe and shield, Gendrin pulled a sort of flute from his shirt. He played, the notes driving and harsh. Danger pounded beneath Caelia's skin. Her head throbbed in time to the beat. It was the sound of death waiting, coiled and ready to leap. She ached to run. Flee. But she was frozen in this useless body.

And the beasts ... stopped. Their tongues flickered out, tasting the easy prey before them. Gendrin stepped toward them. The creatures took a step back. He took another step. The creatures turned and went back the way they had come.

Gendrin continued playing, driving them back. Caelia writhed, desperate to escape a terror that had no source. The moment he stopped playing, so did her fear.

Panting, she looked from him to his flute. "How—how did you do that?"

"Magic."

She would have dismissed his statement as a joke. Except she'd seen it and felt its effect. "What are you?"

"An enchanter." He bent down and lifted her over his shoulders like a lamb—arms on one side, legs on the other. Hooking one arm around her limbs, Gendrin picked up the torch. The forest blurred as he ran, her side jarring into his shoulders with each step.

She didn't know what an enchanter was. But he had saved her at great risk.

"The beasts," she choked out. "Will they follow?"

"Those aren't the beasts."

Everything in her stilled. "What do you mean?"

"Those are just gilgad."

She swallowed her rising horror. "There's something worse?"

"Quiet now." He glanced furtively at the shadows closing in on them. "They will have heard your screams."

Five

Venom

GENDRIN'S WORDS ECHOED THROUGH Caelia, *They will have heard your screams.*

The true beast. The one who stole girls from their beds at night. *Never again to hear their screams,* the old rhyme echoed through her head. The monster Caelia had sworn to kill. But when confronted with what she thought was the beast, she'd run.

She was a coward. A coward and a fool.

She could hear the river now, rushing and deep. Gasping for breath, Gendrin dropped the nearly spent torch. They'd reached the base of a tree that looked no different from any other. He set her down, her head lolling to the side opposite him. She couldn't lift it.

Through brush, moonlight shone on water. Gendrin dug around for something. In a pack, maybe? His hand cradled the back of her head and lifted. Something smooth and cool parted her lips. Something like the medicine vials the apothecary used.

"Swallow," he whispered. "It will counter the venom."

Venom? Liquid trickled into her mouth, tasting so strong of pepper she nearly choked.

He pressed his hand over her mouth to keep her from spitting it out. "You have to swallow, Caelia."

Fighting back a gag, she managed to work the muscles of her throat, the liquid flowing down. He reached into his pack and hauled out a rope.

"You had a rope!" she slurred, her mouth not working right. Why hadn't he brought the blasted thing?

He tied it around her chest. "I didn't know I would need it. I heard someone screaming for help and I ran." There hadn't been time for him to go back for it.

The weakness slid up her face, her jaw going slack, mouth hanging open. "What's happening to me?"

He swung the pack on his back and tossed the rope over a sturdy bough. "Gilgad venom."

The lizard that had bit her arm, wet blood trickling down her leg. The gilgad had raked her with its teeth. "Am I going to die?"

"No," he said simply. His steadiness soothed her. He left her, his steps shushing through thick, fallen leaves. "This is going to hurt."

Unable to brace herself, she whimpered as the rope went suddenly taut, digging painfully into her ribs and armpits and making it hard to breathe. He hauled her up. Her feet dangled like a hanged man's. The forest floor receded until her forehead smacked into the branch.

"Urmph!" Lights exploded behind her eyes.

He stopped. She couldn't turn to look, but the rope tugged as if he were tying it. Moments later, he climbed up beside her.

"This is so much easier with a team," he muttered.

Team? What was that supposed to mean? Instead of asking, she drooled. It was utterly humiliating.

Hands under her armpits, he pulled her up and shifted her over his shoulder. Her faced mashed against the pack on his back. She looked at the ground—far enough away that she would break something if she fell.

Ancestors, she wanted to curse or at the very least clutch him, but she was as helpless as that goat pegged beside the fire. As helpless as when the pains had ripped through her belly. As helpless as when she'd watched her son struggle to take his first and last breaths.

The muscles of Gendrin's shoulders shifted beneath her. He pulled himself up onto a higher branch. He was climbing the tree. With her slung over his shoulder. A better way to die than falling into a gilgad nest, but dead was still dead.

He shifted, and a branch stabbed at her cheek before shuddering past her chin. She would bear the mark of that in the morning.

Finally, he stopped, the bough swaying beneath their combined weight. His arms fussed with something she couldn't see. She was suddenly falling. Plunging to her death. She would have screamed and cinched her arms and legs around him, refusing to ever let go. But something caught her, cradled her. She could make out cloth beneath the bare skin of her hands. She swayed gently. It was like a hammock tied high in the trees.

You could have warned me, you fool man!

Gendrin let out a shaky breath. "All right. You're safe now."

He started undoing the rope around her chest. The knot didn't want to give. He worked at it, fingers grazing her breasts. "Sorry," he kept mumbling.

She wanted to bat his hands away and do it herself, but of course she couldn't. Finally, he had the thing off her and she could breathe without pain. He shifted her legs inside the hammock and straightened them.

She could feel him looking down at her. "I have one blanket and one pod. I don't want to freeze. So I'm climbing in with you."

What? No you are not!

The pod vibrated, then his weight made it dip. If the thing broke, they would both spill to their deaths.

But it didn't break. He swung his legs into it, so they were lying side by side, fetched up together like Widow Morin's seven children squished into one bed. He wiggled and shifted her until they were both centered. Then he wiggled some more as he pulled a blanket over them, tucking the edges around her muddy dress.

When he was finally still, she lay, her cheek mashed up against his shoulder. She was exhausted, but too tightly wound to sleep. Judging by the sound of his breathing, he wasn't sleeping either.

He tugged something out from inside his shirt. His pipes. The source of his magic. Fear reared again—she didn't understand how his magic worked. Didn't know how to fight its effects.

He played. The song wrapped around her like her mother's arms. Her fear abated, replaced by the smell of hearth fire and laundry soap and drowsy sunshine. She felt her mother's body curled around her. And in Caelia's own arms, she held her son, his sleepy sighs filling her with peace.

Caelia fell asleep to the feel of her mother rocking them both.

Magic

CAELIA WOKE TO THE smell of roasting fish. Her belly clenched hard, making her nauseous. She tried to sit up in the hammock and instantly fell back. Her sore muscles tore a groan from her throat. But she had sat up! The forest take her—which she supposed it had—she would never take her body for granted again.

"You'll loosen up the more you move," Gendrin's voice called from somewhere below.

Gendrin. The enchanter who had saved her with magic.

Her leg ached. She glanced down, neck screaming. Blood crusted her leg from when the lizard's teeth had grazed her. She groaned again. "I hurt too much."

The boughs shifted, though there was no wind; Gendrin was climbing up. He peered down at her from above.

She hadn't had a chance to take a good look at him before. He was deeply tanned and barrel-chested, his head shaved—save for one long, thin braid behind his right ear. His prominent nose and brows framed his dark eyes. His beard was thick and wiry, with the faintest hints of auburn.

Not an especially beautiful man, but not an ugly one either. And yet there was something about him. A steady presence that made it hard to look away.

He studied her too. She wondered what he saw. "You have magic?"

He shrugged. "Where I'm from, all men have magic."

"Not the women?"

"No," the word was heavy with emotion she didn't understand—sadness and anger and bitterness. "Not women."

Of course not. The world seemed intent on keeping women utterly powerless. "Why?"

"The same magic that lends my music power over emotions also binds my tongue. I can't tell you more, Caelia. You'll have to figure it out on your own."

He reached into his pocket and withdrew a wooden box. He slid it open, revealing six vials packed in straw. He took out the second one and held it out to her. "Here. This will cleanse the remaining venom from your body."

She drank the antidote, not caring if it tasted like pepper if it made the pain go away. She eyed him warily. "Are you manipulating my emotions now?"

He replaced the empty vial in the box. "Only when I play my music. And you can stop looking at me like that—I have a feeling you'd stick me with a pitchfork if I ever tried to manipulate you."

"Or break the flute over your head before you even got started."

He laughed. He looked nice when he laughed. "I promise I won't use it on you without your permission first."

She let him pull her into a sitting position, biting the inside of her cheek to keep from groaning again. She took stock of their surroundings. They were in an enormous tree, bare of most its leaves. Forest surrounded them, the river rushing past. Below, a small fire let off lazy smoke. A little pot boiled and fish sizzled on a rock nesting in the coals.

"The River Weiss?" She pointed with her chin.

Gendrin followed her gesture. "Yes."

Which meant her town was downstream, though she could only see more forest. She couldn't have gone too far in the few hours she wandered. Less than a day's walk and she would be back with the rumors, sharp and piercing, that would surround her like an angry cloud of hornets for the rest of her life.

"Where are you from?" He had a strange, precise accent—one she'd never heard before.

"Hamel. You?"

He glanced upriver. "A place far different from anything you could ever imagine. Or believe."

Longing and pain were at war in his gaze. A woman, maybe? "There's nothing upriver but more forest."

"How would you know?"

Could such a thing be possible? But then, she supposed no one had ever really been able to go into the forest and find out. Yesterday, she would have scorned anyone who believed magic was real. That was before she'd seen it. Felt it.

She looked him up and down. His tunic, trousers, and cloak were all finely woven, pied fabric. The design and making were foreign from anything she'd ever seen before. A pan pipe and some sort of flute hung from around his neck. Those things coupled with his strange hair made it clear he wasn't Idelmarchian as she was.

"Why were you in the forest?" he asked.

Harben's words echoed through her, *I'm going to find you, and when I do . . .*

Shuddering, she rubbed at the bald spot on the back of her head; Harben had pulled out a chunk of her hair. "I—I saw a man murder my friend." Her voice choked on the last, a sob rising in her chest. "He chased me in."

Gendrin swore.

Caelia pushed the fear and horror and sorrow deep—she wasn't out of the forest yet. "Will the beast and the gilgad hunt us now?"

"They winter in the hot springs. You happened to fall into their nest. As for the beasts—they hunt at night."

She was safe, at least for now. She sagged in relief, though guilt still ate at her for her cowardice. "Why are you in the Forbidden Forest?"

He eyed her, his gaze seeing far more than she was comfortable with. "You're not the only one running from something."

"What are you running from?" she whispered.

He looked away. "The fish are going to burn." He held out his hand.

She understood the need to keep secrets, perhaps better than anyone. She took his offered hand. He braced himself and hauled her up. The pain surged, but she forced herself to ride it out. After a moment, it eased.

It took far longer than it should have to get down the tree, and far too much holding hands with a man she barely knew. By the time she'd reached the bottom, she collapsed against the trunk, her whole body aching.

He went to the fire and used a stick to push the cooking rock out of the coals—when had he woken up this morning? Leaving them to cool, he wrapped a bit of leather around the cookpot handle and brought it to her along with the pack. He rummaged around inside and pulled out bandages, salves, and the like.

"I'm no healer, but I can clean and stitch." His dark eyes asked permission.

She winced but nodded. He pulled up her shredded, filthy skirt, revealing her pale legs coated with soft, dark hair and a fine layer of dirt and blood. Embarrassed at her state, she braced herself and looked. Long parallel lines began as puncture wounds and ended as welted scratches on her outer thigh, above her knee. Not as bad as she'd thought.

Gendrin hummed low in his throat. "This won't even need stitching, though I'll have to clean it. Gilgad bites tend to fester."

He used his knife to extract steaming bandages and let them cool a bit before laying them on the side of her leg. She sucked in a breath at the heat.

"That'll soften the scabbing." He went back to the fire and tested the cook stone with his fingers. Finding it cool enough, he set it between them with the larger fish facing her. Using his knife, he scraped the meat off the bones for her in one clean swipe.

She ate all of it—the fish hot against her cold, filthy fingertips.

When they'd finished, he tossed the stripped bones into the fire and watched her. "Are you ready?"

Teeth gritted against the coming pain, she nodded. He dipped his hands in what had to be scalding water, pulled them out, and rubbed them together for a full minute before dunking them again. They came out looking a painful red. Pennice had done the same when she'd tried to clear the festering from inside Caelia.

He pulled away the bloodstained fabric from her leg and hummed low in his throat. He poured some too-hot water over the wound and scrubbed until it bled fresh, the pain raw and sharp. Worse than when it had happened.

She gritted her teeth and tried not to moan. "Tell me— tell me something. Anything. Distract me."

He hesitated. "There is a place where the trees grow so tall, they snag the bottoms of the clouds. Up from the depths of the turquoise waters, they grow. Waters that team with fish pulsing with color. Winter never touches this place. And even on the darkest nights, there is light and music so beautiful it can make you weep or curse or forget everything that has ever hurt you."

Music like what he'd played for her last night. Music that could make her forget. The words awoke a longing that vibrated from the top of her head down to her feet—feet that ached with the need to take her there.

She resented him for painting such a glorious picture. "Places like that don't exist."

"How would you know?"

She started to reply, but then he tugged at the punctures, peering inside. She gasped, eyes tightly shut.

"You'll have an amazing scar to tell stories to your children about." He tossed the rag into the still-steaming pot.

Fingers digging into the loam, she cried softly. As if sensing she needed privacy, he left quietly, his steps leading toward the river. She distracted herself with thoughts of the place he had described. A place with no winter. A place with colors and light and music to make her forget. Such a place couldn't exist. But then, magic wasn't possible either.

He came back into camp with a pot of fresh water, which he placed over the fire. He crouched down and packed up his pack. "If we start now, you'll be home before dinner."

Home. Where her father would look at her like he didn't know who she was anymore. Where children would continue to torment her brother. Where the rumors would sting her for the rest of her life. Rumors that would prevent her from marrying. From ever having a job.

But the beast only took maidens. If she never went home, the town would be certain of her innocence. Her father and brother would be spared any further humiliation.

"What if I don't want to go home?" she whispered.

He carefully packed the antidote. "Where else would you go?"

"The place you described, is it real?"

He slowly nodded.

She eased herself to a sitting position, wincing as the movement tugged at her fresh scabs. "I could come with you."

"It's two days' journey. And every night, you will face the beast. You're safer going home."

She looked to the west. Toward her small town with its small people. Atara had been right. "There's nothing for me to go back to."

She felt his gaze on her. "You don't understand what you're asking me."

She wiped the tears from her cheeks. "So tell me."

"Our people do not mix with yours. It's the law. Once you set foot in the Alamant, you can never leave again."

"My father and brother ..." She fought back a sob. "They'll be better off without me."

"Surely there's someone else?"

Atara, Joy, the baby. "They're all dead." She sniffed. "Is there some kind of work I can do? I've been learning to cook, and I know a little about farming." Mostly that one should put plants in dirt.

"Yes, but—" He rubbed his face in frustration. "Caelia, I'm trying to help you. Someday, you'll miss your family so much you'll wish you'd never made the choice to go to the Alamant."

Caelia used to think she was strong. That she had control over her life. She'd learned in the worst possible way that she controlled nothing. "You don't know what it's like to lose everything. To bury the pain so deep it turns to acid and eats away all that you were."

He stared into the dying embers. "Don't I?" The

heaviness he bore—he had clearly suffered something. He crouched down by the fire and pulled a set of pipes out of his shirt. She tensed. "Let me show you."

Because he asked first, she nodded. He played. The first note wrapped around her, bearing her away to the memory that haunted her every moment.

She was holding her baby again. He was tiny, so tiny he fit in one hand. He was sticky and red with her blood. He'd been perfectly formed, his skin fragile, the delicate tracery of veins visible beneath. His tiny chest rose and fell frantically, his ribs vibrating with the beat of his heart.

She'd never wanted him, not from the first moment. Until she did. As fiercely as she had ever wanted anything. And so, after hours of silent agony, she'd called for her father.

He'd stumbled into her candlelight room. He'd gaped at her, at the blood, at the baby. Comprehension had come over him. Comprehension and bitter disappointment.

Through her tears, she'd begged him to go for the midwife.

What felt like hours later, Pennice had rushed into the room, taken one look at the infant in her arms, and stopped short. She started again, her movements smooth and gentle as she knelt beside the bed. "He's too little to survive, Caelia."

The song released her, slipping away like water to go back to wherever it had come from. Slowly, Caelia came back into the here and now. Gendrin stared into the fire, tears streaming down his face.

"What was that?" she cried.

He shifted to look at her. Their gazes locked. He didn't look away as another might. Instead, he saw her. Saw the tears streaming down her cheeks that matched his own, and he didn't look away. This man had known pain. Known it as she had. She saw the same realization come over him.

When she'd been dangling over a pit of gilgad, she'd thought Gendrin's eyes reminded her of her father, which had given her the strength to fight away her fear. She'd been wrong. What she saw reflected back at her was a grief as deep as her own. It was that shared grief that had made her trust him.

He took a ragged breath. "My friends and I were part of a supply line delivering food to one of our outposts when we were ambushed near sunset. We became separated from the group. We were beset by two beasts. All my years of training, all that preparation ... I froze. My best friend, Serek, died saving me.

"I'd thought I was powerful, strong. But in the face of his wife's grief..." He held out his empty hands. "I couldn't face her. Couldn't tell her the truth. To my shame, I let one of my other friends, Denan, take the blame for Serek's death, when all he'd done was save him from the shadow." Gendrin choked, unable to continue.

He'd lost a friend to the beast, as she had. Caelia wanted to reach out to this man she barely knew, comfort him. But she held back, unsure how he would receive it.

He wiped his face. "I couldn't stay in the Alamant. Not knowing what I'd done." He was running. The same as she. "But after nearly two years ... I'm tired, Caelia. I'm going home." He met her gaze. "Someday, you'll be tired of running and ready to return to your family, only it won't be an option anymore."

She let out a long breath. *You were right, Atara. I don't want to live in a place where I have to pretend my son didn't exist.* Unable to bear his judgment, she turned away. "My son died. He was born too early and he died." That had been the worst of the rumors—that she had done something to end her pregnancy when she hadn't. She opened her mouth to say the rest, but it wouldn't come.

Stunned silence. "Surely your husband—"

"I don't have a husband. I never did." It felt good to say it. To own it. "Mal . . . When I got sick, he left me. My own father barely speaks to me. The entire town suspects." Suspicion alone was enough to ruin her. "And the worst part is that I wanted him to die, from the moment I realized I carried him. I even wrote it on a ribbon for the Curse Tree."

She'd been relieved when she'd gone into labor—she wouldn't have been able to hide her growing belly much longer. It was far too early for him to survive. Even she knew that.

And then she'd held her baby and everything had changed. She took a cleansing breath. "I don't know how it is in the Alamant, but in the Idelmarch, unwed mothers are shunned." She felt the sharp whispers, the knowing looks. Her title had insulated her, but it wasn't enough to save her.

Defiant of the judgment that was surely in Gendrin's eyes, she squared her shoulders and forced herself to face him. "I told you, there is nothing for me to go back to."

He didn't look away. Not once. Neither did he say anything. Not for a long time. The hope inside her wavered like a new vine before a bitter winter wind. And then he spoke, "What is his name?"

She blinked in surprise. "Whose name?"

"Your son?"

She opened her mouth, but nothing came out. "I-I never gave him one."

"You should name him." He held out a hand to help her up. "He deserves a name."

Warmth slid down her face, falling against her collarbone and seeping through her skin to land with a plink into the hollow, brittle nothing inside her. Together, they turned away from Hamel and toward the Alamant.

Storm

GENDRIN GAVE HER HIS belt and knife. "No one should be in the forest without a weapon."

She took it, the leather warm from his body, the tooling worn. The knife was as jewel-like as the sword. It didn't fit. Gendrin pushed the knife through the leather to make a new hole. Caelia wrapped it around herself and tightened the buckle. He nodded in approval.

He took the pot of water from the fire and left while she washed up as best she could. There wasn't much she could do about her dress—not unless she wanted to spend the day naked or wet. But her skin and hair were mostly clean. When she'd finished, they started out.

The forest encased Caelia in a living wall, blocking away the sky and making her feel small and vulnerable. Anything could be hiding just out of sight, watching her. She jumped at an abrupt bird call. Then again as another burst out of some brush to her right.

"That sound is a copperbill," Gendrin said. "The other bird is a forest hen—they're delicious. If I'd been paying better attention, we could have had it for lunch."

He named each forest sound and pointed to edible plants and poisonous ones. With the steady litany of his voice, her fear gradually abated. The pain eased too. The more she moved, the more her muscles limbered up.

As the day went on, the wind picked up until it gusted, the trees swaying violently above her, fall leaves ripped away en masse and tripping over each other on the ground.

They stopped for lunch, huddled between the roots of a tree as they ate dried bread and meat. The warm sunshine had been replaced by a bitter wind. Caelia kept tight hold of her cloak, her fingers numb with cold.

By the time evening came on, black clouds boiled over the blue sky, leaving them in perpetual twilight. Thunder cracked and lightning sizzled. The rain sheeted in a downpour that left Caelia soaked in seconds. *At least I'm cleaner,* she thought miserably.

Gendrin stopped, his mouth fixed in a grim line. He shouted to be heard over the wind, "Wait here."

Before she could protest, he shimmied up a tree. She watched him, the tree cavorting about like a drunk man tethered to the ground. He tied up his pod and fixed his pack to a branch. When he finally dropped back down, his expression was grim.

She backed away from him. "Are you mad? We can't go into a tree in a storm. It will be blown down or struck with lightning."

"We don't have a choice."

She shook her head, rain streaking down her face. "There has to be somewhere we can shelter. An overhang or cave."

"The beasts can't sense us in the trees."

"Surely they're as eager to escape the storm as everything else."

He looked about nervously and held out his hand. "Trust me, Caelia."

He'd already saved her life once. He'd learned her

deepest, darkest secret and hadn't treated her any differently because of it. She did trust him. How could she not?

She placed her hand in his. He boosted her onto the first branch. The tree shifted beneath her. His pod was halfway up, and each bough swayed more than the last. She held on tight, her whole body locking up with fear. Gendrin came up behind her.

"Can't we pick a lower branch?" she shouted.

"Not if we're to be beyond the beasts' reach."

He went first, stretching back to pull her up beside him. She strained for a branch that shifted out of her grasp, leaving her leaning too far toward. Unbalanced, she cried out. His hand snaked around her hips, steadying her against him.

"You all right?" he asked.

No. But she would never admit it. She looked up to find him close and looking down at her. He felt warm and solid and real. She didn't pull away. He didn't let go. The storm suddenly seemed far away.

A blush heated her cheeks. What was she doing? She'd just escaped a bad relationship. She had no desire for another. She shifted slightly back. He dropped his hand.

Clearing his throat, he turned and climbed. She was more aware of his hand gripping hers, of his body's proximity. When they finally reached the pod, he pointed to her borrowed belt. "Take it off. Get inside the pod."

The pod must be what he called the hammock. She did as he asked. He strapped the belt to the tree along with his baldric, sword, and shield. He held open the pod for her. She sat and then shifted her legs inside. She scooted over as he came in after. The pod mashed them together, the edges of their arms and legs touching, and both tried to pretend they weren't.

He shut the pod, which was surprisingly waterproof,

though they were both soaked, so it didn't matter much. He spread a blanket over them. She pulled it up to her chin. It was coarse and smelled of damp wool. She shivered hard, trying, and failing to fight off the chill.

"This is ridiculous," he chattered. "We need to get warm."

She stiffened before giving in with a sigh. "Try anything, and I'll find a pitchfork."

He chuckled, deep and low. He maneuvered his arm under her. She shifted until she wrapped around him. Gradually, their body heat mingled. The shivering stopped. The storm settled a little. Finally, finally, she relaxed.

She nuzzled into him, liking the way he felt against her, the size of him. She splayed her fingers across his chest. He was brave and kind. He understood her. He hadn't judged her. He—his heart was beating too fast, and he held himself far too stiffly.

She froze, realizing that she hadn't been curled around him for warmth. She'd been cuddling him. With that realization, a different kind of heat built in her—heat fueled by embarrassment and trepidation and more than a little longing.

"Would you like to rescind your threat of a pitchfork?" he asked, voice thick.

She wanted to say yes. Wanted it very badly, fool that she was. She'd only known the man for two days. Anyone could be charming for two days. Mal had managed it for months. "I can't—I'm not—I didn't mean . . ." She trailed off before she could make a bigger idiot out of herself.

"I imagine it's hard to trust anyone, after what you've been through."

She relaxed. "I just met you."

"It's all right, Caelia. Go to sleep."

They lay for a long time, neither sleeping.

"Gendrin?" she finally asked.

"Yes?"

"How do you kill a beast?"

He stiffened. "It takes a team to bring them down."

But they could be killed. "Could I do it?" She'd promised Atara she would, after all.

He was quiet a long time. "To my knowledge, no woman has ever managed it."

Her mind spun for what felt like hours, until she gave up on ever going to sleep on her own. "If you put me to sleep like you did last night, would I wake up if there was danger?" *Danger like you.*

"Still don't trust me?"

"It's not that." Although it was.

He chuckled, clearly unoffended. "Only if I kept playing, which I promise not to do." She could feel him looking down at her. "Would you like me to put you to sleep?"

She nodded.

"At times like this, I wish it worked on me." He pulled his flute from inside his shirt. It sounded gentle and sweet. Caelia fell asleep, but this time it wasn't her mother whose arms she imagined around her. It was Gendrin. And he was very, very real.

Eight

Beast

CAELIA DREAMED OF HER family's outhouse. But the door stuck fast, no matter how she pulled. She woke, her bladder demanding immediate attention. She pushed up and looked down at Gendrin. Judging by the dark circles around his eyes, he hadn't slept much.

She reached to pull the pod open, revealing thick clouds and a light drizzle. But it was morning, which meant it was safe to leave the tree. Not wanting to wake him, she tried to extricate herself without rolling on top of him.

"Where are you going?" His voice was rough with sleep.

"I have . . . needs to attend to."

He grunted. "You can't leave the tree until morning."

"It is morning. And I can't wait." Her cheeks flushed with embarrassment. But she really, really couldn't wait.

He pushed himself up.

"No, go back to sleep. I can manage. I'll even start a fire."

He flopped back down, clearly exhausted. "Take the knife."

She managed to extricate herself. She tied on the belt, gripped each bough firmly, and eased from one slippery branch to another, going faster and faster as she neared the lowest.

It was still quite a jump to the ground. She eased onto her backside and pushed off. She landed off kilter in the mud and tipped forward, catching herself at the last second.

She almost lost control of her bladder then and there. Brushing leaves and mud from her hands, she hustled far out of sight—she didn't think Gendrin would peek, but she didn't feel like taking chances.

After she'd finished, she sighed in relief and gathered wood. The wind picked up, bringing with it the smell of death—some animal rotting. She pulled the edge of her cloak over her face and breathed shallowly. The smell grew stronger. A strange smell—like the crypts she'd visited in Landra.

Foreboding slithered along the ground toward her, pooling around her feet like vapor. Like something otherworldly. Like death.

Like a beast.

The sticks clattered from her hands.

"Caelia!" Gendrin cried. "The sun hasn't risen yet. Get in a tree!" Sounds of branches shaking as he dropped.

But . . . he'd told her morning. He'd never said anything about sunrise. Had he? The fear lapping at her ankles reared back and struck. She turned to run back to Gendrin and stopped short.

Before her feet, shadows ripped apart and thrashed like dying snakes. They rose up, forming a mist in the shape of a man, his cloak made of torn shadows.

The beast. The thing that had killed Atara.

She staggered around it, unable to look away, desperate to reach Gendrin.

The mist became solid. Eyes, yellow and malevolent, fixed on her. "A bird has slipped her cage," it chittered.

She ran, her feet churning through the mud. She felt the creature getting close. Felt it in the icy cold that spread from her back, around her ribs, before penetrating her core. She caught sight of Gendrin between the trunks as he sprinted for her. His gaze shifted to the beast behind her.

"Get down!"

She dropped. The beast loomed over her, his sword cutting through where she'd just been. Too late to run. The beast recalled his swing and brought his blade above his head. She lifted one useless arm to block the blow.

Gendrin leaped over her, the full force of his body tucked behind his shield. He slammed into the thing, knocking it back. Both man and creature rolled away from each other.

"Get in a tree!" Gendrin cried.

She shot toward a tree with a low-enough bough, leaped into the branch, and hustled up. From behind, a thud echoed through her. She whipped back. The beast's sword slammed into Gendrin's shield, biting off a chunk. Gendrin backpedaled and jabbed. The beast caught the blade in a mind-numbing parry and delivered a vicious kick to Gendrin's leg.

Gendrin limped back. The beast pressed its advantage, delivering a diagonal swipe that tore another chunk from Gendrin's shield and had him scrambling.

It takes a team to bring them down, Gendrin had said.

But he'd attacked it alone. To save her. Knowing the beast would kill him. Like it had killed Atara. Atara who Caelia had sworn to avenge.

If she cowered again, she would lose the only other person who'd known about her past and hadn't judged her.

Not again. Instead of running from the fear, she embraced it. Embraced that she might die.

She slipped the knife from the sheath, dropped from the tree, and stalked forward. Gendrin's gaze flicked to her. He gave an infinitesimal shake of his head—clearly not wanting to alert the beast to her presence.

That lack of focus cost him. The beast caught Gendrin's blade in the hook of its axe and wrenched it from his grasp. It fell to Caelia's left. Gendrin shifted toward it, but the beast cut him off, driving him back while Gendrin could only parry with his shield.

Shifting the knife to her left hand, Caelia took the sword in her right. A snapping sound. Gendrin fell to the ground, his shield broken in two. The beast stood over him, sword raised above his head. Caelia ran, the sword cocked back.

As if sensing her, the beast turned, its blade slamming into hers and knocking it from her numb fingers. Stunned, she could only watch as it pulled the blade back to drive it forward.

Gendrin lunged at it from behind, wrapping his arms around the creature's legs and wrenching. He screamed in agony even as they fell.

They rolled. The beast came out on top of Gendrin, who was still screaming. Caelia lifted the knife still in her hand and ran at the creature. Its sword appeared in its hand, summoned from the hell it had disappeared to.

She slammed the knife home between the beast's shoulders. The creature let out a guttural cry. Shadows escaped like steam—so icy cold they burned her hand, forcing her to drop the knife to the ground. The consuming black of the creature's robes flickered to moth-eaten gray. It looked back at her, rage seething from its being, and then turned again to Gendrin.

No time to pick the knife back up. She didn't think. She just jumped on the creature's back. And then she understood why Gendrin had screamed.

Shadows, oily and dark, slid into her. Shadows that filled the aching hollow inside her with ice and thousands upon thousands of screaming deaths. Her death was simply one more.

She screamed, but she did not loosen her hold. Even as the creature slammed his elbow into her sore side. Gendrin's scrabbling fingers found the knife she'd dropped. He lunged forward, the blade sinking into the creature's gut. It flickered even more, becoming less solid beneath her.

They could do this. They could kill it. Feral joy broke free something wild inside her. She bent forward, biting down on the creature's neck. Shadows and blood flooded her mouth—blood that tasted of iron and rot.

Against her will, her body went limp. She slid off the beast's back and landed in a crumpled heap. On her side, she watched as the beast and Gendrin wrestled, Gendrin struggling to keep the beast's sword from his throat.

It takes a team. Fighting the strange weakness that had come over her, she gathered her knees under her. The movement seemed to wake up her sluggish body. She coughed suddenly, blood spewing from her mouth—if just touching the creature had made her sick, what could the poison do? Her muscles locked up as she coughed again. She spit, her body growing stronger.

Strong enough to crawl to the sword she had dropped. Pick it up and stagger toward the beast, each step growing stronger until she was running. She thrust. The sword pierced it as though it were made of spider webs. It threw its head back, screaming.

Caelia nearly dropped the sword. Nearly covered her ears and cowed. Instead, she wrenched the sword up, straight through its center. The beast imploded, writhing shadows sucking inward until an outline of ash remained.

Alamant

FIGHTING THE NAUSEA THAT suddenly roiled in her gut, Caelia met Gendrin's gaze. She dropped the sword, stepping through the drifting ashes to sink to his side. Then she leaned over and vomited onto the ground.

"Ancestors," Gendrin said. "You got its blood on you."

He ran back to the tree and came back with a waterskin. He washed her chin and made her rinse and spit three times before he searched her. He found her burned hand. She winced as his hands pressed against the bruise in her side.

"Did he cut you? Even a scratch?"

She shook her head.

"Are you sure? Their blades are even more poisoned than their blood."

"I'm fine." She wasn't, but the blade hadn't come anywhere near her.

He gripped her arms, forcing her to meet his gaze. "Do you have any idea what you've done? That was a wraith. Caelia—they've three hundred years of training."

Wraith. The beast is called a wraith. And I killed it. The forest take her. Whatever fleeting courage had seized her abandoned her entirely. She sat down hard on her backside.

"You said it took teamwork," she managed weakly.

He pulled her into a hug. "I'm glad you listened."

She laughed, giddy with relief. "Me too."

He got to his feet, favoring his right leg. "Come on. It's hard to tell when the sun has crested the horizon when it's stormy. There might be more."

"There are more?" She stood, her side aching. She felt all-over shivery and detached.

He grabbed his sword and the knife she'd abandoned. They scrambled up the same tree they'd spent the night in. They split what remained of the dried meat and soggy travel bread. Gendrin loaded his pack.

She swallowed hard. "We're cursed, aren't we?"

"Cursed to be apart. To live in ignorance or death." He pivoted to look at her. "You don't know everything there is to know about the Alamant. The curse. You're not going to like parts of it."

She frowned. "Am I going to be angry with you?"

"I don't think so. Maybe?" He shrugged. "It's not too late to go home."

Not yet. "Is the Alamant really all you described?"

"The beautiful parts, yes. But there is darkness too."

"There is always darkness," she whispered.

He held out his hand in question. She took it, allowing him to help her down.

By that afternoon, Caelia's wound felt hot and tight. She huddled in her cloak, shivering with fever and struggling to keep up. Gendrin kept casting nervous glances at her and the sun in its inexorable arc across the cloudy sky.

At lunchtime, he made her sit beneath an overhang. "How bad is it?"

Her head ached, her back ached, her leg ached. Not to

mention her bruised side and the weeping blisters on her hand. "It's fine. I'm fine."

"Liar." He pulled up the hem of her skirt, revealing the teeth-marks, which were red and shiny and swollen. Though honestly, Caelia thought it looked better than it felt.

Gendrin passed a hand over his head in frustration. "I can do field dressings, but this . . . You need a healer."

"Then we better make it to the Alamant."

He swore, clearly debating.

"I'm not spending another night in a freezing tree," Caelia chattered. Much as she'd grown to enjoy cuddling with him, she didn't think her body could take it.

Gendrin offered her some food he'd managed to gather, but she wasn't hungry. He wolfed it down instead and took his belt back, strapping his sword to one side. He pulled her up, slung her over his shoulders, and started off.

The shadows were back. The same shadows that had swum above Caelia's sick bed after her baby had died. Now and then, they dove down, gnawing on Caelia's bones. On her leg. She was so tired. She wanted to sleep, but she couldn't. The pain and the shadows tormented her.

"I want my baby," Caelia cried softly.

"I know," Gendrin said.

"They're hurting me. Make them stop hurting me."

He picked up the pace. "We're almost there, Caelia. Hold on."

She fell back into her nightmares, true rest eluding her. She woke again to Gendrin shouting for help. She wished he wouldn't be so loud. Her side and neck hurt from being carried in such an awkward position.

Blearily, she peered up at the sky. The clouds had parted

enough to reveal the sun cut in half by the horizon. Now the shadows really would come. The beast would devour her.

It couldn't hurt any more than her leg.

When next she woke, many hands carried her. They were sloshing through water. Purple water. She was caught in a nightmare again, surely. The water splashed her too-hot skin. She gasped at the shock of it. They passed her up. She was with Gendrin again. She curled into his chest even though he smelled like he hadn't bathed in days. Not that she was any better.

She was in a boat with many men in beautiful armor. An enormous white wall made of trees with elegant arches and gray-green foliage rose up before them. Everything shimmered suddenly, a taste like stardust on her tongue. She blinked, sure she was dreaming again. But then the gates opened and what lay beyond made her mouth fall open.

It was as Gendrin had described it. A city of trees grew out of the water. Trees untouched by the coming winter. Lights in the shape of stars grew all over the boughs. People crowded the edges of the platforms to get a good look at her. Fish pulsing with colors darted through the water—water that was purple where it splashed against the hull.

"This can't be real," she murmured.

Gendrin smoothed her hair from her face. "It's real, Caelia. We're taking you to the healers."

She caught sight of something through the layers of trunks. Something white and opalescent, with gold edges. Then everything went dark.

Caelia awoke fiercely thirsty. She felt groggy and heavy, as if she'd been drugged. The fever was gone. She looked down at her leg, at the bandages there. It ached dully but felt better.

She'd been changed and bathed—even her nails had been cleaned. That might have embarrassed her once, but she was well past that now.

Beside the bed, a five-petaled flower gave off light like a fallen star, a cup of water beside it. Even as she reached for it with a bandaged hand, she looked around the room with a strange, star-shaped roof. The walls were even stranger, like mist frozen in place. Magic. Had to be. Lying on another bed in the corner was Gendrin. He'd found time to wash up and change into clean clothes.

At the sight of him sleeping, something softened inside her. He was beautiful, she realized. How had she ever thought differently?

She picked up the glass, her pasty tongue working over the roof of her mouth. In her haste, the cup bumped against the flower, sending ripples of color along the seams. She gasped.

Gendrin instantly sat up, his gaze locking with hers. "You're awake."

She gulped the tepid water. Thirst satiated, she dropped back to the pillow as he sat beside her. "How long did I sleep?"

"A couple days. The healers thought you needed the rest."

She remembered bits and pieces of the wonders she'd seen. "Was it real? Is this real?"

He seemed to understand what she meant. He slid his arms under her and carried her to the misty thing at the room's edge. With a twist of his hand, he banished the swirling vapors. The breeze pushed her hair back from her face. She had a full view of an opalescent tree, larger than anything she'd ever seen.

The colors shifted, drawing her in. Magic sounded in her head—singing crystals and falling rain and drums. She could feel herself dancing, her skirt tightening and flaring around her legs, the emptiness inside her filled up to the brim.

Suddenly, she wasn't afraid anymore. "Dayne."

"What's that?" Gendrin asked.

"My son's name."

Her father and brother's names combined. A way to honor them. Remember them.

His gaze softened. "It's a good name."

The gentleness in his eyes undid her. Using her hand around his neck for leverage, she pulled herself up and pressed her mouth to his. His lips were soft, but his body stiffened.

Confused, she pulled back. His eyes were still closed. He sucked on his bottom lip, as if he was tasting her. He opened his eyes and looked down at her reverently, like he'd been waiting for this moment his entire life.

The forest take her, how was she supposed to keep from falling in love with this man?

"Caelia, you don't know everything. I would never take advantage of—"

"I kissed you," she said firmly. "And I want to do it again. You're going to give me what I want, Gendrin."

He rested his forehead against hers. "Caelia, you're making it very hard to keep my distance."

I know exactly how you feel. She slipped out of his arms, keeping the weight off her bad leg. She wrapped her arms around his neck. "Your protests are noted."

She pulled his mouth down to hers. He let her. Their lips met. Once. Twice. His palms cradled her face. She slid her hands up his arms and back down again. To his broad shoulders, down his back.

She paused, thinking about going farther, but she hadn't completely lost her senses. Though she wasn't far from it—her head was swimming, and she felt light and floaty. She pulled back.

He wrapped her in his arms, holding her tight. "Ancestors, Caelia."

She rested her head against Gendrin's chest. He tucked his chin over her temple. They both looked out at the city, so beautiful in the fading light. Caelia basked in the possibilities before her. Possibilities she'd never thought she'd have again.

Epilogue

CAELIA PUSHED HER SWEATY hair out of her face with the back of her wrist. Leaning heavily on her cane, she forced herself to take another step. One more, and she reached the window. She banished the magical barrier, as Gendrin had taught her, with a twist of her fingers.

Birdsong immediately flooded her room, as did the morning light. Below, a boat rowed toward the healing tree. Gendrin, coming to take her back to his treehome—she could still taste his kiss. She bit her lip, trying to keep her broad grin under control.

There were two more people in the boat: a man and a woman. The woman looked up. Caelia's smile slipped. It wasn't possible. It couldn't be possible.

She pivoted and limped to the doorway, stepping through the magical barrier and down the wide bough. Her leg ached fiercely as she reached the spiraling stairs and started down. Halfway to the base of the tree, Gendrin met her.

She stopped in her tracks, panting. "It can't be. She's dead."

"She's waiting for you."

Tears blurred Caelia's vision as he confirmed the truth of what she'd seen. Atara was alive. "How?"

"I wanted to wait until you were better, but it felt too

much like keeping secrets. It's time you figured out the truth, Caelia. Atara can help you do that."

The truth he couldn't speak because of the curse.

The ache in Caelia's leg had shifted to a burn. Gendrin let her climb on his back and carried her to the base of the trunk—a dock made of the tree's spreading roots.

Caelia stepped down at the sight of the woman pacing. She had the same build. The same hair. Then she turned. Caelia made a small, animal-like wail. Atara sprinted, closing the distance between them, and they wrapped arms tightly around each other.

Caelia breathed in the scent of wind in her hair. "Atara?"

Tears streamed down their cheeks as Caelia pulled back to look at her. Not even a scratch marred her rich skin.

"How did you escape the beast?"

"I didn't."

"What?"

Atara sniffed and smoothed Caelia's hair. "First, tell me your story. Everything."

Caelia did. About the candles they'd sent down the river for Atara. How Harben had chased her into the forest, and Gendrin had saved her. How Caelia had chosen to go with him and killed the beast.

The man who'd come with Atara hung back, listening with his hands folded. Who was he?

Atara glared at Gendrin. "You weren't lying."

"I told you," he said.

Bewildered, Caelia looked between them. "What's going on?"

Atara linked her arm through Caelia's. "Do you recall when we were young and we found that honey?"

"Honey?" But then Caelia did remember. When they were twelve, they had opened a new jar of honey. Stark bitterness had chased the sweet, the back of her throat itchy and tight. Within the hour, they had started seeing things that weren't real.

Mad honey, Papa had called it. Gathered from toxic flowers. "Poisoned honey," Caelia said. "It made us sick."

"Bitter beneath the sweet," Atara murmured. Gendrin led the way to the boat. They followed him.

"I don't understand," Caelia said.

"Come." Gendrin reached back, holding out his hand for her. "There are so many things I need to show you."

Bestselling author **Amber Argyle** writes young-adult fantasies where the main characters save the world (with varying degrees of success) and fall in love (with the enemy). Her award-winning books have been translated into numerous languages and praised by such authors as NYT bestsellers David Farland and Jennifer A. Nielsen.

Amber grew up on a cattle ranch and spent her formative years in the rodeo circuit and on the basketball court. She graduated cum laude from Utah State University with a degree in English and physical education, a husband, and a two-year-old. Since then, she and her husband have added two more children, which they are actively trying to transform from crazy small people into less-crazy larger people. She's fluent in all forms of sarcasm, loves hiking and traveling, and believes spiders should be relegated to horror novels where they belong.

To receive her starter library of four free books, simply tell her where to send it: http://amberargyle.com/freebooks/

Fire and Fountain

by Luisa Perkins

23 June 2019

IT WAS GOING TO rain any moment.

Lucie glanced at the sky as she came to the closing lines of her "Spinning Tales and Yarn" presentation. The light of the setting sun gilded a mass of dark, heavy-bellied clouds to the south, and lightning had shimmered at the horizon off and on for an hour.

Lucie hoped the storm would hold off a little longer. The Saint-Jean-Baptiste Fête was Québec's New France Historical Museum's biggest fundraiser of the year. Good income from the festival meant funding for children's activities, guest lectures, and traditional craft classes for months to come.

Lucie turned her attention back to her audience. "The princess awoke at the kiss of the prince and, opening her eyes, immediately recognized her true love. And they lived happily ever after." She concluded Perrault's classic fairy tale with a little bow of her head. "Merci, *mes amis*! Enjoy the rest of the Fête."

There was scattered applause as her audience dispersed. Lucie stopped the treadle of her spinning wheel and wound her newly made yarn onto a spool. Though it was midsummer, the evening wind was chilly. She wrapped her shawl around her shoulders and stretched her feet toward the bonfire at her side. It had been burning since late afternoon, but with what looked like serious rain on the way, it would likely all go to waste.

"Lucie! You should take a break. I brought you some poutine."

Lucie turned at Olivier's voice. Her colleague in the Special Programs Department held two paper plates of fresh, golden french fries smothered in cheese curds and rich gravy. The smell wafted through the air, and Lucie's stomach rumbled uncomfortably against her tight corset.

"How sweet of you. Thanks!" Lucie accepted a plate, took a bite, and tried not to moan with pleasure. It was even more delicious than it smelled. She hadn't eaten since noon, and it was close to nine o'clock already. She tried to chew and swallow slowly. "How have things been at your booth?"

"Good. I sold several puzzles, and it seems like there's a lot of interest in the new cabinetry class. I had about ten people sign up."

"I'm not surprised. You're so good at what you do." Lucie looked up and caught a hopeful gleam in Olivier's eye. For weeks, the other historian had hinted he'd like to take her out to dinner. On paper, it would make sense to date him. They worked well together at the museum and had everything in common: a love of books and Québec history and culture. But Lucie felt zero chemistry when they worked together or chatted.

An old French-Canadian legend held that something significant always happened to a woman just after her thirty-first birthday. Lucie wasn't superstitious, but being single and having turned thirty-one the week before, she wouldn't mind a reason to change her social media relationship status in the near future. It just wouldn't be with Olivier. She should nip his enthusiasm in the bud; it was kinder that way.

Lucie swallowed her bite. "You're such a good *friend*," she said, leaning slightly on that last word. "What do I owe you for the poutine?"

Blink. Out went that glimmer. "Oh, nothing," Olivier said, staring into the flames of the massive bonfire. "You can treat next time." Just then, raindrops the size of pennies started falling. Olivier looked up and then flinched as his eyes got splashed. "I should run and put my tools away. I'll see you later?"

Lucie nodded. "I'll be at the dance."

"Save a gavotte for me?" Olivier called over his shoulder as he hurried off toward his booth.

Lucie put away her wool and then folded up her portable maple spinning wheel. It broke down compactly and fit into a special leather case, which Lucie quickly zipped up. It was good she'd worn her wool damask costume instead of the lighter but more fragile silk. She could hang this gown in the bathtub to air and not worry about the fabric getting spotted by the rain.

It would probably storm all night. On second thought, she pulled out her phone and texted Olivier her regrets. She'd skip the dance. Instead, she'd hurry home to her apartment, get out of her corset and petticoats, and curl up with some thick, rich *chocolat chaud* and a good book next to the—

Lighting flashed much closer this time, with a tremendous crack of thunder following immediately afterward. Costumed docents and festival patrons started scurrying in earnest for shelter.

Another bolt of lightning struck so close that Lucie smelled ozone. A horse whinnied in Lucie's ear, and she whirled. Yves, the museum's managing director, stood in the cab of his newly restored calèche, struggling to control his horse. Another peal of thunder made the horse rear, its front legs flailing in the air. Lucie jumped back to get away from the iron-shod hooves—and stumbled into the enormous bonfire. The flames roared up all around her, and Lucie screamed.

Two

"*Il y a longtemps que je t'aime, jamais je ne t'oublierai . . .*"

A rich baritone lingered over the refrain of the melancholy old folk song. Lucie opened her eyes and then winced at the throbbing pain in her head. She had sung "À la claire fontaine" with the youth volunteers at the museum just the week before. Who was singing it now? Where was she? She squinted against the harsh morning light and tried to moisten her furry-feeling mouth.

A campfire ringed with stones burned merrily near her elbow. She sat up, brushing pine needles out of her tangled braid. A rough blanket lay over her; where had that come from? Her wheel case and bag of wool sat on the other side of her. She was in a small clearing with thick woods all around.

"Ah, *la belle au bois dormant* has awakened. Bonjour, madame."

Lucie scrambled up and pivoted, slipping slightly on the thick layer of spruce needles. A tall man stood at the edge of the clearing. His long, brown hair was tied back, framing his sea-gray eyes and high cheekbones. His linen shirt hung untucked over stained breeches, and his beard looked like it hadn't been trimmed in a few days. Still, he was gorgeous. Lucie felt heat pulse up her breastbone. He held a trap in one hand and a dead rabbit in the other. He must be one of the hunting guides the museum employed for paid excursions.

But where was Québec City? And why was she in the middle of the woods?

"Good morning," Lucie finally returned, groping for her manners amid her confusion.

"I am relieved to find you awake," the man said. "I did not want to abandon you here all alone, but I did not know how one would pack you, either. I have enough to carry as it is."

"What's going on?" Lucie demanded. "Where is everyone? The festival . . . ," she trailed off.

"I beg your pardon, madame. I do not know what festival you can possibly mean. There's no one around for miles. Who are you? And how did you get into the middle of the forest in those ridiculous shoes?"

Lucie lifted the hem of her gown and looked down at her feet. Her dancing slippers weren't the most sensible hiking gear. But they'd been fine on the grassy field next to the museum . . . which had disappeared, along with the rest of the city.

Lucie gulped back a wave of nausea and dizziness. She sat back down on the ground. "Do you have any water?" she managed.

The man set down the trap and produced a cheesebox canteen. Taking it, Lucie noticed the beautiful woodwork—much finer than even Olivier's. Had this hunter made it? If so, he was talented. Lucie unstoppered it and drank. The water was warmish but fresh tasting. She took several long swallows and sighed as the vertigo passed.

"Thank you." She passed the canteen back to the man.

He bowed slightly. "Nicolas Beaubien, at your service."

"Lucie Tremblay. *Enchantée.*" The pleasantry fell out of her mouth automatically. She looked around. There were too many trees. Everything looked wrong—too wild, too empty—of people, that is. Masses of vegetation that shouldn't have been there were there—along with what sounded like a million songbirds.

"I don't understand any of this," she murmured.

"Nor do I, madame," said the man. "How did you come to be so far from where any damsel should be?"

"Damsel?" Monsieur Beaubien was taking his docent role too far, with his formal manners and archaic French. "I'm not sure that's a compliment."

"To be sure, madame. I find myself in a similar position. I am not sure of anything."

"Can you break out of character for a minute and tell me where we are?"

"We are in New France, of course, just outside Québec settlement."

Now Lucie was getting mad. "Listen, let's stop the games, okay? The last thing I remember, I was celebrating Saint-Jean's Eve on the Plains of Abraham near the museum."

"Today is Saint-Jean's Day, madame, but perhaps you indulged too greatly in your celebration last eve. I know these woods better than any Frenchman, and there are no plains of Abraham or any other prophet to be found on this untamed continent."

Saint-Jean's Day—June 24th. So she'd blacked out only overnight. Had she been kidnapped? She remembered something about a horse ... Yves's horse! It had reared at a peal of thunder, and Lucie had fallen ...

"Into the bonfire," she whispered. She examined the full skirts of her costume. They were a bit smudged, but there was nothing like soot or singe marks anywhere to be found.

The man squatted down near the campfire across from her and began skinning the rabbit. By the looks of it, he'd done this a million times before. *Way to embrace the ancient ways,* thought Lucie.

He set the skin aside, threw the gut sack into the bushes,

and spitted the rabbit, holding it low over the coals until it started to sizzle. The aroma made Lucie's mouth water and gut clench; wherever she was, she hadn't eaten since Olivier's poutine the night before. After propping up the carcass over the fire, Beaubien took another wooden box out of his pack and sprinkled some of the contents on the rabbit's flesh. Sea salt, from the looks of it.

Lucie looked at Nicolas for a long moment. "You're not a docent?" she asked.

"I am no Parisian *professeur*, I assure you. Before I came to New France, I was a farmer in Lorraine. Now I hunt and trade. I've bought a lot inside the settlement and am building a house as I can afford. But this life in the woods is mine for now."

New France. Settlement. Trapping and hunting for a living. Lucie's mind was chasing itself in circles trying to figure out what was going on. "It sounds lonely," she said lamely, trying to keep the conversation going.

"It is, except for my men." Nicolas indicated behind her. Lucie turned around and flinched. A tall First Nations man in full buckskins stood less than an arm's length from her, and she hadn't heard him at all. The man inclined his head slightly. Two others were coming down the hill just behind him.

"Mebkis is my guide and translator. He speaks fluent French. He is teaching me Algonquian, but I confess it is easier to let him perform our negotiations for now. I'm lucky to have found him. There is my business partner, Jean-Claude Dufour." Beaubien nodded at a heavy, slightly older man. "And that is Michel, my son." A lanky teenager growing into his father's image waved awkwardly. "Gentlemen, I present Madame Tremblay. And now you have the advantage of us, madame." Steel glinted in the man's gray eyes, and he raised his eyebrows.

"I work ... I live ... in Québec City." Lucie's vision shimmered, and her knees went wobbly. She leaned her hands on the ground to steady herself. "I'm really struggling," she said finally. "Can you give me a minute?"

But Beaubien persisted. "How did you come to be here, well fed and without a scratch on you? Your slippers are not worn or dusty. Your frock is remarkably clean—and far too fine for everyday wear. You clearly come from money, yet your French is ... vulgar. It is as though you were dropped here from heaven."

Vulgar? Lucie fumed. She had a doctorate from McGill University. But the hunter was waiting for an answer.

"I ... I can't explain it."

This couldn't be real. Had she been spirited away to the middle of the Laurentides forest? Had the museum contracted to film a reality television show—and somehow forgotten to inform her she was the star?

Lucie stood, brushed past Mebkis, and climbed the small rise above the camp to get a better view. The foliage was too thick. Her ridiculous skirts were in the way; she wanted nothing more than to climb the pine tree next to her to get above the tree canopy. If she could only orient herself, she could find her way home.

Failing that, she didn't know what to do. She looked down at the men, who were conversing quietly next to the fire. Mebkis glanced at her and then shook his head. Dufour huffed a laugh and said something, of which "brazen" was the only word Lucie could make out. She stomped back down the hill. If they were talking about her, she had a right to know what they were saying.

"Did you find what you were seeking?" Beaubien asked.

"No, monsieur," Lucie said. "I did not. Look. You claim you know these woods well. I will happily pay you to lead me to the city. I'm sure there are many people who are very worried about me."

That was a lie. No one at all would likely miss her until Monday, but she was confused and frustrated, and the sooner these men helped her home, the better. Despite what Beaubien had said about her cleanliness, her dress felt stale, and her mouth tasted like a rubbish heap. She wanted a bath and her toothbrush as soon as possible.

"The city," Beaubien repeated. "Québec settlement, you mean?"

Lucie wanted to scream. Instead she took a deep breath. "Leave off with the jokes, okay? I'm tired of this."

Mebkis said something in Algonquian to Beaubien, who then looked at her and nodded slowly.

"We shall escort you to the fort," he said. "If you cannot admit how you came to be here, so be it. I will help you home. We will strike camp and then lead you where you want to go. But first we must eat."

Beaubien carved the rabbit and divided it five ways, which made for a meager meal. They rounded out breakfast with water and some flat biscuits Mebkis produced from his pack. The meat was tough and the biscuits were stale, but Lucie was glad to have both.

After breaking camp, Beaubien was as good as his word. They followed a streambed, where the underbrush wasn't quite as dense. A while later, a rushing sound grew in Lucie's ears. They must be close to a river, which Lucie fervently hoped was the Saint-Laurent. Once they passed a last fringe of trees, she could suddenly see for miles—and got yet another shock.

It looked like the entirety of Québec City had been photoshopped out of the otherwise familiar landscape. The Cap Diamant lay peaceful and pristine, surrounded by the mighty Saint-Laurent river. But almost everything indicating the presence of humans was gone. No office buildings, no highways, no Château Frontenac. Instead, a tiny log fort sat at the river's edge. Smoke arose from several chimneys behind its wall.

"What year is it?" Lucie gasped, looking at Beaubien.

He frowned uneasily before replying, "Madame, to be sure, it is the year of our Lord 1640."

Three

LUCIE'S VISION TUNNELED TO black. She bent over and put her head between her knees to keep from hyperventilating. She couldn't have gone back 380 years in time. She must be dreaming.

But what a vivid dream it was. Gnats buzzed around her face, and the morning dew had wicked from the tall grass into the skirts of her dress, making them soggy and even heavier. Her feet were cold, and her leather slippers chafed at the heels. She could smell the wild bergamot that grew in clumps all around the edge of the hill on which they stood.

"We don't have time for this, Beaubien, not if we're to meet our quota and finish the rest of our shipment before *Le Moulin d'Or* sets sail," Dufour said. "Let's take the damsel to the Ursulines and be done with her."

"That might be best," Beaubien said. "My sister will know what to do. Perhaps the nuns have a remedy that can clear her addled mind."

"My mind isn't addled," Lucie protested. "I . . ." How could she explain that she was from the future? "I need some privacy," she finished lamely. Her cell phone was at the bottom of her bag of wool along with her wallet and car keys. "If you will excuse me." She rolled her eyes at herself. She'd been with these men for less than an hour, and she was already starting to talk like them.

She walked into the trees and leaned against a thick rhododendron bush. After making sure no one had followed her, she dug out her cell phone, which winked to life in her hands. No 4G, no Wi-Fi signal bars ... but she opened her email, anyway. Unavailable—as were the GPS and all her social media apps. She clicked on her photo reel; at least her pictures were all there. She had enough battery to last a while, but with no immediate sign of charging potential, it would be smart to power the phone down. She did so and shoved it deep into her bag.

Sixteen forty. Impossible ... yet the things Beaubien had said suddenly made sense. Having a degree in Canadian Studies and working at the New France Historical Museum, Lucie knew more than most about Québec's history. This early, there would be almost no women in the colony other than a few nuns—the Ursulines, as Dufour had said. For these men to have come upon her must have been as great a shock as waking up to them had been for her. It was like a scene out of one of the fairy tales Lucie told to school groups.

And none of the men had likely seen a woman in weeks, if not months. No wonder Michel's and Dufour's eyes had kept straying to her bodice.

And something about Lucie's attitude had already caused Dufour to label her "brazen." Too direct and demanding; not deferential enough, probably.

She had to be careful. While the French hadn't matched the English Puritans' zeal for witch hunting, there was no doubt that the fuchsia spandex bicycle shorts she wore under her petticoats, the zippers on her dress and bag, and especially her phone would raise serious questions. She had to muster her best acting skills and cultural knowledge and fit in until she could get to civilization and then—somehow—find a way back to the twenty-first century. And soon. She'd often daydreamed about living in a simpler time, but suddenly things like indoor plumbing and refrigeration seemed awfully attractive.

"Be careful what you wish for," she muttered as she returned to Beaubien and his men. "Thank you," she said aloud to Beaubien. "I apologize for causing you delay. I would be forever grateful for your escort to the settlement, and I will find a way to repay you."

Out of the corner of her eye, she saw Dufour sneer, his eyes glued once again to her bodice. She suppressed a shudder. Getting away from these men became more urgent by the minute.

Beaubien's son stepped forward. "I would be honored to carry your luggage," he offered.

The dreamy look in his young eyes reminded Lucie of Olivier. Despite the fact that by seventeenth-century standards, she was old enough to be this teenager's mother, it appeared Michel had a crush on her.

Lucie considered giving him the spinning wheel case but remembered the zipper. She clutched it a little more tightly. "You are a true gentleman," she said, and watched his cheeks flush at the compliment. "But, no, thank you. It isn't heavy at all."

Four

HIKING WASN'T LUCIE'S FAVORITE way to spend a day under the best of circumstances, but hiking through trail-free woods in a replica of a seventeenth-century gown was a special kind of torment. Her skirts, which kept snagging on bushes and weeds, were now covered with burrs. She'd swatted away hundreds of mosquitoes but had missed several others, judging by the bites on her arms and neck. Blisters had made their presence known on both feet, and a warm stickiness on the backs of her heels meant her shoes had chafed to bleeding. She'd given up being embarrassed at the sweat stains that were growing under her arms, hoping only that a thorough session at the dry cleaner's would put her gown right again.

She refused to complain and tried to keep her pace up, but it was obvious she was slowing down the band of experienced—and more lightly clad—trappers. All three of the Frenchmen glanced back at her frequently—Beaubien, concerned; Michel, lovestruck; and Dufour, either annoyed or lecherous, or somehow, both. Ever silent, Mebkis followed Lucie, frequently releasing her dress and bag from the undergrowth that seemed to clutch at her.

At one point, Michel fell back to walk by her side. "You will like my Tante Anne," he said. "She entered the order of the Ursulines when she was widowed. She is very wise, and I am sure she will find a way to help you."

"Tell me about her," Lucie said. "When did you move to New France?"

"We arrived last summer on Saint-Junian's Day. Nine years ago, plague struck our village in Lorraine. Most everyone died, my mother and sisters and grandparents among them. My Tante Anne's husband and children died as well. Of our family, only my father and aunt and I survived."

"I'm so sorry," Lucie whispered, calculating. Yes, plague had decimated France in 1631. "What a tragedy."

Michel nodded. "We did our best to carry on with our lives, but when my aunt decided to take the veil, my father had the idea to come with her. We could build a new life for ourselves here, free of the memories that kept our grief fresh. We sold our land and bought passage last spring. And now we are here."

"Do you ever miss France?"

The boy shrugged. "This is our life now. I am learning to call Québec settlement home."

"I understand. I'm very far from ho—"

And then she tripped.

Rump over teakettle, she tumbled. Flinging her arms out to stop her progress down the rocky hill, she slammed her elbow against a granite outcropping and fell on top of her spinning wheel. She lay there for a moment, conscious that the breeze on her thighs meant she was more exposed than was modest.

Then the pain hit—a pounding roar from her left elbow and an answering wet throb across the arch of her right foot. She struggled to pull her petticoats down below her knees with her right hand. She ground her teeth and held back the sobs that threatened to burst out of her.

Beaubien and Mebkis knelt at her side. "Michel, get a length of linen out of your bag, quickly," Beaubien directed.

Fabric in hand, he bound Lucie's foot tightly. Despite her pain, Lucie was reassured by his quick, sure touch. "Thank you. I'm so sorry," she breathed.

Mebkis handed Beaubien a piece of deerskin, which he then tied around her linen bandage. Then he wrapped Lucie's dancing slipper in another scrap of fabric and handed it to her. Lucie was glad the blood had obscured the stamp of the designer's brand on the insole.

Beaubien watched her fumble to put the shoe in her wool bag with one hand. "Your arm—it is hurt as well, yes?"

Lucie ducked her head. "I'm sorry," she repeated.

Mebkis gently took Lucie's left arm, and Lucie bit back a scream as he tried to straighten it. "Broken," he said.

Beaubien sighed and rubbed his forehead. "Dufour, find me two straight sticks, if you please? Michel, more linen. It is fortunate we did not trade away all our textiles this run." He helped Lucie sit up, his hands at her waist and shoulder temporarily distracting her from the agony that was her elbow. "I apologize," he said, taking a knife from his belt and slitting open her sleeve. "We will splint this, and you will need to be brave, because the pain will be considerable. If you can endure this and we can get you to the nuns, my sister will be able to give your injuries more thorough care. All right?"

"That would be great," Lucie said. "Could you . . . ," she trailed off, embarrassed.

"Yes?"

"If you could hold me while Mebkis does the splinting, I think I could bear it better." Lucie's face blazed as she forced herself to meet his eyes.

Their once-stormy gray was calm. "Absolutely, madame," he said.

The pain was more than considerable. Lucie pressed her face against Beaubien's chest so that his blouse would muffle her shrieks. She came close to passing out, but the comfort of strong arms around her kept her conscious. When the splinting was done, Lucie's hair stuck to her sweaty forehead. She wiped her face with her sleeve and tried to force her lips into a smile. She was probably grimacing like a gargoyle. "Thank you," she said, looking at each of the men in turn. "Thank you all. I don't know how to express my gratitude for your kindness."

Dufour huffed a laugh as he shouldered his pack. A chill passed through Lucie, but as Beaubien and Mebkis helped her to her feet, she forced fear away. As long as she stayed close to these two, she would be safe.

"Michel, carry madame's baggage," Beaubien said.

"No, I'm fine," insisted Lucie.

Beaubien's eyes turned to steel again. "Madame, whatever you are, you are most assuredly *not* fine. We must make haste to get across the river and to the fort before sundown. Allow me to determine what will best suit our needs, if you please."

Stung, Lucie started limping forward behind Dufour. "Yes, of course, monsieur," she said. "As you wish."

Five

THE NEXT SEVERAL HOURS were a blur of pain, hunger, and barely suppressed panic. Lucie felt as if she were outside her body, watching her poor, broken self stumble on and on through the wilderness. A persistent rattle made her suspect she'd broken her spinning wheel in her fall, but she didn't have the time or the privacy to unzip her case and check it.

Michel had passed some sliced dried apples around on a short water break, but the group did not stop for a more elaborate meal. As the midsummer sun set over the far hills, they came to the bank of the Saint-Laurent River. Mebkis produced two canoes from under cover of a deadfall, and the men slid them through the tall grass to the water's edge.

Beaubien helped Lucie into one of the canoes. "You'll travel with Mebkis and Michel," he informed her. "Dufour and I will man the other boat to keep the weight evenly distributed."

Lucie couldn't help but shiver in the humid air. Beaubien noticed and removed two pelts from his pack. He draped them over her. Lucie wrinkled her nose at the smell of the half-cured fur but was grateful for their warmth. "Thank you very much," she said through chattering teeth.

The canoe was clearly made for two people, not three. The boat wallowed low once Mebkis pushed off the shore and jumped in. He and Michel paddled after Beaubien, fighting to keep the canoe workways to the strong current. To Lucie, the river she'd known all her life had never looked so vast, so dangerous. She ducked her chin under the stinky pelt, closed her eyes, and prayed they'd get across safely.

Despite her fear and discomfort, she must have drowsed, because the next minute, Mebkis and Michel were dragging the boat to shore on the Cap Diamant. The fort that had looked so tiny earlier in the day now loomed overhead. Stiff with chill, Lucie tried to lever herself up and out of the boat. In a moment, Beaubien was at her side, lifting her up. "Not long now, madame," he said softly. "You have proven yourself very brave today. If you can endure but a few moments longer, we will have you safely in my sister's care." He turned to his men. "Dufour, would you be so kind as to take Michel and our wares to our lodgings? I will meet you there shortly after I deposit Madame Tremblay with the Ursulines. Mebkis, with me, if you please."

Lucie leaned heavily on his arm as they made their way slowly through the fort toward a long, low building with a wooden cross nailed to the gable. "We're here to see Soeur Anne," Beaubien said to the nun who opened the door.

They were ushered into a small room lit only by a fire in the hearth. Beaubien helped Lucie to a seat at a table near the fireplace and paced the length of the chamber. Mebkis stood like a statue near the window, the contrast in his demeanor highlighting Beaubien's restlessness. Lucie slipped the elastic from her messy braid and ran her fingers through her tangled locks but realized too late that she couldn't rebraid it one-handed. Knowing that loose hair was considered seductive, she twisted it and shoved the ends down the back of her gown so she'd look a little less wanton.

Moments later, a woman opened the door. Her hair and

eyes were the same as her brother's, her cheekbones softer but still prominent. Lucie would have recognized them as related even if she hadn't known beforehand. Soeur Anne's eyes widened when she saw Lucie, but she said nothing until she turned toward the others.

She took the First Nations man's hand in both her own and squeezed it warmly. "Mebkis! *Kwey widjiwàgan.* God's blessings on you; I am glad to see you." Then she hugged her brother, saying, "Nicolas. Saint-Christophe has brought you safely back to me. I shall sleep well this night. Now. Come, sit. I've asked that food be brought to us. In the meantime, tell me about your guest." She sat down at the table and looked at Lucie expectantly.

"Anne, may I present to you Madame Lucie Tremblay?"

Lucie dipped her head in what she hoped was a reverent bow. "I'm honored to meet you, Soeur."

Soeur Anne looked at her keenly. "Madame, or Mademoiselle?"

"The latter, Soeur. I'm singl ... unmarried." Lucie couldn't help but look at Beaubien for his reaction to her admission. His face remained still, but she thought she saw his eyes brighten.

"And how did my brother come to meet you? I thought I knew all the women in our settlement." Soeur Anne glanced at Lucie's filthy dress. "Though you are somewhat worse for wear, it is clear that you are a lady of refinement and standing."

"I . . ." Lucie hesitated. She'd been pondering a cover story but hadn't come up with much through her haze of pain and fatigue.

The door opened, and two other nuns brought in a candelabra and trays laden with food and clean dishes. They set out the dinner, poured what looked like cider into four pewter goblets, and left the room.

Soeur Anne took up her goblet. "To your health," she said to Lucie before drinking. "Which seems to be in some question. What misfortune has befallen you?"

That was easier to answer than the nun's first question. Lucie sipped the flavorful juice, which felt like a balm on her dry throat. "I fell early this afternoon," she explained, trying to match the formality of the other woman's speech. "Your brother and Mebkis were kind enough to bind up my wounds and bring me here to you. I'm afraid I'm at your mercy, as I am quite lost and do not know how to find my way home."

"And where is your home?" Soeur Anne, asked, dishing up venison stew and passing out plates. "Have you come from the east, from Tadoussac? Or Trois-Rivières, perhaps?"

Lucie took a large bite of stew and chewed, racking her brains for accurate historical information. Which was the more convincing lie? Ville-Marie, which later would become Montréal, or Trois-Rivières? The latter was closer . . .

"She is from this place, but not from this time."

Lucie, Soeur Anne, and Beaubien all looked at Mebkis in surprise. "I beg your pardon?" said Beaubien.

Mebkis held Lucie's gaze. "She is not from this time," the First Nations man repeated. "She has come here through fire."

Beaubien and his sister both crossed themselves. Lucie sat in shock. "How did you know?" she finally managed.

Mebkis grinned for the first time since Lucie had met him early that morning. "The trees whispered it to me when we first found you. Also, you smell wrong." He fell to his stew with gusto.

Lucie became acutely conscious again of her underarms and bad breath. "Excuse me?"

"It's not a smell, exactly," said Mebkis around a mouthful of food. "But I do not know the French for what I mean. The fire you light at the summer solstice. It brought her here."

"She came through the *chavande?*" Beaubien and his sister exchanged a glance.

"What's that?" Lucie asked.

"At home in Lorraine," Soeur Anne explained. "We call the midsummer's eve bonfire the *chavande*. It represents the hope that though the light lessens, it will return."

"But traveling through the fire? How is it possible?" asked Beaubien. "It sounds . . . diabolical."

Mebkis shook his head. "She is not *madji-manidò*. There is no evil here."

I'm glad to hear it, thought Lucie as she ate, but held her peace. It was vital that she not be locked up—or worse—as a witch, if she was to find her way back.

"No," agreed Soeur Anne, looking into Lucie's eyes. "It is not witchery that has brought her to us." She took her rosary from around her neck and held it out to Lucie. "But just to be sure. Kindly say an 'Our Father,' if you please?"

Lucie took the string of beads. She hadn't told the beads of a rosary since middle school, but once she started, it was like getting on a bicycle. When she finished the prayer, Beaubien and Sister Anne both visibly relaxed.

"Come now, Mademoiselle Lucie," Beaubien said. "Tell us your story."

Lucie related the details of the previous evening—had it been only twenty-four hours ago? When she finished, she took up her bag and made a show of unzipping it. All three of the others gasped at the noise it made, and Lucie laughed at their wonder. She'd been taking zippers for granted all her life.

She held the bag up to the candelabra so they could see the zipper's tiny teeth and how they fit together as she moved the slider. Then she removed her spinning wheel. As she'd suspected, it was broken: the treadle had snapped in half. But she set it up for them next to her on the bench.

Beaubien came around to her side of the table and knelt beside the wheel. He ran his hands lightly over the smooth wood and pushed the levers that moved the wheel. "It's marvelous," he murmured. "If you wish, I believe I can repair it for you."

Lucie warmed at his offer. For the first time, she felt a pang of regret at the idea of getting back to her own time. "I would be grateful, but I hope I'm not here long enough for that to happen."

Beaubien stiffened and looked away. "Of course."

To cover the awkwardness of the moment, Lucie pulled her cell phone out of her bag of wool and turned it on. Its screen flashed cold white, blinding eyes accustomed to candlelight. Once they all adjusted, Lucie showed them a few photos. Sister Anne crossed herself repeatedly, and even the unflappable Mebkis looked . . . flapped. Finally, Lucie powered down her phone again and put it away.

"And from how far into the future have you come to us?" asked Beaubien.

"From 20—" Lucie corrected herself. "The year of our Lord two thousand nineteen."

"Nearly four hundred years," whispered Soeur Anne. "That seems impossibly far away. You poor child."

"I'm not exactly a child," returned Lucie. "I'm thirty-one years old."

Beaubien laughed in astonishment. "That cannot be true. That is my sister's age. Begging your pardon, Anne."

Lucie glanced at Soeur Anne. She'd thought the nun was twenty years older. It made sense, though. Uneven access to high-quality food, exposure to the elements, childbirth, and tragedy all had aged pre-Industrial women. Lucie had learned as much in her studies, but being confronted with this reality was a different thing altogether.

Soeur Anne smiled faintly. "Well, then. We have all had enough excitement for one evening, have we not? I suggest that we take our rest and reconvene on the morrow. Would that be acceptable, mademoiselle?"

Now that her stomach was full of savory stew, Lucie felt fatigue blanketing her mind. "Yes, please."

Beaubien stood, squeezing his sister's shoulder fondly. "We will all think more clearly after some rest. We'll take our leave. I have business to which I must attend in the morning, but Mebkis and Michel and I will meet you at midday, yes?"

"Yes," his sister answered. "I am most anxious to see my nephew."

Beaubien moved to the door, Mebkis at his heels. "Until tomorrow, then, sister. Mademoiselle." The trapper bowed to each of the women in turn and left.

"Have you eaten and drunk your fill?" Sister Anne asked.

"Yes, Soeur, thank you very much for your hospitality."

"Charity is the watchword of our order. Let us find you a bed, then, and something to wear. I'll clean and dress your wounds and make you as comfortable as possible. Some willow bark tea with plenty of honey is in order, yes? With perhaps some valerian to help you sleep."

Lucie smiled gratefully. The throbbing of her arm and foot were the only things keeping her awake, and the salicylic acid in the willow bark should help take the edge off the pain. If only she'd had some ibuprofen in her bag of wool . . . "Yes, please." She followed after the nun.

In a room no bigger than a broom closet, Soeur Anne unwrapped Lucie's foot. She inhaled sharply when she saw the cut, which now looked puffy and inflamed. "Bring me some goldenseal from the infirmary," she directed the novice who had come in with them. The girl returned with some withered roots a moment later and handed them to the nun. Sister Anne set a shallow wooden basin under Lucie's foot and poured vinegar over the cut. Lucie winced at the sting but held her leg as still as possible. Once the wound was flushed clean, the nun spread honey on Lucie's skin. Next, she sliced open the roots, pressed the cut sides against Lucie's flesh, and wrapped the foot, roots and all, with clean linen.

She surveyed the splint on Lucie's arm, smiling approvingly at Mebkis's work. "We'll leave that for now," she said. She helped Lucie out of her gown, murmuring amazement at the zipper set in the side of the bodice. "I'll clean and mend this myself," she told Lucie as she bundled up the fabric. "It wouldn't do for others to see it."

Once Lucie was down to her bra and bicycle shorts—she noticed Soeur Anne trying not to goggle at her twenty-first-century underwear—she gratefully sponged her body off and donned the clean nightgown the novice had brought her. The large bell sleeve just fit over her splint. She'd have to move carefully to avoid tearing it.

"Now, drink your tea, say your prayers, and rest." Soeur Anne smiled and shut the door behind her as she left.

Lucie curled up on the short, narrow cot after drinking her tea. Her splinted arm felt like a log, but it was wonderful to lie down. Despite her exhaustion, she was afraid to go to sleep. After all, it wasn't necessarily the bonfire that had brought her to this time, no matter what Mebkis thought he knew.

And curiously, the thought of waking up at home without another chance to see Nicolas Beaubien, a man she barely knew, troubled her more than she wanted to admit.

Finally, though, Lucie slept.

Her body was one massive muscle ache when she woke up the next morning. Her splinted arm was all over pins and needles, and Lucie felt sure that if she looked at her foot, it would be visibly pulsing with each beat of her heart. Almost as bad, she could barely stand her own smell. *I'd trade at least a week's pay for a hot shower*, she thought.

Someone rapped softly at the door, and a moment later, Soeur Anne popped her head in. "Bonjour!" she sang out.

Lucie levered herself up to sitting as the nun bustled in with a tray of food and medicaments. Nuns kept grueling schedules; Soeur Anne had surely been up since well before dawn. "Good morning. What time is it?"

"It's past nine. You slept for almost twelve hours. There's

nothing like sleep for healing." Soeur Anne set down her tray and moved to Lucie's bedside. "May I?"

Lucie nodded.

The nun turned back the covers to expose Lucie's bandaged foot. Once it was unwrapped, Lucie could see it looked better. Soeur Anne repeated the wound care she'd performed the night before and wrapped Lucie's foot back up. "It will leave a scar," she said. "If someone could have sewn it up shortly after you injured it, it might have healed more cleanly."

"I don't mind the scar," Lucie said. "Thank you for your help."

Soeur Anne handed her a plate with bread and cheese on it. "Break your fast while I fetch your gown. I did my best to clean it last eve. It might smell somewhat of smoke. I hung it to dry at my own hearth. I left the sleeve open for your splint, but turned the edges under to prevent the fabric from fraying. It's a surpassing fine weave. What looms you must have in your time."

You have no idea. "You are too kind," Lucie said aloud. Smelling like smoke was far better than the alternative. "Would it be possible to get a basin of water and a cloth? With more vinegar—and perhaps a comb? I would like to wash."

"Yes, of course."

Once the nun left, Lucie wolfed down her food, thinking as fast as she chewed. Vinegar would cut the smell and the greasy feel of her skin somewhat—and would also make a basic mouthwash. Lucie wished that during their journey the day before, she had thought to gather some bergamot or teaberry to scrub her mouth with.

After eating, Lucie took some wool roving and her drop spindle out of her bag. Spinning with a drop spindle was much slower and laborious than using a wheel, but it was all she had at the moment to keep her hands busy and her mind focused.

Soeur Anne soon returned, Lucie's gown over one arm. "I'll leave you to your toilette. Once you've finished, come out to the hall, and we'll sit in the garden. Fresh air and sunshine will do you much good, and I plan to receive my nephew and Mebkis there."

The garden—perfect. Lucie could hopefully pick some mint or parsley and chew it. It would be nice to see Michel and Mebkis. Was it too much to ask that Nicolas Beaubien might be able to accompany his son?

She was disappointed; the boy and the First Nations man came alone.

"Father and Dufour are overseeing the loading of our furs onto the ship," Michel explained. "They have much to do before it sails. They'll leave tomorrow."

"Your father is going to France?" Lucie tried and failed to keep disappointment out of her voice.

"No, madame. He sails only downriver to the Atlantic to see off the ship. It has become a tradition."

"Oh." Lucie bit her cheeks to keep from smiling. What was wrong with her? She was acting like a silly teenager. She looked down at her spindle to hide her face.

"When they return next week, Father will host a dinner. He asked me to extend an invitation to you. Please say you'll accept."

Oh, that hopeful spark. Lucie should put the boy out of his misery sooner rather than later. "I would be glad to. I've just had my thirty-first birthday, and I would love to celebrate it with you." She smiled as Michel tried to cover his shock.

"Madame . . . I . . . we all will be so glad of your company," he finished lamely.

Soeur Anne laughed. "I am sure she will look forward to it. Michel, you should go help your father now," she suggested. "Mebkis and I need a word alone with Madame Tremblay."

"Yes, of course." The boy stood, bowed, and left.

"The poor boy," the nun said, looking fondly after her nephew. "Well, Mebkis," she said, returning her attention to the crewelwork in her lap. "What think you of our poor lost Lucie's quest to find her way home? Saint-Jean's Day is past, so we cannot build another *chavande* and hope for that strange magic to repeat itself."

"If there was a way here, there must be a way for me to get back," added Lucie.

"I know of nothing that could send a person forward through many thousand tomorrows," the First Nations man said. "I wish to return to my people and consult the elders. If anyone in all of Kanatà can solve this riddle, it will be them. They have some powerful magic, but it is guarded closely. I cannot promise they will give you any aid, but I will try. I will be gone at least seven days, but I will make haste."

"Thank you," Lucie said. "That's very generous of you."

Mebkis took his leave. A week—at minimum—seemed a long time to wait, but what else could Lucie do?

Why had this happened to her? Was it just a random blip in the normal functioning of the universe, or did this strange turn in her life have a purpose?

"Patience is bitter, but its fruit is sweet," said Soeur Anne, seeming to have read Lucie's thoughts. "Time will tell us the meaning of all things."

Lucie thought about that as she let the roving twist through her fingers until it was a single ply of yarn. Finally, she said, "I'll just have to trust you on that."

Seven

THE DAYS IN THE monastery were quiet, punctuated only by meals and prayers. Lucie spent much of her time in the herb garden in the shade of the porch, spinning awkwardly on a borrowed wheel and watching bees pollinate the flowers. There wasn't much else she could do; the only books the nuns owned were precious copies of the Bible and collections of music. She did beg some paper, pen, and ink so she could record her observations of daily life. Once she got home, she thought she might write a book and set straight some misconceptions that had persisted down through the centuries. How she'd support her assertions was another matter, but she could worry about that later.

Paper was scarce, however, and there was only so much writing Lucie could do. Needlework was impossible. Lucie fairly ached to knit or do some kind of embroidery. But she'd have to wait until her arm was healed, and that would be another three weeks, at least.

So she sat in the shade and spun, daydreaming about flush toilets and refrigerators. More often than she would have liked, she found her thoughts straying to Nicolas. *Monsieur Beaubien,* she corrected herself. The way he'd held her when her arm was getting set. The wonder in his eyes as she showed off the relics from the future. His changeable eyes—one minute the soft gray of a kitten's fur, the next, bleak granite.

His pride in his son; the grief over his lost family; his aspirations for remaking his life in New France.

Why weren't there any men like him in the twenty-first century? Circumstances shaped character, Lucie decided. He'd been given a hard lot in life and had refused to let it define him. He'd certainly confirmed Lucie's suspicions that good men existed. If she could only find one in her own time.

But did she want one like him? Or did she just want *him*?

The day of the dinner party finally arrived. Lucie overheard Soeur Anne talking to a younger nun about the fact that her brother had returned from Gaspésie.

Lucie washed as best she could and asked the young novice Soeur Madeleine for help with her hair. Her dress had stayed pretty clean; bless wool for its stain-resistant properties. Lucie picked some mint from the garden and tucked it into her bodice along the neckline to keep herself pleasantly fragrant and to help keep the odors of others at bay.

Though she was dismayed to find she was noticing smells less and less. *Noseblind*, she said to herself.

She had joined a gym after college and remembered being overwhelmed by the smell of sweaty bodies and chlorine for the first few days. After a week or so, she stopped noticing it and assumed that the gym had been thoroughly cleaned. But then one day, she met a newcomer on the neighboring treadmill who complained about the room's reek—and Lucie realized she had become immune to it.

Lucie hated the thought of becoming used to the odors around her in the settlement, but she had to admit it made it easier to eat and generally enjoy life when not continually plagued by seventeenth-century stenches.

Michel came at six o'clock to escort her to the Beaubiens' house. It was a short walk across the inner fort. Like all the other buildings in the settlement, Beaubien's house was a *piece-sur-piece* log cabin. But Michel led her around back before taking her inside.

"See? Here my father is building a grand house," he said, pointing to a stone foundation more than three times the size of the original cabin. "It will be a home for our family for generations to come."

They walked back to the front and entered the crowded cabin. It comprised a single room about the size of the monastery's chapel, with a big hearth on the wall opposite the door. A few small windows lined with parchment blocked most of dying light, but candles stood down the length of the long trestle table that dominated the room. Chairs and benches lined either side, and hay and lavender were strewn liberally on the floor. Nothing matched; Lucie guessed that to have a dinner this size, Beaubien had borrowed table linens, plates, and furniture from most of his guests. What it lacked in elegance, it made up for in cheer.

Beaubien turned from a group of men he'd been talking with. Lucie hoped she wasn't imagining how his face lit up when he saw her. He came around the table and greeted her with the traditional kisses on either cheek. "*Bienvenue*, mademoiselle. You are looking very well. I trust your wounds are healing?"

"Yes, thank you. Your sister has taken excellent care of me."

"I am delighted but not surprised. Anne is a skilled nurse."

Lucie looked up into Nicolas's eyes. He smiled down at her. She should really say something instead of staring back and grinning like a fool.

"Your business went well, then?" she asked.

"Yes. We sailed to Gaspé Bay, where the Saint-Laurent empties into the sea. We bid the ship Godspeed on its journey back to France and made our way back on foot, trading along the way. It was a profitable and productive week. We stopped at Trois-Rivières to deliver a letter for my sister."

Lucie chuckled inwardly as she thought of her most vivid memory of Trois-Rivières—a roller skating party with cousins at a discotheque-style rink, complete with flashing mirror ball, arcade games, and snack bar.

"You must have been relieved to encounter no more strange women along your route," she said.

"Who says I did not?" Beaubien's eyes twinkled. "At any rate, welcome. I'm glad you are here. These ruffians need to be reminded that the beauties of civilization still exist." He bowed. "I'll call the group now. I think we're ready to serve dinner now that you're here."

Lucie sat at Beaubien's right. Michel was at the other end of the table, with Dufour next to him.

Dufour raised his glass. "A toast from our host," he cried.

A cheer went up as the guests raised their glasses.

Beaubien grinned and raised his as well. "Thanks to you all for your company. Here's to a prosperous summer and a short winter."

Another cheer, and then everyone drank deeply. Beaubien sat back and fingered a religious medal he wore around his neck on a leather thong.

"Your patron saint?" Lucie asked.

Beaubien's eyes grew melancholy. "That of my wife, Marie, God rest her soul."

"I'm so sorry." Lucie drank more cider. "Your son told me of your loss."

"It has been nearly nine years, and yet sometimes ... sometimes I still wake up in the morning expecting her to be at my side. And when she is not ..." Beaubien stared into his goblet. "But enough. I need not burden you with my grief. How do you find our settlement?"

Lucie thought about the past week, how fascinating it had been to see in real life what she had only read about for years. The rhythm of the days, the social interactions. "I confess, I've enjoyed it more than I thought I would. It seems a quiet life, but a satisfying one."

Beaubien raised his glass. "Here's to satisfaction," he said.

As they drank, Lucie looked into Beaubien's eyes. The cider was cool, so why were her cheeks growing so hot?

Dinner lasted for hours. The food was delicious but heavy, especially on such a hot summer night. Thick fish chowder, peppery roasted venison and potatoes, ripe tomme cheeses and crusty wholemeal bread. It was a display of wealth for Beaubien to serve so much rich food. The nuns ate much plainer and lighter fare: roasted trout, fresh-picked *dent-de-lion* and *mâche* dressed in vinaigrette, stewed dried apples and cranberries, porridge. Lucie wished for a salad or at least some fruit, but there was none in sight. She thought for the thousandth time about the air-conditioned, bug-free Intermarché near her apartment, with its lavish aisles of fruit and vegetables from around the globe. Once she got home, she'd never look at avocados or bananas the same way again.

The smoke from the fire and the candles thickened the already-humid midsummer air, and Beaubien's cabin got ever stuffier as the evening progressed. At the other end of the table, Michel had fallen asleep, his forehead pillowed on his arm. Lucie smiled at the sight, then sighed and wished she could do the same.

"Will you excuse me?" she asked Nicolas. "I need some air."

"Of course. I'll accompany you."

Lucie laid her hand on his arm, ignoring the zing under her collarbone as she touched him. "No, thank you. I'll be fine. Stay with your guests. I'll be back in a moment." She arose, made her way around the crowded room, and slipped outside.

The outside air was still humid, but at least it was fresh. She stared up at the stars, remembering an old legend that if you counted nine stars for nine nights in a row, the last star would point toward your future husband. She loosened her lace scarf so that the faint breeze could cool the back of her neck.

The settlement lay quiet, only the outlines of buildings and the stockade visible. There was no denying the primitive beauty of the seventeenth century. The stars were as thick as gravel, and the virgin forest whispered with life just outside the fort walls. Lucie paced around the small yard. How strange these past days had been. She was grateful Mebkis had gone to his council of elders for help. When would he be back? She worried about her work and her apartment. Her plants were likely dead by now, and her rent was a couple of days past due. Did her colleagues miss her?

The crack of a snapped twig brought Lucie back to the present. She turned, peering through the darkness. "Who's there?" she called softly, wishing she didn't sound like a mouse.

Someone stepped forward heavily. Dufour.

"Good evening, monsieur." Lucie tried to adopt the modest but firm reserve of Soeur Anne.

"There you are," the man said, his words slurring. "At last, I find myself alone with you."

The last thing Lucie wanted was to be alone with him. "I was just going back inside," she said.

"Pray do not hurry away," Dufour said, stepping forward to close the distance between them. "Do not play the coy mistress. There is no one else present, so kindly drop your maidenly act. You can be honest with me. I know what you really are."

Lucie had resisted retreating as he advanced, thinking

that showing her fright and aversion wouldn't help. But now he was inches away, his foul breath bathing her face. She stepped back, but he lunged and grabbed her arm.

"You are no lady, it is clear," he murmured. He was strong; Lucie twisted in his grasp in vain. "But you *are* a woman, and it has been a long time since I've been close to a woman. Play nicely, and I will reward you handsomely." As he bent toward her, Lucie turned her face away so that his fleshy lips landed just below her ear.

Then he was wrenched backward, still clutching Lucie, so that she stumbled over his legs and landed on her hurt arm. Dufour finally released her, and she rolled away across the grass, squinting through the shadows to see what was going on.

Beaubien had come to her rescue. He and his business partner exchanged several blows. Dufour was bigger, but his bulk slowed him down. Finally, Beaubien broke free of Dufour's grasp, reared back, and hit the other man in the jaw. Dufour fell to the grass unconscious.

Beaubien turned to Lucie, wiping his bleeding nose with the back of his hand. "Are you all right?"

Lucie nodded, trying not to cry. "Thank you," she whispered. "He was . . . presuming."

"I could see that. I am so sorry, mademoiselle. Most of the men here count themselves deprived of female attention, but that is no excuse for depraved behavior. I submit to you my deepest apologies."

"I'm fine," Lucie said, silently vowing she'd take a self-defense class when she got home. "But I'm tired, and I'd like to go back to the monastery, if you don't mind."

"Of course. I shall escort you." Beaubien drew her unhurt arm through his and walked slowly through the streets. "I had hoped tonight would be a pleasant experience for you."

"It was, really. Except for Dufour, your friends are gentlemen, and I enjoyed getting to know them."

"I am glad."

They fell silent as they made their way to the monastery. At the door, Beaubien bowed. "Again, I apologize for Dufour's behavior. I'll see to it that he never bothers you again."

"Thank you." Lucie looked at Nicolas's face, shadowy in the moonlight. "And thank you again for inviting me to dinner."

Nicolas pressed her hand and took a step closer. "The pleasure is all mine," he murmured. His gaze dropped to her mouth, and for a breathless moment, Lucie thought he might kiss her. She gasped a little at the way her heart started pounding. How different this was from being close to Dufour. All was still. She leaned toward him and closed her eyes.

Then Nicolas turned away and sighed. "Good night, mademoiselle," he said gently. He turned and left the monastery's porch.

Lucie watched him go, embarrassment and disappointment warring for territory in her heart. She'd been a fool; Beaubien was clearly still devoted to the memory of his beloved wife. Lucie had to remember not to get too attached to any of these people. With any luck, she'd be leaving them very soon.

Eight

MEBKIS AND BEAUBIEN JOINED Lucie and Soeur Anne in the monastery garden the next morning.

Beaubien spoke first. "Mademoiselle, I wanted you to be the first to know that I have canceled my contract with Dufour and strongly advised him to take up residence in Trois-Rivières. He shouldn't bother you again."

Lucie felt as if a boulder had just fallen off her back. "Thank you. I hope you have not been inconvenienced."

"Not at all. A man without honor is not someone with whom I want to do business. We will be better off without him." He settled back in his chair and gestured to his friend. "Now, Mebkis. Share your news with us."

Mebkis leaned forward, eagerness enlivening his usually grave features. "I have met with the elders, and I believe there is a way I can help you."

Lucie stopped the treadle on the nuns' spinning wheel and stared. "Truly? Oh, Mebkis. That would be a miracle."

"And like the miracles of your saints, it will take much faith and work. We will need the help of Nicolas as well."

Lucie looked at Beaubien. "Will you help me?"

Nicolas's eyes were distant even as he smiled. "Of course. I will contribute however is needed. Tell us more, Mebkis."

"There is a cave a half day's journey from here, hidden by the tall waterfall we call Gondawakamigise."

"I know the place," said Beaubien. "Champlain named it Montmorency Falls. But I did not know about the cave."

"It is a mystical place, usually unable to be reached. But at the height of summer, sometimes the water is low enough that one can risk the climb and enter the cave.

"We must go behind the water to the cave and build a fire of birchwood. Each person present must sacrifice an object very dear to them in order to feed the sacred fire. My elders have given me the words that must be spoken and the motions that must be made—all very precise, so I will practice. If we perform each step correctly and our wills are strong enough, the elders say we can open a pathway through time—a door to your home, Lucie."

Hope flooded through Lucie. "Thank you, Mebkis! When can we go?"

"We must wait another fortnight, at least. The water is usually at its lowest near the end of the month you call July."

"July twenty-sixth is Sainte-Anne's Day," volunteered Soeur Anne. "As the patron of unmarried women, my namesake might grant you your heart's desire on her feast day. Perhaps that would be an auspicious day for this endeavor."

Mebkis thought for a moment. "The light of the full moon would favor us on that night," he said. "We should plan to go then."

"We must speak of this to no one," cautioned Soeur Anne. "To anyone else, this would speak of witchery. To the undiscerning, there has ever been a fine line between the miracles of the saints and the craft of witches."

You don't know the half of it, thought Lucie, thinking of events in Massachusetts still fifty years in the future. "And you're sure it will work?"

"Nothing in life is sure, but it should work if we believe it will work," said Mebkis. "Desire and imagination will be the forces that bring it about."

"Desire and imagination—we call that combination 'faith,'" said Soeur Anne. She turned to her brother. "Nicolas, you have said little. What think you of this plan?"

Beaubien shook his head. "I trust Mebkis with my life and more. If Mademoiselle Lucie wants this, I will help all I can." He looked out across the garden, his face unreadable. "Well," he said, standing. "I must get back to work."

Mebkis stood as well. "Mademoiselle, think of the possession most precious to you. That is what you must be willing to sacrifice to the sacred fire. It will be wasted, otherwise."

Lucie nodded. "I don't have much, so it shouldn't be hard to figure out," she said.

Beaubien walked toward the door but then came back to where Lucie sat. "May I renew my offer to fix your spinning wheel? It looked to be a fairly simple repair. Michel and I would love the chance to examine its workings. We have three weeks. It could be my parting gift to you—something for you to remember me . . . us by."

"I would like that very much," said Lucie, her traitorous heart thudding. Why did she let him have this effect on her? "I'll go fetch it now."

A moment later, she returned, her leather wheel case in her arms. "Thank you. You've done nothing but help me. I'm afraid I've been a terrible burden."

Beaubien took the case and bowed. "Not at all, mademoiselle. Not at all."

Nine

26 July 1640

IT WAS STILL OPPRESSIVELY hot at four o'clock on the afternoon of Sainte-Anne's Day, but it was time to go. Standing outside the monastery with the rest of the traveling party, Lucie smoothed the patched breeches she wore. Mebkis had warned that the climb to the falls was treacherous under any circumstances, definitely not to be attempted in a gown and petticoats. Nicolas had given her a set of clothes that Michel had outgrown before they were worn to utter rags. Soeur Anne had contributed a pair of battered riding boots she'd found in the monastery's storeroom.

Now that her splint was finally off, Lucie had been able to braid her own hair for the first time in weeks. Her long plait was tucked into the back of her shirt, and her gown and twenty-first-century belongings were bundled into a linen knapsack. She carried it and her spinning wheel's leather case on her shoulders.

She embraced Soeur Anne. "Thank you for everything," she whispered, sorrow closing her throat.

"I will fast and pray in the chapel until my brother returns," said Soeur Anne. "Though it pains me to bid you adieu, I know you must be desirous to return home after all this time. I wish you safe journey." She pressed something into Lucie's palm. "Keep this as a remembrance," she urged.

Lucie opened her hand to see an oval medal on a fine ribbon. She held it up and saw that it bore the face of Saint-Anne. Tears spilled freely from her eyes. "I shall never forget you, Soeur." She put the medallion around her neck.

Soeur Anne turned to Nicolas. "Hasten here and inform me of your success," she said. "No matter how late the hour. I will not rest until I know all is well."

Nicolas nodded. "Come, let us begin," he said to the others. "It will be far easier for us to approach the cave while there is still daylight in the sky. I would prefer not to be burdened with lit torches if we can avoid them."

As Mebkis led them northeast into the woods, Lucie couldn't help but think of their journey toward the settlement a little over a month before. In some ways, it felt as though she'd been in 1640 for far longer than five weeks. Yet as she walked behind Beaubien, she wished this day hadn't come quite so quickly. She imagined bringing Nicolas home. He had bravely begun a life in a new land; was there a way he could start over yet again in a new century? Likely not. There wasn't much call for trappers in her Québec. And surely the noise and people and technology would be overwhelming.

Now that she thought about it, after her weeks of peace—no television or internet, no cars or airplanes, no schedule other than the passing summer and the Ursulines' daily round of prayer—she wondered if *she* would be able to endure the city furor she'd taken for granted her entire life.

Nearly four hours later, they stood at the base of Montmorency Falls. Lucie had visited the massive cataract many times, but seeing it unframed by any concrete stairs, suspension bridge, or tram wires made it look even grander and untamed. Mebkis was right, of course; there was far less water falling than there would be after spring or late summer storms. This was their best chance of reaching the cave.

They kept to dry ground as they climbed. After a few dozen meters, Lucie's newly healed arm ached nearly as much as it had the first few days after the injury. She tightened her jaw and kept climbing. Beaubien, Michel, and Mebkis were doing all this for her. She couldn't breathe a word of complaint.

It grew dark. The silver lining was that now Lucie couldn't see how far down the base of the falls was. She focused on Beaubien's feet just above her head. Finally, Beaubien reached out his hand and lifted her up to a narrow ledge on which he and Mebkis stood. Michel clambered up last of all.

"Now we'll need light," shouted Mebkis over the roar of the waters.

Taking out his flint and steel, Beaubien lit a torch he'd prepared earlier. By its flickering light, the entrance to the cave was just visible behind the cascading water. Though at their ebb, the falls were still mighty, and Lucie tried not to think about being smashed to a pulp on the rocks dozens of meters below. Beaubien held the torch steady so that Mebkis could see to cross the slippery rocks. Once the First Nations man had made it to the slight lip of stone that marked the cave's threshold, Beaubien reached around Lucie and handed the torch to Michel.

"Wait here until we're safely across," he shouted to his son. "Once Mebkis has the fire going, hopefully it will cast enough light so that I can lean out and help you."

Michel nodded, gripping the torch tightly. Slowly, Beaubien followed in Mebkis's footsteps. His boots weren't as flexible as moccasins, and his feet slipped once or twice as he inched toward the cave. Finally, he made it. He pantomimed to Lucie to take her boots off. That made sense; she pulled them off and stuffed them into her knapsack. Hugging the face of the rock, she felt her way forward centimeter by centimeter.

Even though the summer heat still lingered in the air, the wet stone felt chilly against her face and body and positively icy on her sensitive feet. She forced down a shiver and continued with her eyes closed.

After an eternity, she felt strong fingers envelop her own. Beaubien heaved and pulled her across the remaining distance and into a tight hug. Lucie held the embrace, reveling in the feel of his hard, broad chest and strong arms. Then she forced herself away, waving back at Michel.

Mebkis had been busy in his few minutes in the cavern. He'd already made a small heap of tinder, kindling, and wood he had brought. Now, shielding the pile from the misty cave entrance, he worked his bow drill to produce a spark. He nursed it carefully until it was a flame, gradually feeding the fire until it burned brightly. Quartz sparkled and winked in the cavern's moist walls and low ceiling.

Beaubien looked out at his son, motioning for him to douse the torch and come across. Michel frowned and shook his head.

"Why won't he come?" asked Lucie.

"I don't know. Maybe he can't see well enough and doesn't want to chance it. No matter. He can wait there, and it will be that much easier for us ... for Mebkis and me ... to make our way back to the bank." Beaubien waved and nodded. Michel sat down, still holding the torch, his legs dangling over the edge.

"Now we begin," said Mebkis. He sat near the fire and pulled out a rolled deerskin. Once he smoothed it out on the floor, Lucie could see it was covered with pictograms. The historian in her itched to take a closer look at it. There was no way she could take it with her, but she felt professional envy all the same. Murmuring in a low voice, Mebkis added some strong-smelling herbs to the fire. "Through fire and fountain, flame and water, I will see only what you envision," he told

Lucie. "That is how I will hold the door open for you."

The smoke swirled around Lucie, making her dizzy. She leaned against Beaubien for support. He held her shoulders lightly, as if afraid he would break her.

"*Jamais je ne t'oublierai,*" Nicolas said softly in her ear.

I will never forget you. The first words she'd ever heard from him. "À la claire fontaine," the old folk song he'd sung when she'd awakened at his campfire on Saint-Jean's Day.

Her eyes teared up, and not just because the smoke had gotten thicker. She coughed a little and then stared. The flames had begun to spiral like a miniature cyclone. Mebkis raised the pitch of his chanting. "It's time to add the sacrifices," he said in French, then continued his monotonous song. He pulled the shaft of a broken arrow out of his pack and cast it on the fire.

Beaubien gasped. "The arrow that killed his father," he whispered. "Be deeply complimented. That is a great sacrifice, indeed." Then Beaubien himself tossed a small object into the flames. Lucie's throat tightened as she realized what it was: his dead wife's medal of Sainte-Marie. That he would give up such a precious thing for her . . .

The melting lead dripped down into the ashes. The whirlwind of fire grew stronger and taller. Now it was Lucie's turn.

She took out her wallet. It had been a graduation gift from her mother—a pale-blue calfskin wallet from Hermès, easily the most valuable accessory she owned. Never mind; she could get another. She had already emptied its contents into her knapsack. Now she carefully placed it on the flames.

Instead of increasing, the blaze died down somewhat, and Mebkis's eyes widened in alarm. *"Kawin tabise,"* he said. "Not enough."

Lucie felt stirrings of panic in her gut. What else did she have? She dumped out her sack and put her paper money on the flames. They sank lower. She added her driver's license and credit cards—which made the fire stink even as it subsided further. The air reeked of melting plastic, and Lucie despaired. Those things hadn't meant enough to her to generate the power the magical blaze needed. All that was left was her phone, and that seemed dangerous. She didn't care that much about it, anyway, so it surely wouldn't help.

Then it came to her. "Of course," she whispered. Unzipping her case, she quickly took out the maple spindle, wheel, and treadle. This spinning wheel had seen her through so much and had become even more precious to her once Beaubien had repaired it.

But if this was her only chance to get home, so be it. She set the pieces of her wheel on the fire. Immediately the flames leaped upward once more, and the cyclone became ten times stronger.

"Now make the picture of your home in your mind," directed Mebkis and resumed his chant.

Lucie imagined the Plains of Abraham, the Château Frontenac, the *basse-ville* that housed all of what she used to consider Old Québec—none of which had been built yet in this time. She thought of her parents, her sister, and even sweet Olivier. She thought of poutine and *pouding chômeur* and *chocolat chaud*. She—

Behind her came a crash, and she was knocked forward until she almost fell into the fire. She whipped her head around. Dufour! The odious man had toppled Nicolas from behind and now grappled with him on the cave floor. Where had he come from? Lucie looked out to the place Michel had been sitting, but the boy and the torch were gone.

"What have you done?" she screamed, launching herself onto Dufour.

"Get off me, witch!" The stocky man threw her off easily,

and she landed in Mebkis's lap. His eyes unseeing, he continued chanting. She stood up and prepared to attack Dufour once more.

"Lucie, stop," Nicolas gasped. "I can handle Dufour. Go, now, or all this will have been for nothing."

He was right. Once Lucie was gone, Mebkis could let go of the spell and help him. Dufour was no match for both men. Leaving immediately was the best way to help Beaubien.

Lucie looked back at the flames. The fiery column reached to the cave's low ceiling now, but there wasn't much of the spinning wheel left, so she didn't have long. She had to steel herself to step into the fire. *You didn't get burned coming through the chavande,* she reminded herself. *Trust Mebkis.* She took a deep breath, closed her eyes, and jumped.

She landed on cool grass and heard sirens, the rumble of trains, and a million other sounds of the twenty-first century. She smelled car exhaust, frying sausages, and tar. She had made it.

But then she looked back through the portal still hanging in the air and gasped. Nicolas now hung over the edge of the cave, clutching the wet stones with slipping fingers. Dufour knelt beside him, pounding and slapping at Nicolas's fingers. "No!" she screamed.

She dived back through the bridge connecting the centuries. Her momentum carried her forward into Dufour's wide back. With a cry, he fell headlong into the dark falls. Lucie teetered and slid on the narrow stone lip. She fell hard on one knee but ignored the pain that rocketed up her leg as she grasped Nicolas's wrists.

And then Mebkis was next to her, hauling his friend up to safety. The magical fire had died down to embers; the portal was closed, likely forever.

Once Beaubien sat safely on the cave's floor, Mebkis looked out where Michel had sat. "I'll go in search of the boy," he said, and made his way swiftly back to the bank.

Lucie threw her arms around Beaubien. "I thought you were dead," she whispered.

He coughed a ragged laugh. "I thought you were gone forever," he replied.

And he kissed her.

As their lips met, joyous energy surged through Lucie. "My home is here now," she said.

Nicolas chuckled. "Dufour was right about one thing. You are far too brazen for your own good," he murmured in her ear.

"For shame, monsieur!" Lucie chided mockingly. "My brazenness just saved your life."

Nicolas wrapped his arms around her and held her close. "Indeed, it did. And now that it did, my life belongs to you."

Ten

13 December 1640

WRAPPED IN FURS, LUCIE sat next to her sister-in-law in front of the bonfire burning merrily in Québec settlement's small square. Lazy snowflakes hissed as they fell into the flames. Residents milled around, laughing and talking. The autumn ships had brought a few more women to New France, and Lucie welcomed their civilizing influence. She set down her knitting—a set of tiny wool stockings—and clasped her hands over her slightly rounded belly.

"Nicolas said he'd arrive in time for the fête," she said.

Anne smiled. "He and Michel will be here soon. I think they have a surprise for you. It's your feast day, after all."

Staring into the bonfire, Lucie thought of her namesake, Sainte-Lucie, who had lit her path with a wreath of candles on her head so she could carry more food to the poor. Her very name meant light. It made sense that Christians would co-opt a day near the winter solstice, the darkest day of the year, to celebrate the return of the sun—just as they celebrated the summer solstice as Saint-Jean's Day.

Michel sat down clumsily next to her, jostling her out of her reverie. He'd grown another six inches since summer and still wasn't used to his gangly limbs. "Papa has something for you," he announced, holding his hands out to the flames.

Lucie stood and wobbled as she kept from overbalancing. Talk about changing bodies. Lucie had yet to grow accustomed to her constantly shifting center of gravity. She turned to greet her tall, handsome husband, who had a large bundle in his hands.

"This is for you," he said, reflected firelight dancing in his eyes.

He held out the bundle, and Lucie took it and sat down.

Slowly she unwrapped the layers of cloth as Michel and Anne looked over her shoulder. She gasped as she uncovered her gift—a spinning wheel nearly identical to the one that had burned in Mebkis's magical fire back in July.

"How—"

Michel interrupted her eagerly. "Mebkis and I went back to the cave and pulled the metal pieces out of the ashes the week after you were married," he said. "I wanted to go sooner, but Papa said I couldn't go until Tante Anne took the bandages off my head."

Michel had miraculously suffered only a concussion when Dufour knocked him down the cliffside. Thank heaven for the resilience of the young. That fateful evening, Lucie and Nicolas's joy hadn't been complete until Mebkis had discovered the boy dazed but otherwise unharmed.

Her stepson continued his explanation as Lucie unfolded the wheel and set it up on the snowy ground. "We've been working on it in secret for months. See?" He pushed down on the treadle, and it ran as smoothly as the original had.

"Thank you!" Lucie hugged Michel tightly and then stood to kiss her towering husband. "I cannot wait to use it. I feel terrible that I did not have a gift for you on your feast day." Saint-Nicolas's Day had been the week before, and Lucie had forgotten until then how much more important feast days were than birthdays in this century.

Nicolas laid his hand softly on Lucie's belly. "You have given me a great gift already, *ma belle au bois dormant.*"

Lucie leaned into his strong arms. *Happily ever after isn't reality,* she reminded herself. In four months, she'd give birth to her first child, far from any hospital. The fierce Canadian winter loomed before them, and their stores of food and firewood and faith would hopefully be enough to see them through until spring. Danger, disaster, disease—these were ever-present facts of life in 1640. But she and Nicolas had each other. That was enough for the present, no matter what the future—or was it the past?—would bring.

Luisa Perkins is the author of the dark fantasy novel *Dispirited*, the conspiracy thriller *Premonition*, and the cookbook *Comfortably Yum*. She has had short stories and essays published in numerous print and online anthologies. Luisa Perkins loves abandoned houses, ancient trees, and graveyards. Reading a great novel while eating homemade cookies is her idea of heaven. She and her family live in a small town in Southern California. Luisa blogs (infrequently) at http://kashkawan.squarespace.com.

Follow Luisa on Twitter: @LuisaPerkins

www.ingramcontent.com/pod-product-compliance
Lightning Source LLC
LaVergne TN
LVHW021231080526
838199LV00088B/4309